VICIOUS CIRCLE

Mark Neild

ISBN: 9798651703920
Cover design by: Art Painter
Library of Congress Control Number: 2018675309
Printed in the United States of America

For Carl, Dave, Ste, Damien and Rob.

CONTENTS

18TH JUNE 2002

T erry threw down his blueprints and marched towards his workforce, who for reasons unknown had downed tools. "The lazy bastards, it's not even ten yet." Halfway up a mountain of mud, he paused and mopped his grimy brow. This job was killing him. The protesters, ganged behind the chicken-wire fence separating the site from the rest of the woods, were not sympathetic.

"You're getting past it, old man. You should pack it in and find something else to destroy."

"What ladies? No, beneath this crumbling façade lies pure steel."

"Oh, I'm sure. Go home and get some rest. Take your cronies with you."

"What, and deny myself the sight of you beautiful girls every day? No, we'll be here for a good while yet."

"Ditto. Remember this isn't a job for us. We live here. You'll be gone long before us. I can assure you of that."

"Fair enough. I'm presuming there's still no hope of that cup of tea then?"

"You'll have a very long wait for that, I can assure you."

Amidst the placards and fair-trade earrings, a familiar face caught his attention.

"Alright, pal? Not seen you for a while."

The man ignored Terry's enquiry and while staring straight into his eyes, spat a ball of spit onto the forest floor.

Just what I need, him starting again.

He pushed through the crowd towards the edge of the pit.

"Murphy, why have you stopped? Colin, what's up?"

"Boss, look at this."

"What is it?"

"Not sure boss, but it looks like a big fucking bone or summat."

"Fuck off."

20TH JUNE 2002

He lay sprawled across his desk, counting the ticks from his Rolex. The office bathed in the warm glow of late-afternoon lethargy.

"Fuck it."

His shift didn't end for another hour but he was calling it a day. On jumping up, he caught his reflection in the mirror he had placed on the top of his filing cabinet. It had previously witnessed many of his greatest triumphs – a familiar routine of thrusting fists and matinee idol poses. Now, it displayed only the sagging ramparts of his belly and the ruthless army of grey overrunning his black hair.

The phone rang. He picked up the receiver as if it was smothered with germs.

"Dave Wrench. How can I help?"

"Hi, it's Jeremy Clarke from forensics. Is Jakes in?"

"No, I'm afraid he's out at the moment. He should be in later though."

"Is Light about then?"

"No, he's not in either."

"Jesus, tell them this is no time for the golf course."

"I will do, Jeremy."

"Yeah thanks. Sorry, who am I speaking to again?"

"DS Wrench. Dave Wrench."

"Oh, hello hotshot. Sorry, it's a crap line. How's tricks?"

"Oh, you know, still living the dream."

"Ha, me too son, me too. You're being sarcastic, right?"

"Yes."

"Of course you are. Right, when are they due back in?"

"It says not back."

"Not back! They never bloody change do they?"

"Nope."

"Cheating a living, son. Oh well, I'll catch them in the morning then. If they're in that is."

"They should be. Can I help at all?"

"I was just ringing to tell them that I've got the prelim report on the body in the woods."

"The body in the woods?"

"Bloody hell Dave, don't tell me Jakes hasn't briefed you on it yet?"

"Sorry, yes, Light spoke to me earlier, the body in the woods."

"Oh yes, just when you thought that new housing development couldn't cause any more controversy."

"What's the story then?"

"Well, it's a bloody shame. It's a smashing bit of green belt."

"Sorry?"

"Oh, you mean the body …You've got a real one here son."

"Go on."

"How does a middle-aged male, with more holes in his chest than a block of Swiss cheese and a cavity in his skull so big I can nearly put my fist in it, grab you?"

"Shit, really?"

"Oh yeah."

"Any ID?"

"Not at the minute. We're seeing whether dentistry can come up with anything. If not, we're struggling … unless someone comes forward with a name."

"How long has he been there?"

"Well, judging by the level of skeletonisation, I'd probably estimate mid-seventies."

"Really?"

"Yeah, he's been down there a good while. The press will lap this one up, son."

"Absolutely. Any evidence on the perp?"

"We're still searching but the body is in a hell of a state. I wouldn't hold your breath, son."

"Okay. Fuck …"

"Yes, it's definitely a 'fuck' kind of case."

"It certainly is. Well, right, shall I get Jakes to ring you?"

"Tell him I'll drop the report off tomorrow morning around ten."

"Okay, I'll let him know."

"Good man. Right, I'll let you go then. Listen, don't take any crap from Jakes; he's getting a right miserable sod in his old age. You can tell him I said that too."

"Right, I will do."

"Speak to you soon."

"Okay, bye."

He rubbed his palms over his face. *Do something. Take back control. These corrupt bastards know nothing about policing. You've forgotten more in a day than they've learned in a career.*

The phone rang again.

"Just fuck off ...Hello, Wrench speaking."

"Dave? Tell Jakes that he better get Sally at dental a good drink. We've got a name."

13TH JANUARY 1975

Sarah never had a problem getting up for school. She didn't relish it but nevertheless, she could manage it. Getting up for work though was another matter; she was just so tired.

Last night, the layers of her bedclothes were in sharp contrast: her flannelette sheets temperate and smooth, her woollen blankets full of prickly heat and anger. Now though, within the ethereal daze of half-sleep, they were in perfect harmony, heating and caressing her every fibre. She lifted her head and peered through a hole in her condensation-soaked window. A coating of frost covered the terraced street from top to bottom. The icing on the cake.

"Sarah, time to get up. It's half seven."

"Oh Dad, no. Please no."

"C'mon love, your breakfast is on the table."

I can't get up. No way. The bathroom yesterday was like a bloody igloo and his porridge and the bloke at the bus stop and—

"Sarah. C'mon love, you'll be late."

"Dad, I'm not going in. I've been sick. Ring in and tell them. Tell them I'm sick."

"Sarah, you'll lose this job. You're never in."

"I don't care. I can't help being sick. Please Dad, I'm ill. Ring in for me."

"No way love, ring in yourself."

"Please Dad. Honestly, I'm not well. I have a temperature. I've been sweating all night."

He wasn't stupid. She was lying through the back of her teeth. There was something though in that tone; a familiar quiver, carrying reminders of all their forged precedents and fixed narratives. Daddy's girl.

"Dad, please. I'm really bad."

"Ok. But don't tell your mum for God's sake."

15TH JANUARY 1975

S he skulked into the gape of the garage, her stomach flip-ping like a tossed coin. An unholy symphony of clangs, bangs and expletives greeted her without ceremony. This was definitely the worst moment of her life. Nothing else came close.

Why does he want to see me? Peter should be doing this. He's my manager.

A young garage native – a bad teenage moustache just visible behind his oily war paint – stopped brushing the floor and stared at her with unbelieving eyes.

"You've missed a bit …Sorry, I'm only kidding."

She moved onward, passing the other mechanics working on a wounded artic. She knew most of them from their forays into the admin offices, where they would always try to entice the secretaries into town after work for a steak meal and a few in the Star. Clive, the West Indian guy from Longsight, was there. The only mechanic she could stand. He would talk to the secretaries, but never in a sleazy way. He didn't take shit either: the word was he'd hammered Doyle in the Kings, after he called him a black bastard.

"Be careful Sarah. Be careful of the Big White Chief."

"I will do, Clive."

"Tut blondie, you've been a naughty girl."

"Piss off, Doyle."

She climbed up the cast iron steps towards the managing director's office like a condemned woman walking the plank.

New Direction Catalogues – or NDC for short – were once market leaders, mainstays of UK retail. The early seventies though had not been kind to them. A vicious circle of industrial unrest and poor-quality service had left them moribund and the transport department, with their lost days and botched deliveries, were undoubtedly the main culprits: A virulent strain of the British disease.

James Dolby disinterred the corpse of NDC and shook it back to life. His methods were uncompromising and on occasion brutal; but the consensus was that he had saved the company. Clive had given him the nickname the 'Big White Chief' and everybody agreed it was perfect. Everybody but Sarah: she had far worse names for him.

She knocked on his door and waited for a response.

There's no answer. It's the right time. Peter said half nine.

She knocked again.

He's not in. He's not in. Thank Christ for that. If I keep my head down, he might forget—

"Miss Gregory?"

She turned around and faced an older woman dressed in a mauve turtleneck sweater and tartan skirt. Her hair pitch black and poodle clipped.

"Oh, hello. I'm here to see Mr Dolby."

"Yes, I know. I'm Ruth his secretary. He's running late. He told me to show you into his office. He said he won't be long."

"Oh, okay then."

Ruth grabbed the handle of his door before pausing and knocking.

"If this job has taught me one thing, it's that you can't be too careful."

"Er, yeah, I'm sure."

She inched open the door.

"Okay, all clear. Take a seat then Miss Gregory. Like I say, he won't be long. Would you like a drink?"

"No, I'm fine thank you."

"Okay, well make yourself comfortable."

"Yes, thank you. I'll try my best."

She'd distracted herself from the fact that she'd been waiting for at least half an hour by studying the pictures hanging on his office wall. With his glue-pot side parting and POW frame, he was an ugly man. Judging by the number of images of him arm in arm with beautiful girls though, she thought he must have something about him. A rouge image burst through the fleapit of her mind: his naked skin, pallid and pockmarked, barely covering the severe contours of his bones. It was a very unattractive image. There was little doubt about that. So why in the depths of her gut were butterflies congregating?

The door flung open. He marched in and hung his grey mack-intosh on the aged-browned coat stand; the flat of his palm smoothing away any creases.

"Er, hello sir."

"Jesus … you scared me half to death. Who the bloody hell are you?"

"Sarah Gregory, sir. You wanted to see me."

"Did I?"

"Yes sir. Peter told me this morning."

"Ah, that's right. The vanishing secretary."

"Sorry sir?"

"You heard, Gregory. I'm surprised you know where this place is."

He swaggered towards his wooden drinks cabinet and poured the contents of a crystal decanter into a squat glass. He took a hefty swig and moved towards the window situated behind his desk. A commotion had erupted. Clive and the lads had commenced a kickabout on the field of concrete where the packed containers stood. His fingers drummed on the headrest of his black leather chair as he surveyed his motley crew.

"The people of the North hold a particular fascination for me Gregory."

"Er, do they sir?"

"Yes, their fortitude in the face of living in this city. I mean, look at Bailey over there. Do you know how long he has worked here Gregory?"

"No sir."

"Thirty-five years. In all that time, he has only had four sick days. I dropped him off at home once. He was waiting at the bus stop and I drove past him, so I gave him a lift. Do you know he still lives with his mother? They live in perhaps the most depressing flat in the whole of Manchester. In Hulme, Gregory; quite an extraordinary dive. Then every day he comes in here and counts boxes. It's remarkable really."

"Er... Reg loves his job sir."

"Quite."

He span around.

"That's not you though is it? The discipline, the commitment – you're not made for all that. No, that isn't your bag at all. This was your fourth absence this year and we're only in bloody mid-January."

"I've been unlucky sir. I've picked up a lot of bugs."

"Unlucky! That's one word for it. You've certainly got chutzpah, I'll give you that."

"I've not heard of that sir, what are the symptoms?"

"Ha, another marvel of the comprehensive education system. Chutzpah means gall, audacity …In other words Gregory, balls."

"I don't follow, sir."

"Presumably you're aware of my reputation, Gregory?"

"Yes, si—"

"Do you know that this wasn't supposed to be my office? When I came here, this wasn't an office. This was the mechanics' staff room. I changed all that. I wanted to be where the awkward squad prevailed. I wanted to be sat right on top of them, crawling up their arses. I got rid of more people in my first six months than the company had lost in all the time it's been trading. I didn't just concentrate on this depot either. Morley, Liverpool, Bristol, Stoke, Coventry, Huntingdon, York …I visited them all and I told them straight: things were going to change or they were out. It was my way or the highway. And they did change, they changed very quickly indeed."

"Yes, I heard that sir. People say that if it wasn't for you there would be no such thing as NDC."

"Very true Gregory, which makes your behaviour all the more baffling. I mean, how did you expect all this to end?"

"Er … I'm not sure. Like I say, I've been really unlucky with my health."

"That word again. I don't believe in luck. I believe in commitment to a cause. I believe in blood, sweat and tears – attributes that you've shown a complete lack of."

"I don't know what to say sir."

"Well, you can start by giving me one good reason why I shouldn't sack you."

"Er … well …I'm committed to this job, I promise I am. It's just like I said, I've just been …I've just been, I've had a few knock-backs. I'm feeling good now though. And Peter says I'm the fastest typer in the pool. Well, second behind Mavis but I'm still—"

"Where do you live Gregory?"

"Sorry sir?"

"Where do you live?"

"Eccles sir."

"And do you plan to live there for the rest of your life?"

"Erm, well … I'm not sure sir. I'll probably get a place of my own when I get a bit older."

"What does your father do?"

"He's a chippie, I mean a carpenter, sir. He's not in work at the moment."

"Hmm, lot of it about. Gregory you're lucky; you have me on a day when I'm feeling charitable. I'm not going to sack you. In fact, I'm going to do the opposite; who says a strong man cannot be compassionate, eh? Tomorrow morning you will clear your desk and come to work for me in my office. Ruth's months from her retirement and I need a replacement, some-one I can rely on. I may live to regret this but I think you have potential, Gregory. I see it in you. You're not feckless, you're understimulated. That bloody typing pool is sapping your soul. You're bored. Am I right?"

"Er … yes sir. Spot on."

"Yes, you're like an exotic bird in a manky old cage. Well, I'm going to unleash your wings. You no longer answer to Peter Davies, you answer directly to me. We've got an important convention next week in Luton. You'll be accompanying me there. We will be staying in a hotel overnight, so pack a bag. I need you to do two things and two things only – look good and manage my paper work. Okay? Good. See you tomorrow eight o' clock sharp. And remember, this is your big chance. Don't even think about letting me down."

He returned to his desk and began searching through some documents.

"No, I won't sir. I promise. Thank you. "

She stumbled towards the exit.

He's messing around. He's got to be. He can't promote me – I'm never in.

"Oh, and Gregory ..."

"Yes sir."

"How tall are you?"

"Er ... I think about five foot ten, sir."

"Yes, you are aren't you. Okay, off you go then."

"Okay sir."

9TH NOVEMBER 1996

Adam Grimes was sitting in the Jobcentre. A brutalist toilet overflowing with human waste – crack-heads, green-heads, trigger-heads – it was the single greatest impediment to him joining the ranks of the employed. Or so he said. In reality, his heart wasn't in it. He wanted to work insomuch as its status would assuage his guilt at the stuff he was doing out of work, but not enough to truly get his hands dirty. Carole was on this morning. Her undulating black hair and understated make-up the perfect balance of grammar and glamour. She was once of great comfort: her repertoire of empathetic gestures, seemingly recognition that oleaginous red hair and spots in his thirties were not antithetical to a life of meaning. He almost asked her out on a date – seeing her on Salford precinct with her walking bicep of a boyfriend ended that particular dream. Now though his constant failure to provide evidence of his commitment to job seeking – bus tickets, letters, interview dates – had filled her with such contempt towards him that he half expected her to start addressing him simply as knobhead.

"Next. Next!"

"Sorry, I was miles away Carole."

"Please sit down Mr Grimes."

"Right, yes. How are you?"

"What?"

"How are you?"

"Aside from working thirty-seven hours a week in this place, Mr Grimes, I'm golden."

"Tell me about it, I was—"

"Had any interviews this week, Mr Grimes?"

"Er … yes, one. There were a couple of others that I could have gone for but I decided to concentrate on this one."

"Okay, where?"

"McDonalds."

"Any luck?"

"Not a sniff. They've nothing available, full staff compliment they said."

"But you went for an interview."

"Yes."

"For a company without vacancies."

"Well there are different types of interviews aren't there."

"No, not generally, Mr Grimes. To have gone for an interview there has to be a job on offer."

"Well, I thought I'd use my initiative and ring to see what they had available. Just on the off chance, like."

"So, let me get this straight …You didn't go for an interview; you didn't prepare for an interview; you didn't iron your best shirt for an interview; you didn't comb your hair in a nice little side-parting for an interview; you didn't turn up on time for an interview. You simply rang them 'on the off chance.'"

"Yes, that's right."

"Unbelievable …Right, last-straw time Mr Grimes. I have warned you before that we have the power to suspend your payments if we feel that you're not trying to find work and I think it's about time that we utilised these powers."

"Why?"

"Because of your pathological reluctance to look for a job."

"I've been on interviews."

"That's just it Mr Grimes, you haven't have you? You just lie or make ridiculous excuses."

"No I don't."

"Like you told me you didn't have a driving licence, so you couldn't take delivery jobs, then the week before last your excuse for not attending the interview at that paper merchant's was that your car had broken down."

"I meant my mate's car."

"Rubbish, Mr Grimes. Stop insulting my intelligence.

"No I'm not."

"Yes you are Mr Grimes. You're talking the piss but no more. I've put this off for too long. The hint's in the title *Jobseeker's Allowance*."

"No Carole, please don't stop my dole. I want to work, honestly I do. Just give me one more chance. Please, I promise I won't let you down."

Carole tapped her pencil on her desk.

"Okay, but only on the understanding that this is your final chance. One more episode like this and I will stop your dole."

"Absolutely."

"Right, there's a job here that I think will be perfect for you – it's unskilled and not that physical."

"Er, okay where?"

"New Direction Catalogues, their warehouse is in Eccles."

"New Direction, I thought they'd gone bust."

"Evidently not Mr Grimes."

"Right. I mean, I'll definitely go but …"

"What Mr Grimes?"

"I'm just not sure it's for me."

"Mr Grimes, have you forgotten what I just said? You're in no position to be fussy."

"I know but warehouse work at my age …It's a bit degrading. Do you know what I mean?"

"Frankly Mr Grimes, no I don't. You're a thirty-eight-year-old man with the work experience of a schoolboy. What do you expect? And remember, Mr Grimes, there's a lot more degrading things than warehouse work. Selling *The Big Issue* or rooting in the bins outside *Greggs*, for instance.

"When would I start?"

"Unfortunately, you've a bit of a wait but you can look for other stuff in the meantime. No reason why not eh? Not like your time is barely your own. If you get it, which you will, you start on the 19th of November. They've got a bit of casual labour in at the minute and they don't finish until the Friday before."

"Okay, fuck it, yeah."

"Mr Grimes, you could sound a little more enthusiastic about this. It's a very good opportunity for you."

"I'm sorry. I'll go."

"Good. I'm pleased. It will be good for you. Right Mr Grimes, I will send you the details in the post. Are you still at the same address?"

"Yeah, okay. Yep, I'm still there. Thanks for that. Bye now."

27TH JUNE 2002

It was becoming his default position. Outside Jakes' office, sitting on hard plastic, the noise from the ornamental water cooler gnawing at his equilibrium. It was a sign of the times. You never saw Keith Light here. Jakes would never keep him waiting. They were always in there though: Light rocking on his chair, his beard and sunglasses redolent of a terrible disc jockey; Jakes with his head rooted in the biscuit barrel, identifiable only by his overlapping jowls and sloppy grey peak. They were to blame for all of this. Them, and the government, of course – Dave was keen not to forget the government's role in his downfall.

"Sorry I'm late Dave. Bloody rush-hour traffic; and what are those roadworks about on Regent Road? Absolute fucking joke."

"No problem sir. It's getting ridiculous."

"You're not wrong. Right come in, sit down. Drink?"

"No thanks sir."

"Sure?"

"Yeah, I'm fine thanks."

"Well, I'm going to pour myself a little dram. I've got a bloody interview with the regionals and then the London media later."

"Don't envy you that one sir."

"I know, bloody vultures. For some reason, they've gone mad

on this one. We've got murders left, right and bloody centre in Ordsall and Little Hulton and no one gives a shit. Find a stiff in the fucking woods and there's a fucking frenzy. Bastard press … they want shooting and I'd gladly pull the trigger. Anyway, that's my rant over. They tell me we've got a name."

"Yes sir, Gordon Lundy. He was forty-five years of age when he went missing in late seventy-five. Born and brought up in Hastings, Sussex. No kids, no known connections to the North and no previous. Successful man by all accounts, bit of a furniture magnate. Went on some convention, according to his wife, and never came back. His missus still lives in the marital home apparently."

"Let me have a look at him."

Dave passed Jakes the picture of Lundy he had cribbed from missing persons.

"Looks a bit of a hard-nut sir. Look at that boxer's nose and cauliflower ears."

"Yeah, hulking-great shoulders too. Whoever killed that big bastard must have had a lot of company. What do you think?"

"Maybe sir."

"Nothing else found on the site yet Dave?"

"Not yet sir. We're going over the whole area bit by bit though."

"And we've made no connections as to why he was down here …Business? Pleasure?"

"Not yet sir, but were working on it. We'll hopefully know more when we've spoken to Mrs Lundy."

"Who's informing her?"

"Two from their uniform told her the day before yesterday. I was thinking of going down there myself …Give her a few more days though, let her get over the shock …If that's okay, of course?"

"Yes, good idea. Take someone with you, whomever you need."

"Right sir, thank you. I'll start making the arrangements then."

"Good man."

"Okay."

"Yeah, take it easy son."

"Will do sir."

Dave turned around and headed for the door.

"Oh, Dave."

"Sir."

"Under the circumstances, feed directly back to me, not Keith."

"What circumstances are those, sir?"

"You know son. C'mon, don't be daft, don't be too proud. We know how disappointed you were not to get the inspector's job. We still value you very highly son. You know that don't you? I wouldn't trust you with this assignment otherwise. We based the decision on the interview, just the interview on the day son. Keith was just slightly better, only slightly mind."

"Okay sir. I admit I was disappointed, but I respect the decision."

"You've got plenty of time son."

"Okay yeah. Right, I'll get on then."

He wanted to say that it was all bullshit; that everyone knows Light cannot hold a candle to him; that he could never have matched his interview presentation; that he only got the job because of his mastery of the quantitative dark arts. He wanted to say all these things, but he didn't utter a word. His was a silent fury, burning and seething but ultimately shackled and impotent, unable to breach his very nature – his towering wall of submissiveness.

23RD JANUARY 1975

Sarah only ever left Manchester for the annual Gregory family holiday to Cornwall. These trips were her favourite thing in the whole world. She even relished the twelve-hour journey – this despite being hermetically sealed in the back of a Vauxhall Viva, alongside myriad cardboard boxes and the flatulent family Alsatian.

Her trip with Dolby was a world away from this. The whole of Hartington Road appeared at their front windows when his car glided into view – a bright red Triumph Stag, the same model Georgie Best drives. His cashmere scarf, tweed cap and string back gloves confirmed that this was a different way of doing things: brains not brawn, cheques not cash. As she climbed into the motor, with its cream interior and oak-panelled dashboard, she recalled his words.

"I'm going to unleash your wings."

The Stag turned left out of the street; her head dizzying with thoughts of progress.

I could get my own flat. In town, with a dog.

The Stag was powering down the fast lane of the motorway. Since leaving Manchester, they had barely spoken two words. *God, this is horrible. What can I say? Shall I talk about Bailey? He likes Bailey … I think.*

Her fingers began massaging the rough edges of her brown leather attaché case, anything to stop biting her nails.

"What's in that bag?"

"Note pad and pen, Mr Dolby."

His mouth contorted into a sneer.

"You won't need that."

"Okay."

"I said to you that your job is to look pretty. That's all you need to do. These shit-kickers from Dundee will need something to look at. Very unsophisticated people they are, as I suppose the Scottish are in general. Probably turn up half-cut on whisky. It wouldn't surprise me. Do you know any Scottish people?"

"No."

"No bad thing that. Why on earth are we opening a branch in fucking Jockland? The owners must be finally losing their minds. Personally, I wouldn't piss on them if my life depended on it. No, you just sit there, shuffle some papers and flash that smile of yours. Business is all about image, all about the right image."

They fell back into silence.

Who does he think he is? Like Dad said, 'no better or worse than anyone else.' I'm no one's bit of fluff. I'm no one's fool. He's picked the wrong bloody one for that.

She readjusted her position in her seat. Her posture more pronounced. Her head higher.

No better no worse.

The Stag swung across the lanes amidst a crescendo of horns and squealing brakes.

"What are you doing? Jesus, Mr Dolby!"

He taxied to a stop on the hard shoulder and began gently banging his head on the steering wheel.

"You could have killed us, we could have died. Mr Dolby? Mr Dolby, speak to me."

"Why am I cursed by this affliction? Why am I such a bloody idiot?"

His head banging went into overdrive; the impact shuddering the wooden dashboard.

"Stop it Mr Dolby. You'll hurt yourself."

"Such a bloody idiot."

"Mr Dolby. Stop!"

He slumped back into his seat.

"Sarah, I am so, so sorry. You didn't deserve that. Look, this is not an excuse for what I said but I'm terribly old-fashioned and … no, be honest, man. Tell the bloody truth for once. Okay, if you must know, I've never been comfortable around women … and I tend to hide behind stupid comments like those last ones. A lot of it is from the army. The bloody bravado certainly is. It's because I'm scared to show my feelings and admit that I'm shy and very self-conscious. It's always the bloody same. When I'm trying to impress someone, I end up saying the exact type of thing that will make them run a mile. It's like a curse."

Oh my God, I'm winning. See Mum, I'm winning. He likes me. He fancies me.

She placed her arm on his shoulder, a slight smile emerging across her face.

"Mr Dolby, did you say you were trying to impress me?"

"Sarah, I'm only human. The whole of the male staff at NDC spends a frankly ridiculous amount of time thinking of ways to impress you."

By midnight it was all finished, that is, the business element of the trip. A movie was playing in Sarah's head regarding this whole journey – the hotel, the meal, the business meeting. As a prophetic piece it made an impressive French farce. The hotel was not a large neo-gothic monolith with a frenetically busy reception area filled with harassed concierges, florid old women and penguin-suited waiters; it was a Victorian guest-house, situated in a residential street near Luton Airport. The meeting was not held in a sombre boardroom, participants sat around a large brown oak table – faces vexed and furrowed, the air veneered with a film of cigarette smoke – but instead took place in a small, grim taproom masquerading as a hotel bar.

Her final disappointment was Dolby's performance, which was nowhere near as impressive as his film portrayal. The two Scotsmen, Mr Docherty and Mr Cleary, scorned his loose grasp of specifics, mocking his concerns regarding the militancy of the highland workforce by evidencing how many more man-hours have been lost this side of the border and he conceded to their terms, cementing the deal with an over-effusive hand-shake, before a fork had been lifted. They were back on-route to Dundee Airport within the hour.

Dolby though was of a different mind. After the Scotsmen had left, he insisted that he buy the whole bar a drink – the two older, raincoated men who made up the rest of the clientele respectfully declined the offer – and then ordered a bottle of *Dom Perignon*. The fact that the bar only stocked *Lambrusco* didn't dampen his ardour in the slightest.

"Oh what a great evening, a really good piece of work. And I'll tell you something Sarah ..."

"What Mr Dolby?"

"I couldn't have done it without you."

"C'mon Mr Dolby, I barely said a word."

"Hmm, Sarah I don't want to offend you again, but you didn't need to. You sold the company to them with your smile, your charm, and shoot me for saying it … your looks. You may not think so, but I know how these things work."

"They didn't seem very enthusiastic Mr Dolby."

"Who, our Scottish friends? Well, business is like that Sarah. They were a dwindling joke of company until New Direction bought them out. As ever with the Scots, they need their English neighbours but resent this fact. It's a very good deal for us and for them. We're closer to where we want to be. Each year we're making more noise, getting stronger."

The two older men inched past the small wooden tables and stools towards the bar exit.

"Goodnight chaps."

"Goodnight, sir. Goodnight young lady."

"Night."

Dolby and Sarah burst out laughing.

"Salesmen Sarah. A rare breed."

"Sorry?"

"They're salesmen – cutlery, toys, kitchen gadgets …Up and down the motorway, flogging anything and everything."

"Really, how can you tell?"

"The briefcases, the air of defeat …I'm afraid when you have frequented as many of these places as I have, spotting such characters becomes second nature."

"I wonder if they're brothers, they look very alike."

"Sarah, surely a mother would never be as luckless as to produce two offspring like that."

"Maybe they're secret lovers. I bet they're sharing a room."

"Keep your voice down, this is Luton not San Francisco. And anyway, Mrs Chesterton would never allow such things to go on under her roof."

"Who?"

"Mrs Chesterton, the proprietor."

"You mean that old battleaxe who signed us in."

"Oi, that old battleaxe is a family friend! She's put me up on numerous occasions. She can't smile now because of the stroke."

"I bet she didn't smile much before it either."

"Now that is not nice. Hey though, you could be on to something. Did you notice how one of them had his hair parted to the left. That's a sure sign you know."

"What?"

"Having your hair parted to the left. A sure sign that you're, well, you know."

"Who told you that?"

"Listen, in the army my dear, one's reputation could depend on which way your hair is parted."

"Oh c'mon."

"I'm being serious. There was one chap I served with who had his hair parted to the left and …Well let's just say he got some terrible stick for it."

"And was he a poofter?"

Dolby looked at the table and began playing with his napkin.

"Jack? God no. One of the bravest men you would want to meet."

"See."

"Yes, you're right. Certainly if Jack is anything to go by."

Dolby topped up Sarah's glass, his pouring hand betraying a slight tremor.

"Are you okay Mr Dolby?"

"Yes. I'm fine, I'm fine."

"Mr Dolby, are you sure?"

"Yes Sarah. I'm fine."

"You're not, I can tell."

"You could have a job in interrogation. No, I'm being stupid really. It's just that we lost Jack. It's still hard …Still very hard to take."

"Lost him?"

"Yes, in the army. In the trouble in Aden, about six or seven years ago."

"I'm sorry."

"No, please don't be. It's nice to remember; well if you know what I mean, remember the lads at least, not the fighting."

"Do you still see any of your army friends?"

"Yes. Well not as much as one would like – once, twice a year, at functions. I do miss them. When you've gone through hell with people, the bond you have is cast iron. But like everyone, you drift apart. They were good men though. Jack Crossing was my best mate in C Company. A treacherous Arab policeman shot him dead, supposed to be on our fucking side he was. His head and stuff all …Look, I'm sorry."

She grabbed Dolby's hands.

"Listen, don't be daft. You can talk to me anytime. It's a pleasure. Well, not a *pleasure*, if you know what I mean."

"You're such a kind soul."

"No, I'm not. You don't know me."

"I know enough to tell you're beautiful inside and out."

"Mr Dolby, you'll have me blushing."

"I mean every word."

They stared into each other's eyes.

"You know, I can't believe we're talking like this. Most people are so scared of you at work—"

"Who me? The Big White Chief, surely not?"

"You know that they call you that?"

"My dear, it is my misfortune to know everything that goes on in that blasted place."

"But you're a really nice man. I never saw it before, like when you called me into your office and—"

Dolby lifted up Sarah's hands, massaging her palms with his two thumbs.

"Like I said Sarah, I'm a fool when I really like someone. I can't help acting like an idiot."

The night porter breezed into the room prompting them to pull their hands apart.

"Sir, Mrs Chesterton said if you want to stay up, take the key and lock up on your way out. She says that you can slide the key under her door."

"Okay, thank you. Right, well you better give me another bottle of this monstrous stuff then."

"Mr Dolby! That's too much for me, I'm already feeling tipsy."

"Nonsense, we're celebrating. Get me another bottle and a large brandy please."

"Okay sir."

"You're a bad influence. I'm going to the loo."

Sarah stumbled towards the woodchip-covered door. She'd been drunk before but never like this. This was a whole new feeling.

On returning to her seat, her glass was full.

"C'mon, let's share a toast. To a prosperous partnership ... to me and you."

1ST JULY 2002

They had been sitting in a sweltering Mondeo, waiting for Rose Lundy to return home for close to two hours. Dave had chosen Detective Constable Ian Harington, a new arrival at North Manchester CID having transferred from North Yorkshire, to accompany him. Although only a year and a half younger at thirty-six, there was an age between them in terms of knowledge and experience. The trip would be good for him; show him how a true professional works. A man once tipped for very big things.

Dave's initial impressions were not encouraging. Yes it was hot, but taking his tie off and rolling his shirt sleeves up? Combine this with his shaggy blond mop and he looked like a barman from his local Masonic lodge. North Manchester needed many things but another maverick wasn't one of them. That position was heavily oversubscribed. He filed this deliberation into his pending tray. Confrontation would merely sully the atmosphere and this was his best afternoon in ages. Their destination was beautiful: glossed bungalows guarded by a phalanx of yucca trees, and although he had a constant urge to tip him, he had a captive audience for his specialised subject.

"And top brass know all about it, Dave?"

"Fucking right they do. They called Jakes in and told him that our stats needed a bit of padding, so he got straight onto it. Next thing you know, uniform are pulling people in after a bit of handbags for assault and battery, solved shoplifting jobs are re-classified as solved burglary jobs, and Light has prisoners on remand coughing to all sorts for a few bob. Pure unadulterated corruption ...It's fucking criminal."

"That Light's a fucking piece of work."

"Oh, it goes the other way too ...The election last year, right?"

"Yeah."

"This time we're under pressure from the top, and I mean the top – fucking politicians mate, to get our crime figures down. Again, over to Light, who basically tells all departments not to arrest people. Extortion, armed robberies, the lot, just fucking ignored."

"Bollocks, that can't happen. That's not feasible."

"First rule of North Manchester CID – anything's feasible with Keith Light."

"Unbelievable Dave. What have I let myself in for?"

"You'll be fine mate. Just stick with me and a couple of the other cops. We're not all bent. We've got pride in the badge."

"Glad to hear it. Fancy a sandwich mate? My missus has gone a bit OTT on the old stakeout theme."

"What are they?"

"Ham or cheese and chutney."

"Go on then, give me a ham one."

A combination of white bread and processed meat calmed his ire. A feeling of equanimity overcame him; his mind moving onto other planes.

"You know what Ian. I bet if you came to this street every day for a year, the weather would be as sunny as this."

"You reckon?"

"Oh yeah, it's the southern climate, mate. It's a lot more beneficial for your health down here."

"I could imagine that."

"Yeah, stands to reason. Waking up in this environment, you're bound to feel better about yourself."

"Would you not get bored though Dave? It's right out in the sticks this place."

"That's the whole point …"

He rose from his seat, repositioning his rear-view mirror.

"Hang on. Here we go, is this her?"

"Where?"

"There with those two blokes."

Ian span around.

"That can't be her …Unless she's in the Costra Nostra."

"They're heading for her place, 32 Bloom Street, that's right. Are they going in? Yes, it must be her."

"What, with those heavies? It can't be."

"It does look a bit weird. Are they doormen? They're all going in though. Who the fuck are they? The copper I spoke to said she's got no kids, and there was no word of her remarrying."

"Fuck knows mate."

"Right, come on Harington."

They jumped out of the Mondeo and strode towards Rose Lundy's front door. Dave took a deep breath and rattled the door handle. A man in a black flecked suit answered, his bulk filling the entrance.

"Yes, can I help you?"

"Hi, yes I wonder if you can. I'm looking for a Mrs Lundy."

"And you are?"

"My name is Detective Sergeant Dave Wrench and this is Detective Constable Ian Harington, we're from North Manchester CID and we would like to speak to Mrs Lundy please."

"Oh sure, yes, please come in. She's just out the back. I didn't mean to be standoffish, but we got a very unpleasant visit from the local press the other day."

"We could imagine, couldn't we Ian?"

"Yes, not known for their tact and diplomacy, unfortunately."

Gordon Lundy's image covered every inch of the pearly white hallway.

"Nice pictures, very poignant."

"Yes Sergeant Wrench, they are, aren't they."

"Please, call me Dave."

"Okay then, if you're sure. Oh, in case you're wondering, which I'm sure you are, my name is Stuart."

"Thank you, Stuart."

"No problem. Yes, they're very moving Dave. This one here is Mrs Lundy's favourite."

He pointed to a picture above the living room door of Mr Lundy windswept on a moss-covered rock, arm in arm with a long-haired English Collie.

Dave paused and read the picture's inscription.

Be sure, wherever I may roam, my heart is forever in this home.

"If you just want to sit in there and I'll go and get her for you."

"Thank you."

"Would you like a cup of tea, or a cold drink?"

"No thanks, we've just had one."

The two detectives sat down on the floral-patterned sofa.

"Well Ian, he ain't no doorman."

"No?"

"A mullet, slip-on shoes, white socks, at his age? No mate, he's in God's squad."

"You think?"

"Absolutely … and if he isn't, dressed like that, he fucking needs to be."

"Ha, maybe you're right."

"No doubt in my mind."

Ian scanned the walls.

"Fucking hell, this room's a shrine as well. It's a bloody shame Dave."

"I know, yeah."

"She's not moved on at all. Probably the love of her life, looks like it in these pictures …Nothing like me and my missus."

"A picture can hide a multitude of sins, Ian."

"True enough, 'Smile for the camera' and all that …Hey, that's an interesting one above the telly."

"Which one?"

"That one there – him at a black-tie do, with his pals."

"Hmm … yeah, could give us a handle on some of his old acquaintances. We'll ask her whether we can have a look at that one. She may have—"

Stuart walked back into the room with the other man. They looked like twins.

"She won't be long, officers. She's just changing."

"Ok. Thank you."

"You're welcome. No problem. My name is Mark by the way."

"Hi Mark. My name is DS Dave Wrench and this is my colleague DC Harington."

"Nice to meet you Ian."

"Yes, same to you Mark."

Stuart took the remaining place on the sofa, while Mark sat

on an identically patterned armchair. Dave leant forward, his hands tightly clasped together; Ian feigned interest in the ceiling.

She entered the room. They jumped up, Dave taking the lead, his arm outstretched.

"Hello Mrs Lundy. Thank you so much for agreeing to see us."

"Don't worry; it's fine. Thank you for travelling down; it must be quite a drive from Manchester."

"No, no, not at all, no problem. My name is Detective Sergeant Dave Wrench and this is my colleague Detective Constable Ian Harington."

"Hello Mrs Lundy, thanks for seeing us."

"No that's fine Ian. Nice to meet you both."

"Before we start, Mrs Lundy, we would just like to offer on behalf of everyone from North Manchester CID our sincerest condolences on your sad lost."

"Thank you Dave, you've all been so kind."

Mrs Lundy eased into her armchair; her hair long, grey and broken; her floral frock failing to disguise the decay of a myriad sleepless nights.

"Now then, have my boys offered you a drink?"

"Yes, they have. They've been very courteous."

"Yes. I'm sure they have. They don't need to be here, you know. They insist though."

"Family should stick together, at a terrible time such as this."

"No, no Dave, we're not blood family but—"

Stuart jumped in.

"We're part of a bigger, much more important family – the family of our Lord Jesus Christ."

One hundred and eighty. The fucking master.

"Yes, that's it Stuart …A much more important family. Officers, how terrible remiss of me; what with everything, I have forgotten my manners. Let me introduce Stuart and Mark … They are my close friends from church. Since the news, they have been round every day. They're fantastic, the jobs these two do for people. I'd be lost without them."

Stuart leant over and grabbed Mrs Lundy's hand.

"Like you said, we are a family and this is what families do."

"Thank the Lord for you two. I am blessed."

"You're doing a great job lads."

"Thank you, Dave; like I say, it's what families do."

"Yes, very noble of you. Now Mrs Lundy, this is not an easy conversation we're going to be having."

"Right, yes … I know."

"But it's something we're going to have to do. We want to bring to justice the person who did this to your husband, and this will help us in that task."

"Okay, I know. Please carry on."

"Thank you, Mrs Lundy. Just a simple first question for you, and it would really help us if you try to answer as honestly as you can. Did Mr Lundy have any enemies that you were aware of?"

"Gordon? No, not at all, he was a very popular man. I never heard a bad word said against him."

"Are you sure about that Mrs Lundy?"

"Oh yes, without a shadow of a doubt. He was a popular man. I honestly cannot remember ever hearing anybody say a bad word about him."

"Okay fine, Mrs Lundy. What about professionally though? I believe your husband had his own business, in furniture?"

"Yes, that's right. He bought and sold antique furniture. He was very good at it too. When he started, he just had a small, well … shed you would have to call it. Then he worked his way up to owning a shop on Appledore high street. He was very successful."

"I'm sure he was. Were you aware of any professional disagreements that your husband may have had? I could imagine it must be something of a dog-eat-dog business, what with the profits on offer. A lot of money about, maybe some jealously?"

"No. No. Mr Wrench, you must understand that Gordon was a charming man. He was a kind man. Everyone that ever met him loved him. And in his job, he was very professional. He would meet with, well competitors I suppose you could say, all the time. And he never mentioned any problems to me. He never seemed unduly concerned or anything. He would have told me if he was having any problems."

"I'm sure he would have Mrs Lundy, I'm just trying to establish a motive that's all."

"Yes, I know. It's okay."

"Thank you, Mrs Lundy. What was Mr Lundy's social circle like?"

"Well, as I've said, he was a popular man. He was also a very keen rugby player and as you can tell from some of these pictures, he had the build for it. The states that he used to come home in …I didn't know where to start. I would just say, 'Take them all off at the back door.' He loved his rugby. He was in the Territorial Army for years as well."

"Really?"

"Oh yes. He was in for years. In fact, most of his buddies came from there. He was based in West Leonard down the road … He went all over with them though camping, manoeuvres or whatever they're called. He loved it."

"Right …I couldn't help noticing that picture over there of a group of men, all suited and booted, arm in arm with your husband. Are those army colleagues?"

"Probably, which one?"

"This one. Can I show you?"

"Yes, go and get it."

Dave tiptoed to the far corner of the room.

"This one here."

"Yes, just take it down, don't worry. Let me have a look at it."

Dave gently removed the picture from the wall and brought it to her.

"It's a lovely picture Mrs Lundy."

"Yes, these are some of his rugby and army friends. I think this was taken at the Conservative Club just down the road, it looks like it. They were forever having benefit shows and charity nights. Or at least that's what they told me. It was probably just an excuse half the time to get a night out with the boys."

"Do you know any of these men, Mrs Lundy? Are you still in touch with any?"

"Well I'm not in touch with any of them; but let me see if I can remember any of their names. It was such a long time ago. Okay, him I don't know. I know him; he's Charlie Burns. God bless, he passed away years ago. I sometimes still see his wife in the shops ...Cancer, terrible shame. Him, I'm not sure of, I think it's Mr James. I think he was an army friend, but I may be wrong. I've no idea who that chap is. Oh, and I know this one ... oh dear, what's his name—"

"Have any been in touch, Mrs Lundy."

"No, not really. Although Mark, didn't you say that someone had phoned the other day?"

"Er ... yes. I'm sure he said his name was Mr Dolby. He rang to offer his condolences. Said he was an old friend of Mr Lundy's from his Territorial Army days. He said he was back in the area, and would call again to arrange to pop in to see you; but I asked him to give it a couple more weeks yet."

"Was your husband close to ... Mr Dolby did you say?"

"Yes, Dolby."

"Was he, Mrs Lundy?"

"Well ... I suppose so. He came around here a few times. I don't think he's on any of these, maybe the ones in the attic. He didn't come that often though. If I remember rightly, he was away on business a lot. As was Gordon, so I don't think that they saw that much of each other. I didn't know him that well. It was nice of him to call because I've not spoken to or seen him for ages."

"Did he pass on an address or a contact number, Mark?"

"No Mr Wrench, he didn't I'm afraid."

"Okay. Never mind. Okay ... right. Mrs Lundy, I am going to ask you a personal question. It's something I need to ask. Maybe you'd want to discuss it in private."

Dave stared at the suited men.

"No, that's fine. I want them to stay, please."

"That's fine Mrs Lundy, I was just making sure. Mrs Lundy, how was your marriage to Mr Lundy? Was it a happy one?"

Mrs Lundy rolled her eyes towards the heavens and blew out her cheeks before glancing at the numerous pictures of them together on the wall.

"Well, we had our ups and downs, like every other marriage. To be honest, we loved each other deeply. We had such a close bond. But, well, let's just say there were other elements of the marriage that didn't run that smoothly."

"How do you mean, Mrs Lundy?"

Stuart passed her a tissue from his pocket.

"Thank you dear."

"Well, I'm an old-fashioned girl from a small town. I suppose I was a little bit conservative. Well, I suppose I'm still a bit conservative …And a bit naïve about things. Oh dear, I wasn't very passionate Dave, if you know what I mean? I tried to be, but I just didn't know how to be. I had always been taught that, you know, that kind of thing was sinful and I couldn't get that out of my head. I just didn't think that it was that important. But it was important; it was important to Gordon. He was a red-blooded man and it must have been very hard for him. I don't think I really appreciated how hard it was for him. Well … let's just say he met those needs elsewhere."

"Affairs?"

"Yes, I'm afraid so."

"Was there anyone in particular that you were aware of?"

"I never knew names. I never wanted to know."

"Mrs Lundy, I'm sorry to press this point but you just said 'names.' Are we saying that he was unfaithful on more than one occasion?"

"Being older and wiser, yes, I think he was."

"Did you ever confront him about it?"

"I didn't need to. He confessed to me. On his knees, begging me for forgiveness, begging the Lord for forgiveness."

"He confessed?"

"Oh yes, he confessed. As I say, he begged me for forgiveness … On that very spot over there."

"And you are sure that he didn't give you any indication of names, or where they lived?"

"I told you Dave, I didn't need to know names or details. I just knew he was sorry and he wanted to change. And he did change. He changed completely."

"How do you mean change? In what way did he change?"

"He found the Lord. He found Christ."

"Did he?"

"Yes, he was shaken by the Holy Ghost. I'd never seen someone change so quickly. It had a profound effect on him. He changed. A new man reborn in Christ."

"Right, and how long was this before his disappearance, a year, a couple of months?"

"I don't know. Probably about four months or so."

"And in what way did he change, Mrs Lundy?"

"Well, he changed completely."

"In what way?"

Stuart jumped in again.

"If you have ever been touched by the Holy Ghost, you'd know, Dave."

"Right, well, unfortunately I haven't, so could you tell me more about how his behaviour changed."

"Oh, he was always at church. I was sure he wanted to make his peace for some of the things he had done, to me I mean. I'm sure of that."

"So, he converted then?"

"Well, if you like. He prayed. I heard him praying many a time and he stopped going out as much. And like I say, he never missed church. He would, if you pardon the pun, go religiously."

"And you think this was motivated by his guilty conscience?"

"Yes, maybe at first, but God works in mysterious ways."

"Right, what does that mean?"

"It was written in the stars, Dave. It was all part of God's will."

"Mrs Lundy, could we stick to the material facts please."

She turned towards Stuart.

"Spoken like a true non-believer."

"No, it's not that, Mrs Lundy. Like I said, I'm trying to establish a motive for your husband's death and from what you're now saying, the actions of a vengeful husband or boyfriend could be top of the list. Now, I'm not proposing that's what happened but it's our most credible motive at the moment."

"No, I'm sorry Dave. Yes, you could say it was guilt that drove his conversion but that's nothing without a commitment to change; and he had that in spades. Like I say, he was a man reborn, living a completely different life. I just don't want you going down any blind alleys."

"No, I understand that Mrs Lundy. I'm not doubting his conversion but people have long memories. Grudges persist unfortunately. People want revenge not redemption. They want to see their enemy suffer."

"And you think that's what happened to Gordon?"

"Well, I don't know … I certainly hope not but as I said, revenge is certainly one motive we will be closely looking at."

Her eyes began filling, shoulders caving in, reality like dynamite bringing the whole house down.

"Mrs Lundy, I'm sorry. I could have put that better."

Between tearful gasps, she managed some words.

"It's okay. I know what you mean. We're all prisoners of our past."

Mark jumped up from the sofa and put his arms around her shoulders.

"We need to end it for today gentlemen."

"No, absolutely, I completely agree."

He respectfully lifted her to her feet and guided her away.

"C'mon Rose, let's take you for a nice cup of tea and a lie down."

"Thanks again Mrs Lundy."

"Yeah, thank you Mrs Lundy."

She raised her right hand like an injured player acknowledging the crowd, Mark carefully closing the living room door behind them.

"God, I feel terrible."

"Don't feel bad Dave, she's up and down. She's on medication for her mood; it's hit and miss. She never thought he was dead, see. She used to say to me that the Lord wouldn't forsake her, that He would bring him back safe and sound. It was a double blow for her when he was found …Her faith has been severely tested. It's been heartbreaking to witness."

"I bet. I still feel like crap though."

"Don't worry Dave, we'll look after her. We'll see her through."

"Yes, I'm sure you will. She's in good hands …Right, well, if there's nothing else, I guess that's our lot for today. You got anything else, Ian?"

"No, only that picture."

"Oh yeah. We were going to ask Mrs Lundy whether we could borrow that picture we took from the wall. I suppose we'll have to leave it now though."

"No, take it. She won't mind."

"Are you sure Stuart? We'll bring it back."

"I wouldn't worry about it. She's hates that picture. She's always saying it."

"Why? It's a nice picture."

"She says she can't stand the look on their faces, 'like cats that have got all the cream.' I can't see it myself."

Dave lifted the picture towards his eye level.

"She's got a point, I suppose. They all look pretty self-satisfied."

"Maybe. No honestly, take it. She won't mind."

"That's really helpful, thanks Stuart."

"No, no, anything we can do to help …Right, okay then chaps, I'll show you out."

"Okay, thanks."

As they approached the front door, Stuart glanced around and lowered his voice.

"Listen chaps, there's one more thing, another person who may be able to help you with your enquiries."

"Yeah?"

"Yes, but I'd appreciate it if you didn't mention to Rose or Mark that I've given you his name."

"Okay, no problem."

"It's a chap called Reverend James. He mentioned to me the other day that he knew Mr Lundy well – he's been here since the early sixties, see. I've got his number here. I'm sure he won't mind if you gave him a ring."

"Yeah, that would be good. Is he far from here?"

"Just a couple of miles down the road."

"Perfect. A bit of a break, Ian."

"Sounds like it, Dave."

"Just one thing though, why wouldn't Mrs Lundy or your mate approve?"

"You'll know when you meet him."

24TH JANUARY 1975

S he finally prised open her eyes. She'd been labouring within a bleak semi-consciousness for a couple of hours now: a state appropriately soundtracked by the militant barrage of wind and rain still assaulting her hotel window. She tried moving but couldn't do it. It was like she was lying underneath concrete.

During the night, she was intermittently aware of pain. Was this real or a dream? The burning spears assailing her pelvic area was definitive proof: it was as real as you can get.

"Oh no. What's happened?"

There was a loud knock on the door.

"Sarah, Sarah ..."

She lurched forward. The contents of her brain colliding like shards in a snow globe.

"Sarah, we need to leave now. Come on, I don't want to be late."

She grabbed a towel and stumbled to the door. On opening, she found Dolby, his eyes volcanic, his fists clenched.

"Look at you. You've got ten minutes before we leave."

"I can't remember what happened. None of it."

"How very predictable ...You'll be pleased to know that I've had to give Mrs Chesterton ten quid to recompense her for her trouble, after your singing and shouting kept the whole bloody building up. Embarrassing, Sarah, is the word I would have to use."

"I don't know what you're talking about."

"Oh, I'm sure. C'mon, I'll meet you downstairs. Ten minutes."

Singing and shouting? That's not me. I didn't do anything like that.

She closed the door and began gathering her things. She pulled her yellow turtleneck sweater over her head; the wholeness of the acrylic a momentary haven.

It'll be someone else. They'll own up. They'll get found out.

She stood on one leg and wrestled with her tights. Another spasm of pain shot from her vagina. It felt so raw and damaged. The chafing afterheat of bad intercourse? No, she didn't sleep with him. Absolutely not. She would remember if she had.

She grabbed her bag and inspected the room for the final time. A guilty criminal leaving the scene ...*Oh my God, look at the sheet, it's soaked!* She tore it from the bed and tossed it through the bathroom window onto the sodden turf below. One misdemeanour less on her already stacked charge sheet.

Her weighted legs barely negotiated the blue floral stairs. *What's happened to me?* The two travelling salesmen were at the desk checking out. She dropped her head and kept moving.

They're going to kill me. Just ignore them and keep walking forward. Out the door, and home.

"Excuse me miss, are you okay?"

Is he talking to me? He can't be.

"Sorry miss, are you okay? Miss ..."

He is.

"I'm okay, thank you."

One of the men strode forward, placing his hand on her shoulder.

"Miss, take my advice. Get out of this. You were in pain last night and trust me this pain will endure. We should have called the police, but Joseph felt ...Listen, I have been there. I have seen it. Just get out."

"But I was too drunk, I can't remember for sure. I was shouting through the night though wasn't I?"

"Listen to me. Nothing that happened—"

Dolby opened the front door and re-entered reception.

"Sarah come on, we're going to be late. We need to go. Can I help you gentlemen?"

The man stepped backwards and swallowed hard.

"No sir. Not us, but you can help this young lady. Leave her alone sir."

For a couple of moments no one spoke.

"I'm sorry, but what the hell are you going on about?"

"The young lady sir, she—"

Dolby moved closer to the man.

"Listen, you fucking crank. I suggest you and your boyfriend mind your own business and fuck off, before I hurt you."

Dolby stared the salesman hard in the face. He stared back, seemingly determined to match his glare, before blinking and looking down upon his stolid raincoat.

"Now fuck off."

The men turned and walked away.

"Come on Sarah, let's go."

She rested her head on the passenger-side window. Within seconds, a terrible showreel began in her mind's eye.

The hotel bar. She's laughing with Dolby and another man.

The other man's features are distorted, as if they've been broken apart and put back together in the wrong order. A face in abstract, like a Picasso painting.

Next, she's lying in a darkened room; muffled voices surround her, as if she's underwater and they're not. A looming mass covers her. It's dense and solid, far too heavy to be Dolby. He's there though; sat in the corner, the glow of his cigarette lighter illuminating his ravening eyes. The body lies on her like a fallen statue; her desperate pushes only cementing its presence. A scream breaks from the depths of her gut but stalls in her gullet.

Then, another scene. Dolby and the other man dragging her kicking and screaming up the hotel stairs. Her shouting is shriller now but no one's coming to help. No one is taking any notice.

The passenger door flew open.

"Get out. We'll talk about this on Monday morning."

15TH NOVEMBER 1996

A thick glaze of frost covered everything, even the masses of dog shit adorning the pavements. This drop in temperature was provoking the usual hysteria from the huddled masses but not Adam. This weather was right up his street; it evoked in him a sense of frigid detachment – a natural buffer against his daily onslaught of feelings. As he strode through the eddying mist, he began fantasising that this shroud of numbness could be permanent. It certainly looked like it would take some shifting.

"Adam Grimes, you ugly bastard."

I don't fucking believe it. Fucking Flames. Of all the days …

"Oh Grimes, Grimes!"

Why the fuck did I not put my headphones on.

"Oi, I'm fucking talking to you."

No choice.

He turned around and weighed him up. A real street animal: pencil thin with jutting teeth and ravenous blue eyes. His real name wasn't Flames, it was John Fleming. He earned his moniker due to his love of setting fire to things, things like the local primary school and church. The word on the street was you could probably beat him in a fist fight but you would have to kill him. Otherwise, he would keep coming back, with knives, coshes, and ultimately a can of lighter fluid.

"Good job you turned around then Grimes or I'd have banged you out for being ignorant."

"Sorry mate, I was miles away."

"Yeah, you're a docile cunt alright."

"I know, yeah. We're you going?"

"Meeting with my fucking parole officer. Right cunt he is."

"Yeah."

"Yeah, nearly twatted him last week; he was trying to be a smart fucker."

"Was he?"

"Called me a fucking bully. A fucking bully! That close from butting the old bastard I was."

"Right."

"Where are you going anyway Grimes?"

"Just for a walk, I'm right into a bit of exercise at the minute."

"Are you fucking mad, it's freezing."

"Nah, it's better on a bracing day."

"You're fucking nuts. How's that garden furniture you're holding for me?"

"Funny you should mention that, I was going to ask when you're planning on picking it up. It's just I'm a bit short on space at the minute."

"So am I, why do you think you're housing it for me? Just keep hold of it for a bit longer. Don't be selling any of it mind."

"No, of course not mate."

"Good. Anyway … listen I'm a bit short at the moment, could you lend me a tenner?"

I knew it. Either he mugs you or batters you. Fuck this. Over my dead body.

"I swear down, I've not got it mate."

"No?"

"No, honest, I'm really short at the minute mate."

"That's the way it's going to be then, eh. You can't give your old mate a little borrow."

"You know I would Flames. If I had it, I'd give it you."

"Right. Take that you cunt."

The blow was as inconsequential as a feather. *You fucking piece of shit.* His fingers curled into a fist. The resistance starts here. The time was now.

Oh no, not his pocket.

"If you don't give it me, I'll slice you to fucking ribbons. Don't tempt me Grimes, because I'll do it."

"There's no need for that mate. Just chill—"

"Give me the fucking money, now!"

No choice.

He reached into the depths of his trousers and pulled out the last of his dole.

"I didn't think that I had it, sorry. Here you go."

"You know, it comes to something when a mate has to threaten to cut a childhood friend just to borrow a tenner from him."

"I didn't think I had it. I swear down, I didn't."

"You've fucking changed Grimes. There's something not right with you."

"I've not, I've not, I didn't think I had it."

"Yeah, you've got ideas above your fucking station."

27TH JANUARY 1975

A chorus of familiar sounds emanated from above: the creak of floorboards, a wounded cough, the rattle of dry hinges. The clock on the living room wall read a quarter to five. *He can't be. Not at this time. Never in a million years.*

Her bed was intolerable so she'd moved to the downstairs sofa. Despite its velouresque caress soothing her carpet burns, her eyes had stayed open all night. She'd consoled herself with the promise of an early dart for it – she couldn't face him this morning, or perhaps ever again – but like everything else, this looked like it was going down the shitter.

The frosted-glass door opened slowly.

"Hey love, I was going for a wee and saw your door ajar …I got a shock when you weren't in bed. What are you doing down here?"

"Didn't sleep very well Dad, thought I'd have a change of scene."

"Why couldn't you sleep?"

"No reason Dad. Sometimes you're just not tired are you?"

"No, I suppose not. Hey, it'll be all that excitement. You know, now that you're working for the big boss."

"Yeah, probably."

"How was your trip anyway? You've barely said a word about

it. Did it go okay?"

"Fine Dad. It went fine."

"What was the hotel like? Posh I bet."

"Yeah, you could say that."

"And the meeting?"

"Sorry?"

"How did your meeting go?"

"Fine Dad, it went fine."

"Good. Good. Do you want a cuppa?"

"No thanks."

"Are you okay love? You seem a bit down."

"Fine Dad. I'm just tired."

"C'mon sweet, I can always tell when my best girl is worrying about something."

"No, I'm not, honestly I'm not."

"You can't kid me ..."

"Dad leave it, I'm fine. Stop going on."

"'Coz you know that—"

"Dad!"

"Okay princess, if you're sure. I'll put the emersion on, warm the bathroom up."

"Okay Dad. Thank you."

He was once her greatest confidante: she would tell him everything. Her mum wasn't interested – unless delivering censure – then she became very interested indeed. Her dad was the opposite; sheltering her from pain was his life's motivation and he had a sixth sense for when she was upset. In these moments he would take her for a walk in the park and tell her to open up; that he would love her no matter what;

that he would make it all better. And he always did.

Once, she bunked of school, strolling around the boutiques in town, eating her sandwiches in Piccadilly Gardens. She got busted – a rouge fire bell necessitating an afternoon roll call. The headmaster demanded an urgent meeting with her mum and dad. Her mum's response would be all too predictable. Stricken with worry, Sarah confessed to her dad through a fountain of tears. Unable to bear her distress, he rang the school and told them it was all his fault: he had taken her to a medical appointment and forgotten to inform them. He was very sorry and would make sure it would never happen again. And it never did.

This time though, her dad would be the last person she could tell.

The sixty-seven bus sputtered to a halt, reigniting the bonfire in her gut. *Of all the days to have a clear run of bloody traffic.* She pushed through the wall of passengers towards the exit. Last week, on a wave of exhilaration, she was leaving them behind. Now, their denials and disappointments, the emptiness of their routines, would be a blessed relief. That was her rut and she wanted back in.

She inched through the layers of fumes, the eyes in the stalled motors looking her up and down, questions buzzing around her head like irritated bees.

What will he say? Will he sack me? Did we shag? Who was the other guy? Were the salesmen nuts or telling the truth? Why can't I remember anything?

The quietness of the depot panicked her. *Had he told them all?*

Clive strode in through the door leading from the forecourt.

"Hey Sarah, how are you girl? I believe you work directly for the man now, the Big White Chief."

"Who told you?"

"Whoa, easy girl. Just glad to be seeing you every day, that's all …Add a bit of colour to the place."

"I'm sorry to snap Clive. I'm just a bit tired."

"No problem girl. I know Monday. We all know Mondays – the worst of all the days."

"Where is everyone?"

"Out the back like a pack of zombies. They never learn girl, always keep out of The Eagle on Sunday lunchtime, coz you never get out before midnight."

"Is he in?"

"The Chief? Aye he's in. He was here before me …Sat in his rabbit hutch."

The door of his office flung open. He swaggered towards the balcony, his left cheek twitching.

"I'll thank you for not keeping my staff from their work, Jackson."

"You've no need to thank me boss. I'm a naturally friendly guy, just wishing Sarah all the best in her new job."

"Jackson, you never disappoint me. Laid back, like so many of your kind. Will come in useful when you are troubling the doors of the labour exchange; be like a home from home for you and all your mates. By the way, where are the rest of the soon to be ex-workforce?"

"Out the back sir, checking the William Street order."

"Good. All sixteen of them, what a good use of labour. Do you think we'll need some reinforcements to get the dinner-time sandwiches in?"

"Nah, should be okay boss."

"Good. Good."

He turned back towards his office, before spinning around.

"Just one more thing Jackson, before I forget … if you and that lazy fucking shower that call themselves mechanics do not get to work within the next minute, it will be my pleasure to dock you all a morning's pay. Any longer than that and you are all fucking fired …Okay? Good. Now fucking move!"

"Sure thing boss."

"When you're ready Miss Gregory, we've a lot to get on with."

He slammed the door behind him.

"You know girl, spending each day with him in there …Well, let's just say life's too short. If you know what I mean."

"I know exactly what you mean."

She slowly pushed the door open. He was sitting at his desk, eyes fixed on a large jotting pad. She focused on the distant green moors beyond his shoulder on the edges of the city. *I want to be there. Not here. I want to be there. All on my own.*

"I've got some filing that I will need you to do in accounts, please. It shouldn't take long, and then I want to dictate a letter to you."

"Okay."

As she scooped up the mountain of invoices from the corner of his desk, a picture of Dolby and another man with flaxen hair and broad shoulders captured her gaze.

Oh fucking hell, it's him. It's him. Him! The man dragging me up the stairs, the man in the hotel room.

The image on the journey home from Luton was like a jigsaw puzzle: the pieces for his legs and torso were in place, just not his facial features. That piece was missing, until now. She ran into the filing room, vomit curdling in the back of her throat. *What am I going to do? Now that it's all real …Now that it's real life.*

The door swung open.

"Sorry, I forgot I need these doing as well."

She faced the wall.

"Okay."

"And you'll need to sign this admin order as well, please."

"Just leave it on there."

"Sarah, are you okay?"

"Yes, Mr Dolby."

"Sarah, what on earth is the matter?"

He touched her shoulder, his fingers massaging the chiffon fabric of her blouse. That touch, the human touch, was the final straw – like taking the top off a shaken bottle of fizzy pop. A torrent of emotion burst through her, tearing her from her rock of Northern reticence; her trauma echoing around the depot.

"Jesus Sarah, whatever is the matter. Sarah please just—"

There was a loud bang on the door.

"Sarah it's Clive, are you okay? Sarah …"

Clive pushed the door open but Dolby rammed it shut with his shoulder, his oily fringe flailing over his face.

"Jackson, get back to work. Fucking get back to work now."

"Sarah, are you okay in there?"

"Jackson, can't you hear she's upset? …Sarah please, just a minute—"

"Sarah, it's okay, I'm coming in."

"Jackson fuck off, or you're sacked."

Clive won; the force of his weight firing Dolby into one of the filing cabinets.

"Jackson, you idiot."

He carried her out without saying a word.

"It's nothing to do with me why she's crying, nothing to do with me at all. Jackson, you idiot, bring her back. Sarah!"

Her safe place was an empty trailer in which Clive had flattened some cardboard boxes for them to sit on.

"Girl, you don't cry like that for no reason."

"Honest Clive, I've no idea why that happened."

"It must have been something he said, something he did. He's made so many people cry in there but never like that."

"No, honestly Clive, it wasn't. My dad's not been so well. I've tried not to think about it, pushed it to the back of my mind. It must have just got too much."

"Why didn't you say so girl. Is he going to be okay?"

"Oh yes. He'll be okay."

"You know, I lost my dad when I was young."

"Did you?"

"Yeah I did. We had only been in England four years. I went to the shop to get his tobacco and his paper, and when I got back to the house my mother wouldn't let me in. She'd found him dead in his chair."

"How old were you?"

"Just a young boy, I was only fourteen. It was hard, you know, very hard. But I learned to be tough. And so will you girl."

"I don't think he will die Clive."

"Well there you go girl, dry your eyes then."

He handed her a stained, oily rag.

"Ha, no thank you Clive. I've got some tissues in my bag."

"You know girl you're a fine lady, but there's one thing I have noticed about you. Everyone here likes you. The other secretaries like you. And Dolby, well he especially likes you, right? All us lot think you're great. But you don't seem to like yourself. And you know you should coz you are a very good person, you know? And don't let anyone tell you different."

This was true. The root of her low self-esteem was a teenage growth spurt that came out of the blue. A ladder of bones, the other kids nicknamed her the "freak" and this broke her, repeatedly. To negate the abuse, she would wear multiple school jumpers and stuff masses of tissues down her bra. It didn't work. The name-calling continued. In fact, it got worse.

Everyone was looking and laughing at her. She knew this. And even if they weren't, they soon would be. She even stopped going to the Tuesday and Thursday dance nights at the Eccles Palais. No longer could she endure the ritual of the final song – the boys swaggering over to where the girls were sitting and picking a lucky lady to slow dance with and walk home. The feeling of being analysed and graded, weighed and considered but ultimately rejected, was just too much. Damaged goods in a perpetual market place.

"No, no, I do like myself. Well not a lot like, but enough. I'm not in love with myself or anything. I just think I'm okay."

"Girl, you're more than just okay. You're great, you know? Come here."

He wrapped his large frame around her; pulling her head into the vast recess of his shoulder.

"Ahem. I hope I'm not interrupting anything."

Dolby stood outside the entrance to the empty berth.

"What, no man. I'm just comforting Sarah."

"Yes, it certainly looked like it."

"She was upset."

"I bet."

"She was sobbing man."

"And you had to play the big hero. What is it with your lot and white women?"

"Now listen Dolby, don't push me. I don't need this fucking job as much as I need to paste you all round this fucking forecourt."

"No please don't. Mr Dolby, he—"

Clive jumped from the artic and got into Dolby's face.

"Now walk away Jackson. Don't be stupid. Mechanics like you are ten a penny you know."

"Yeah Dolby, but one more bit of shit from you and I will get every man to walk out of here …Leave you all on your own."

"And they'd all do that for you would they Jackson? Are they your, how do you say, brethren?"

"That's right boss, every last one. Then bye-bye William Street order, bye-bye career."

Dolby leant into Clive's left ear, gently whispering and grinding his teeth at the same time, the personification of unhinged affability.

"Careful now, that's two threats in the space of a minute. You really have no idea of what I am capable of do you Jackson. You have not got the slightest fucking clue who you're dealing with."

"Please stop it Mr Dolby. Clive was just comforting me. I asked him to. He's done nothing wrong."

Dolby stared hard into Clive's eyes, before patting him on his shoulder.

"Of course not Sarah. Don't worry, it's you we're both worried about. We just lost our rag, didn't we Clive? Just because we're worried about you, that's all. Isn't that right Clive?"

"If you say so Dolby."

"Yes, anyway, off you go Clive. You've done your bit. Let me have five minutes alone with the girl."

Clive looked towards Sarah and nodded his head.

"Yes, it's fine Clive, you go. Thank you so much."

"You sure?"

"Yes, thanks Clive."

Dolby spoke in that nutcase voice again.

"You heard the girl, Clive. Off you go. I am allowed to speak to staff on their own you know. I'm only the fucking manager around here."

"Shout me if you need me girl."

"Okay Clive. Thank you."

Clive slowly left the scene.

"Mr Dolby, I don't want Clive to be in trouble."

"Don't be silly Sarah; of course he isn't in trouble. Like I say, he's just worried about you, like we all are. Listen Sarah, can we talk about this in the office eh?"

"I'd rather not Mr Dolby. I would rather stay here for a bit longer."

"Would you not be better in a warm office?"

"No, I just want to stay here for a bit."

"Okay then. Here we go."

Dolby clambered into the artic and sat opposite her.

"Oh, it's not too bad here is it? Bit dirty but we'll make do ...Right, I think this has something to do with Luton, has it not?"

"No, it's not. It's nothing to do with Luton. My dad's ill, that's all."

"Oh my God, what's the matter with him?"

"It's his chest. His chest is bad."

"It's not … you know, cancer is it Sarah?"

"No, no. Nothing like that."

"Is he going to be okay?"

"Okay Mr Dolby that's not it. It is to do with Luton. There is something I need to ask you. There's something else."

"Okay."

"What happened that night? Something happened and I can't remember … well I can remember bits but only snapshots."

"Sarah, you know very well what went on."

"No, I don't. I swear I don't."

"C'mon Sarah, I wasn't born yesterday. It's the oldest trick in the book, 'I can't remember.'"

"I can't, only little bits. That bloke in the picture in your office, he was with us."

"That's right, Gordon Lundy. Oh, you got to know Gordon very well didn't you? Close up and very personal. Fine fucking friend he turned out to be and that's all I'll say on that."

"What?"

"C'mon Sarah, *you* know. You both made a fool out of me. All over each other right in front of my face. You humiliated me. By rights, it should be me in tears."

"No. No. I've never spoken to him before, I've never seen him before, I don't know him."

"Sarah, are you seriously telling me you don't remember a thing about that night – is that what you're really telling me?"

"Yes, that's what I'm really telling you."

"Oh come on. Please …"

"The only thing I can remember, after the meeting with those Scottish men, is drinking in that bar. Just me and you."

"Well you did put it back a bit, I suppose—"

"Only because you forced it down me!"

"Whoa, now hang on a second Sarah. I don't like what you're implying here at all."

"You did. I remember telling you I'd had enough."

"Oh, so you remember that then."

"He attacked me and you watched. I didn't want to—"

"I'm sorry, what did you say?"

"You were watching. I saw you in a dream I had about it. You were in the room."

"'In a dream you had about it.' What on earth do you take me for? I was sat in my room, with a pillow over my head, my heart breaking. That's disgusting, it really is. You seduced him in front of my face. You humiliated me. You knew that I liked you, and you knew how hard it was for me to tell you, yet you still did it to me. Now you're blaming me …You're a right piece of work, you are. A champion liar and a champion tart."

Teardrops began falling down her cheeks; compounding the lubricity of the wagon floor.

"I'm sorry Sarah, I didn't mean that."

He scooched closer and draped his arm around her shoulder.

"No Sarah, he didn't attack you. He didn't force himself on you. In a terribly perverse way, I wish he had – God forgive me for saying it."

"He did. You were there watching."

"No, no, no. Sarah listen … listen dear. Please listen. It's okay. I know what's happening here."

"Yes, so do I."

"No. No. Listen. Sarah, please listen. Please just let me speak … Years ago, when I was in the army, I did a couple of tours of Ireland. In Belfast. One day we got involved in an exchange with some delinquent Catholic kids. They had been throwing petrol bombs, some small arms fire – the usual crap. They were Provisional wannabees, small fry really. Anyway, me and my mate Terry Jenkins – proper Welsh lad he was, real valley boy – bumped into these little bastards later in the evening, when they were coming home from their local pub. We decided to teach them a lesson …Nothing too heavy mind, just a bit of a slap. Well, Terry begins to go too far. He starts really laying into this lad. I try to get him off him, but there's no way. He's like a wild animal. Eventually I prise him off. The lad's practically dead. Ends up in a coma, intensive care, but thankfully pulls through in the end. They made some enquiries. The Fenian bigwigs and busybodies from the estate get involved, and the next thing you know our Brigade Commander is interviewing us. Despite my better judgement, we decide to lie about it – we just denied everything. The thing was though, when Terry denied it he genuinely believed that he hadn't done anything. He believed that someone else must have got to them. That's when I first experienced someone being in denial. Have you ever heard of it?"

"What? No, I'm not denying anything."

"You're not *consciously* denying anything – it's a defence mechanism."

"What do you mean?"

"Look Sarah, as soon he walked in I could see there was an attraction between the both of you. It was like a tension in the air. It's the same old story I'm afraid. When he's around, I don't get a look in. It's the blond hair and broad shoulders. And, yes, I was in bad form giving you that much to drink. I just wanted us to celebrate a job well done. However trust me, everything you did that night was not because you were drunk. Well … yes, in a way I suppose you were; you were drunk on lust. I just wish you hadn't done it in front of *me*. The pain of hearing you two at it – his horrid grunts, you screaming like a banshee, him boasting about it to me at breakfast – will never leave me."

"That didn't happen. I'm not like that. How could it happen if I don't remember a thing about it?"

"This is what I'm saying …Because you made a mistake, because you gave in to temptation, because you're not like that, your mind has blocked it out. It's pure self-survival. And well, I suppose as you say, the drink wouldn't have helped. Some people can't remember things the next day. Unfortunately for me, I'm not one of these people; I remember everything about that wretched night."

"Why didn't you talk about it then? In the morning, why didn't you tell me then? You didn't say a thing, you said I fell over drunk and was sick. Why didn't you have a go at me then?"

"Jesus Sarah, what was there left to say on the subject? You picked my mate over me and rubbed my nose in it. I wasn't in the mood to perform an inquest on the subject. It was too painful; I've been hurt too many times before. Stiff upper lip, that's my way."

"No, I'm not like that."

"Sarah, I can only give you my word that I'm telling the truth. My word means a lot. You do not get where I am without having integrity. I'm a man of the armed forces, I'd never do that. Look, there's no real harm done. We've both learnt lessons. We all do things we regret. And don't worry; I will make sure he never comes around to the office, so you won't have to see him. That is, if that's what you want?"

"Of course that's what I want."

"C'mon Sarah, forget about it now. You messed up when you were drunk. Who hasn't done that?"

"What about the dream?"

"Sarah, you had a dream. You saw what you wanted to see. You didn't see the truth, did you?"

"I don't know."

"No, you didn't. Look, come here. Worst things happen at sea you know. It's your own fault for being so damn gorgeous."

He wrapped his arms around her: the barbed fabric of his tweed suit, his xylophone-like rib cage, the cloying odour of *Old Spice*, a very different beast to Clive.

I'm being lifted. Sucked into something I can't stop.

Dolby looked into her eyes.

"Sarah, please kiss me."

2ND JULY 2002

The silver Mondeo roared down a dust bowl of a country lane, past lime-green meadows and unruly thickets, cows and their diffident young, towards St Mary's church for an afternoon rendezvous with Reverend James.

"Fuck, it's too warm."

"Stop complaining Harington. It's bloody lovely."

"There's no air."

"You'd be complaining if it was raining."

"Aye, I suppose so. It certainly beats Manchester."

"Exactly."

"He was pretty keen to speak to us."

"Hmm."

"Wonder what he's going to come up with?"

"We'll soon find out. Now if I'm right, we should be just down here. Yep, here we are."

The Mondeo pulled up alongside a small grass verge.

"God, it's beautiful. Is that roof thatched?"

"I think so."

The scene spoke to Dave of an England he'd presumed dead, or at least on its last legs: A medieval chapel built of straw and stone, its spire towering all the way up to heaven; flocks of birds in huge oak trees chorusing a sweet serenade; a vintage push bike leaning against a pebbled wall.

"God's own country, Harington."

"What?"

"Nothing, hurry up."

They climbed out of the Mondeo, Dave leading the way down the path.

"Hey Dave ..."

"What?"

"I feel like Morse."

"Shut up you dick. I'll knock on the main door, you check out the sides."

Dave strode towards the large gothic door and rattled its brass handle.

Yeah, coming through here, strewn with confetti with Anita from HR ...She'd jump at the chance, low maintenance too. She'll get a part-time job in that tea shop when the kids are old enough. I'll have made Chief Inspector and taken that wine-making course—.

"Dave?"

"Yeah."

"There's a small cottage around this side."

"We'll try there. There's no sign of life here."

Ian now took the lead, walking directly over the graves.

"Oi!"

"What?"

"Walking on the graves of the dead."

"Can you hear them complaining, Dave?"

"Not in this realm maybe, but they'll be sat somewhere very unimpressed."

"Fucking hell, you belong with Mrs Lundy and her mates."

"Fuck off, I'm just saying, always respect the dead."

"I don't worry about the dead; it's the fucking living that bother me. Right boss, I'll let you do the honours."

"Thank you."

"You're welcome."

The bronzed stable door was already open. They inched into a porch area filled with canvas coats and mucky Wellingtons.

"Hello? Is there anybody there? Hello?"

"Knock on the front door."

"Hang on, give me a chance."

Through the glass pane, Dave spotted a swollen-looking man, rocking on a wooden chair.

"He's in. I can see him."

"Knock harder."

"Hang on he's coming. He doesn't look like a vicar."

"I don't think there's a defined look, Dave."

"He looks like that wrestler from the Eighties, you know?"

"What?"

"That wrestler ...Fuck, what's his name?"

"Hulk Hogan?"

"No ..."

"Andre the Giant?"

"No, not fucking Andre the Giant."

"Well I don't know, let me—"

"Mick McManus!"

"Who?"

"Mick McManus. You know, on *World of Sport.*"

"Never heard of him."

"Hang on, hang on, I'm coming. I've just got to find these bastard keys. Bloody bastard keys, where are you?"

"They said he was a card, Ian ..."

"Jesus, he's sounds more like the full fucking deck."

The door unbolted.

"I am sorry about that. Bloody keys, a constant tormentor of mine."

"Right sir, yes."

"Yes, a real pain. Anyway, you must be those two young men from the police – from Manchester, all the way from Manchester."

"That's right, and you must be Reverend James."

"The very same. Please, come in chaps."

"Thank you. I'm Detective Sergeant Dave Wrench and this is Detective Constable Ian Harington."

"Hello Reverend."

"Hello, young man. Listen boys, I'm Bill and if you don't mind I will address you as Dave and Ian. Is that okay?"

"Yes, of course, that's fine."

"Good. I cannot stand formalities. Come and sit down. You want a drink? Tea, coffee, or something colder? It's so terribly hot."

"I'll have a cold drink, please."

"Right you are, Dave."

"Me too, thanks Bill."

"Okay boys, lemonade okay?"

"Great."

"Yes good, thanks."

"Good. Right, have a seat in the drawing room."

"Okay, thanks."

The room resembled a museum exhibition piece. A battered desk and an open fireplace encased within a marbled hearth its most prominent features.

"It's like my auntie's place in Halifax, only that's dustier."

"I don't think anything could be duster than this place, Ian."

"Miles worse mate. My sister's fella runs a cleaning company and last year we all chipped in for a deep clean. She had pictures on the walls that she didn't even know she had. Twelve months on, it's nearly as bad."

"I'd rather die than live in filth."

"You don't need to mate. Not with the prices *Soapy Buckets* charge, I'll get you my sister's number."

"Fuck off."

The wooden door flew open.

"Jesus, I don't know my own strength. Anyway, here we are boys … grab these while they're nice and cold."

"Thank you."

"Yes, that's nice of you, thanks."

"You're welcome. Right … oh excuse me, these bloody bones. Never get old gentlemen. Stay young if you can. This hip of mine has been giving me jip all day."

"Are you okay? Do you want to sit here?"

"No no, I'm okay Dave. I'm fine on old Joanne. That's what I call my chair …You've probably guessed gents, I'm as daft as a brush."

"Right."

"Bill, you said on the phone—"

"Hang on son, just let me get down. Ow … you … bastard."

"Are you sure we can't help you?"

"No, I'm fine now. Just got to get settled …That's it. Right, go on Dave."

"Sure? Okay, you said that you may have some information for us about Mr Lundy."

"Yes Dave, I saw the news. They found Gordon, after all these years. Terrible eh?"

"Yes it is. Did you know him, Bill?"

"Yes, I suppose I did. Just before he disappeared I had some dealings with him."

"Dealings, Bill?"

"Yeah, it was strange really. I mean I knew Rose, I knew Rose well. She was a faithful member of my congregation. Gordon never darkened the door though, not even at Christmas – when even the most ardent sinners in the village are forced to pay a visit. Anyway, out of the blue he started attending. I was flabbergasted to be honest. He came to the Sunday service. He probably came around two or three times, and then one day he simply knocked on the cottage door and asked whether he could come in for a chat. So I said 'yes, of course.'"

"Is that usual?"

"Can be. I mean, if someone especially wants support, and it's outside of normal church hours. Put it this way, I never turn anyone away."

"Why do you think he showed a sudden interest in religion Bill?"

"Forgiveness, I suppose."

"Forgiveness for what, Bill?"

"Initially, I thought it was because of how he had treated Rose. I mean, he was a bit of a shit towards her."

"In what way Bill?"

"Well, it was an open secret in the village he wasn't a faithful man. His affairs were the talk of the town, so to speak."

"I've heard. So, there were a fair few people with a grudge against him?"

"Well yes, silently though. He was a big lad was Gordon. He not only had a reputation as a womaniser but he could also be a bit intimidating, quick to temper, that kind of thing. Handy with his fists. People tended to give him a wide berth. Put it this way, there were many who had grounds to knock his block off – not that I would condone that kind of thing, you understand – but I never knew of anyone trying it. He wasn't liked. However, I don't think anybody would have ever confronted him. Not in this village, anyway."

"Can you remember any names or addresses of anyone who could have held a grudge against him?"

"Well, my memory isn't that great. I remember he was caught with the daughter of the lead in my choir. Joanne Rudge, I think she was called. She was only nineteen. Then there was Geoff Clarke's wife. Word was that he caught them at it, if you know what I mean."

"Do they still live in the village, Bill?"

"I don't think they're around anymore. It was such a long time ago you see. I mean, I'll check with my secretary and let you know. She's got a better nose for gossip and a lot better memory than me. But it's a bit of a long shot."

"If you would, thanks Bill. So, you think that it was guilt about his affairs that pushed him towards the church?"

"Like I said, at the beginning. And to be fair, he did want forgiveness for how he had treated Rose but to be honest, he was more concerned about how he'd treated other people."

"Other people?"

"Yes, other people. Women mostly."

"In what way Bill? Why did he feel bad about how he treated them?"

"Well, it all sounded pretty rough boys, to be honest."

"Go on."

"He'd say things like 'we should never have gone that far.' That's the phrase he would always use, 'going too far.' He said that he had gone too far with a young girl and that really bothered him."

"What did he mean by going too far?"

"Well, perhaps deliberately. He didn't talk in specifics that much. But I remember him saying things like 'I didn't want to hurt her but he forced me to.' Or, 'she didn't want to do it but we made her.' I mean you can use your imagination, can't you? It doesn't take a rocket scientist to work out what he was referring to does it?"

"No Bill, it doesn't. Who forced him?"

"Sorry?"

"You mentioned that he said someone forced him to hurt her, Bill. Who did he mean?"

"Now that was interesting. He would refer to this guy quite a lot. I got the impression that he was a big influence on things."

"How do you mean?"

"Well, he seemed so scared of him. You could see the fear in his eyes when he talked about him. That was a big surprise for me, as I couldn't imagine Gordon fearing anyone. It was like this man had some kind of power over him. I remember him calling this man the Devil."

"What was his name, Bill? Can you remember?"

"No, like I say, he wouldn't go into specifics. I did have a theory that this man didn't actually exist and that it was a personification of his id, but I'm not so sure now. I may have had a lot of sun that day. A bit like today, I suppose."

"Do you think that now Bill?"

"God knows gents."

"So, what advice did you give him? Can you remember what you said to him?"

"Where to start …It wasn't easy, let me tell you. He was a very, very strange man was Gordon."

"How do you mean Bill?"

"Well, I remember talking to him about his childhood. Apparently, his dad left him when he was a babe in arms and his mother had to work like a dog to keep their heads above water. He told me he was pretty much brought up by his grandmother. Anyway, she died when he was in his early teens. I said something like that must have been traumatic but he said he never gave it a second thought. I remember him saying his mum was upset that he never talked about her. And do you know what he said?"

"Go on."

"He didn't see why he should, as he never saw her after she died. Now tell me that's not ice cold."

"Yeah, that's an unusual thing to say …Anything else Bill?"

"Sorry?"

"Did you tell him anything else?"

"Erm…Well, I would have advised him to ask for God's forgiveness, and move on. Get the monkey of his back, because it was destroying him …'Make sure you don't do it again,' that kind of thing. The problem was he thought God was punishing him for all this. He thought that once God forgave him, he would get his daughter back. I mean, it doesn't work like that. He was setting himself up for a big fall in my eyes."

"His daughter?"

"Yes, his daughter. Didn't I mention her?"

"No, you didn't mention it Bill."

"I didn't?"

"No. Trust me you didn't Bill. His daughter with Rose?"

"No, he didn't have any kids with Rose. I presumed it was from one of his many affairs."

"Again, any names Bill?"

"Not a sausage, I'm afraid boys."

"And who had taken her away?"

"Well he never said, and I didn't think to ask."

"You didn't think to ask?"

"Well, I presumed … well I can't remember what I presumed to be honest."

"How old was the girl?"

"Again, he never said."

"But he was affected by his daughter's absence? From what you've said, he was a bit of an emotional blank space."

"Well there you go, another contradiction …You could see the pain in his eyes. I remember him saying that she was very special. He was certainly bothered more about her than his old granny, that's for sure."

"Did all this not raise a few alarm bells Bill?"

"It doesn't sound good, does it? I mean, I'm speaking the words and hearing them, and it doesn't sound good."

"If I'm honest Bill, I'm struggling to get my head around it. To me, it sounds like a group of men physically abusing women. There's a kid in the mix, and he's telling you all about it."

"Yes, I think you're right. It was so long ago though but yes, I'm surprised I didn't do more. But I didn't have any names. I had nothing to go on."

"Tell me about his last visit to you. What are your recollections of it?"

"He seemed focused, but also a little bit altered, a bit out there. He said he was determined to turn things around quickly, to get back on the right course. He said he had been thinking a lot and he knew how to make things right. He seemed determined. He thanked me, and if I remember correctly he'd got me a bottle of sherry, which was rather nice of him. Again, an element of his character that I hadn't seen before."

"Was this the last time you saw him?"

"Yes. It was."

"What about the other man?"

"What about him?"

"Was he going to be involved in making things right?"

"I haven't a clue."

"And you didn't do or say anything when you found out he was missing?"

"The gossip was that he had left town with another woman. I presumed he had left, that he wasn't missing. I just imagined his conversion to have fallen by the wayside, to be honest."

"Didn't you think that there were grounds to speak to the police at the time, Bill?"

"Look gentlemen, you have to understand the context in which he spoke to me. We don't have a seal of confessional or anything like that in our faith, but disclosures of one-to-one conversations are still frowned upon. Especially if there's no specific evidence pointing to, well you know, a specific crime taking place, or anything like that ...And there wasn't in this case. He spoke to me in confidence, he spoke to God in confidence and I didn't think I had grounds to break that bond. But yes, in hindsight, it is a fair point ... maybe I should have been more vigilant. Now, I would be more vigilant. It was a different time."

"I would contest that there were no grounds to speak to the—"

Dave's mobile phone began ringing.

"Oh shit, sorry about this."

A grimace of surprise spread across Harington's face. Wasn't he supposed to be a pro?

"Sorry, I'll have to take this."

He ran out of the room.

"Mum, are you okay?"

"David, David is that you?"

"Yes Mum, are you okay?"

"Not really dear."

"Why, what's the matter?"

"I don't quite know how to say this ..."

"Go on Mum, what's up?"

"Well, it's your father, David ... he's left me."

11TH DECEMBER 1996

New Direction's imperial period of the late seventies, where they shaped the decorative zeitgeist with their revelations in velour and wicker was a distant memory. They were now barely holding a niche in never-never land; their warehouse a refuge for the strays of the commodity class, waiting for less discerning customers to take them home for Christmas.

The building itself was windowless but filled with cheap florescent light – the type the Stasi would use for purposes of state terror. This and the building's heavily glossed white walls gave the place a hyper-real quality. Adam called it Kubrickesque. Which is a definite improvement on some of the things he has called his other jobs.

The job was more pressured than he had expected too, as things were not placed in numbered order, or even in order of type. Ergo, he spent his days running down aisles looking for a chest expander or a juicer, while the shop attendant at the front repeatedly barked out the item's number. After a week, the supervisor asked him whether he would like to go on the night shift. It was a no-brainer.

He shared this shift with four other workers. Three of these were also new starters, school leavers from Adam's estate – Tat, Mat, and Gat. They were largely mute, occasionally communicating through a grunt or a volley of spit. And although they shared the same birthplace, they were like men from different centuries – his post-hippie lexicon utterly incomprehensible to them, the fact they would prefer decapitation to removing their baseball caps, baffling to him. He could only sympathise with them though. This was now their life, forever and forever.

His step ladder swayed like a Hogmanay drunk. This delivery would be on the shelves before the close of play if it killed him. It was a matter of professional pride. Especially since he'd spent half his shift kipping in home improvement.

"Adam? Adam?"

Fuck, Tanner.

"Just in here, Mr Tanner. Just finishing off."

"Adam, it's five past eight, we don't pay overtime you know."

"I know, I'm just finishing this off, then I'm done."

"Hey, I'm not complaining. I like a man dedicated to his work."

"Right, with you now."

He climbed down the ladder and doffed his cap. Tanner was the site manager and a real class act – an exemplar for ageing with his grey mane and cashmere scarf.

"There's something different about this place Adam. What have you been up to?"

"Well, I hope you don't mind but I've just had a bit of a reorganise. It was, if you don't mind me saying, a bit of a mess. Should make it easier to find things, you know, in the morning like. I mean, I don't want to stand on anybody's toes. I spoke to Bailey and he said to get on with it."

"I'm surprised he even noticed, to be honest. I've just seen him leaving. I say goodbye and he looked right through me."

"Er, well he is a bit quiet, prefers to let his actions do the talking."

"Jesus, there's no hope for us then. No, he's a waste of space, a bloody liability. Night Supervisor, what a fucking joke. The gaffer's soft on him for some reason."

"I suppose it's difficult when you're his age. Harder to maintain the enthusiasm."

"Say it like it is son, he's a bloody dinosaur. A fucking relic. No, good work son. I think you're right, it is better. Yeah, I like it. You're proving a real asset lad."

"Thanks Mr Tanner, that's really nice of you to say."

"No, you deserve it son. Credit where it's due I always say. How's the Flem Boy Three doing?"

"Ha, do you mean Mat and Gat and ... the other lad?"

"Don't worry. I don't know their names either."

"That's a good nickname, sir. They do spit a bit."

"A bit! I came in the other day and I thought the roof was leaking."

"Ha, I know, yeah."

"Are they grafting or leaving it all to you?"

"Er, they're grafting like. I mean, people work at different paces don't they? I've always been a grafter, see. Get stuck in. Not everybody is like that though. Do you know what I mean?"

"Very diplomatic son. I get it, don't want to shop them. Don't worry, they'll get found out if they're not pulling their weight."

"I'm sure sir."

"Anyway, what I wanted to speak to you about is that we've got some newbies starting, temp workers for over Christmas. I'd like one to shadow you. You know, so you could show them the ropes, so to speak. I know you've not been here long but I think you'll set a good example. What do you think?"

I knew it wouldn't last. At least with the Special Needs Four I get a bit of fucking peace and quiet. Hang on … what if it's a bird? That'll be brilliant. And she'll have to speak to me coz she's shadowing me.

"Adam, is that okay?"

"Is it a girl?"

"Sorry?"

"I mean a woman, is it a woman? Over 18 like, I don't do underage. No, I mean it doesn't matter, boy or girl. Yes, I'll do it. Of course I will. No problem."

"Er, okay. Good."

The fairy story playing within the fleapit of his mind – a presumed undateable, rescued from permanent soul vacation by a fresh-faced beauty – had brightened his journey to work to such an extent that even the last leg down the fetid canal path was a positive joy. The merest thought of physical contact dousing him in dopamine.

He had only ever had one girlfriend: a middle-class girl called Katie, when he was seventeen. He had the tortured soul of a poet, she said – and less flatteringly the body of a velociraptor. He would spend the rest of his life with her, there wasn't a doubt in his mind. In reality, it barely lasted the rest of the month. He had done nothing wrong; she just didn't want a relationship. Days later, staggering home from the pub, he took a piss down an alley and caught her grappling with a weekend Adonis. He was torn apart but philosophical: he had been beaten by a fitter rival, someone better suited to this terrain of the flesh. His luck though was about to change. The perennial misfirer was about to find his shooting boots. He could feel it in his water.

His reverie was interrupted by the sight of a man crouched under the motorway bridge surrounded by smoke.

What's he doing, walking a fucking dragon? Oh fuck, I know that smell. Just what I need, a fucking crackhead. Do not engage. Do not engage.

He put his head down and quickened his step.

"Oi, Grimes you mad twat!"

Oh please God no, not twice in a month.

He turned and faced his nemesis. Now with added crack.

"Alright Flames ...Fancy seeing you again."

"Tell me about it. Doesn't do nothing for my peepers seeing your ugly kite twice in a month."

"What are you up to mate?"

"On the fucking straight, aren't I man? Knocked it on the head, all that robbing and taxing and shit. Got my head sorted now. Never felt better. Where are you off anyway?"

"I'm just on my way to work. Fucking nightmare."

"Fucking hell, same here mate. Look at me and you both going straight, meeting on the way to fucking work. I'm just having a little smoke, get my head sorted. Do ya wanna toot?"

"Nah, I'm right mate."

"C'mon man. It'll sort your head out."

"Nah honestly, I'm sound mate. Where are you working bud?"

"Just a bit of casual work, get some coin for over Crimbo. At that fucking warehouse, er ... New Direction. You ever heard of it?"

From the corner arch of the bridge he swore he heard someone laughing in the dark.

14TH MARCH 1975

T he French restaurant at the Midland Hotel in the centre of town had become their semi-regular haunt. Dolby had bought her a turquoise gown for these occasions. It was the most beautiful thing she'd ever seen, never mind worn. Her dad said she could be mistaken for royalty and indeed the first time they visited the French (as Dolby insisted on calling it), as she climbed out of the Stag, a passing young girl stopped and stared open-mouthed at her – a novice stargazer viewing her first celestial body. Ignoring his demands to hurry up, Sarah smiled at the girl and gave her the thumbs-up. *I'm just like you love. No better, no worse. I've just got lucky that's all. So can you.*

Lately though, when they went to the Midland they always had company. Tonight, Dolby had all his friends with him: They were dressed in tweed and velvet tuxedos with dickey shirtfronts and black ties. He was wearing his Cuban heals in an effort to be a bigger man.

She had been sitting on her own for at least an hour, staring into the crystal prisms of the restaurant's chandelier, fingering the lump swelling just above her cheekbone. Foundation had helped to conceal the range of its diabolical contours, and partially disguised the blackened reaches of her right eye, but like most lies it could not conceal the whole truth – the full story.

It was great to see Greg again; she'd not seen anyone from her old life for ages. He was her school-yard crush, her secret Valentine. It was his black mop-top and ocean-green eyes – just like Bobby Sherman. She was on route to Dolby's when he came out of the chippy. They embraced like old soldiers, her heart banging like a bass drum. Amidst the swirl of nostalgia and vinegar fumes, she'd lost track of time. The Stag pulling halfway onto the pavement rapidly reorientated her.

"James?"

"Jesus, careful pal …Pavements are for walking on. You know him, Sarah?"

"Yeah, he's my boss. What time is it?"

"Quarter past eight."

"Oh fucking hell, Greg."

"What's up?"

The driver's window slowly wound down.

"Get in."

"Hi James, I thought I was meeting you at yours."

"Get in."

"James, this is Greg, we grew up together, best friends through primary school, weren't we."

"Yeah, we were. Nice car, mate."

"I said get in the fucking car!"

She hadn't seen him like this since that morning in Luton. His face bent and fulminating.

"I'm sorry?"

"Are you deaf as well as dumb? Get in the fucking car."

Greg moved towards the Stag. Her worst nightmare.

"There's no need for that pal."

"I'm giving you five seconds, Sarah."

"Hey pal, I'm talking to you."

"Leave it please Greg."

"One."

"You shouldn't talk to your girl like that."

"Two."

"Please Greg."

"No Sarah, it's a point of principle. A man should not speak to a woman like that."

"Three."

Greg placed his left hand on the roof of the Stag and leant into his face.

"Four."

Dolby lifted his right hand, ignition key protruding from his gripped fingers, and jabbed sideways, as if throwing a dart.

"Argh, fucking hell—"

"Greg!"

"He stabbed me! In the eye …He's stabbed me in the eye. Help me."

"I will ask you one more time Sarah, get in the fucking car."

"He's hurt!"

"Right, that's it."

Imbued by blood and adrenaline, he sprang from the Stag and grabbed her by the arm.

"No, get off me."

"Come with me."

"You're hurting my arm."

"I'll hurt more than your fucking arm. Get in."

He launched her into the passenger seat and locked the door

before turning to Greg, writhing on the floor, and extending his right hand. Confused, Greg reached out in reciprocation, only for Dolby to retract his offer and boot him in the gut. After delivering another kick, he dived back into the Stag and wheelspinned into the night.

"Why? I ... I can't believe you did that. He was my friend, my old school friend. You stabbed him. Stop the car."

"I didn't stab him Sarah, I jabbed him with my key and anyway, he deserved it. Looking for trouble and didn't like what he got when he found it."

"Pull over. I want to go back and see if he's okay. Pull over!"

"No. Fuck off."

"He's crumpled on the floor."

"Why do you care? Are you fucking him or something?"

"No, of course not."

"I fucking bet. Fucking slag."

"Pull over I said, pull over!"

Sarah made a grab for the wheel.

"Fucking bitch!"

The Stag blurted onto the wrong side of the road, narrowly missing a passing truck. He wrestled with the steering wheel, locking his elbows and holding on for dear life, before eventually taming the motor and pulling over to the roadside. Then there was silence. An eerie calm amidst the dust and debris.

"I'm sorry James, I'm so sorry. I was upset ......Say something, James. Please say something."

He turned towards her. His face empty, his eyes dead. Dead like a shark.

"No please don't. No please ... James, no, no ..."

Nobody had ever punched her before. The girl who lived across her street had slapped her once when she was ten but this was in another league: the numbness of her jaw, the crack of bone on bone, the cold sweat of violation. The car was as quiet as a graveyard; her finger tracing a raindrop down the passenger-side window the only sound.

There is no one worse than I am. I'm the most pathetic, weakest person in the whole world.

"You know, I'm really angry about this. All of a sudden, I'm the bad guy. I had the day from hell so I booked the Chinese restaurant for the two of us. If you must know, it's the anniversary of the passing of a good friend of mine from the army … Four years to the day that we lost Jimmy Swords. Good soldier and even better man, ambushed by the fucking Provos. Anyway, I thought I'd surprise you but no, you had to be late. Talking to another man. And when I catch you, he turns out to be an old school friend …How sweet, how convenient …I mean, don't get me wrong, that doesn't excuse what I did – that was really bad form. I have a temper, there's no doubt about that … Do you know what one of my triggers is though? …Selfishness …I simply cannot abide selfish people. The army teaches you that. You can't be a lone wolf in the forces. No way …Do you want to know what really gets my goat though? Selfish people who don't think they're selfish …I mean you, little miss goody two-shoes, would probably baulk at the description. You can't see it at all …Only child, you see – a classic case. Yet you're one of the most selfish people I've ever met. If it's not you, you, you, then you're not interested. Well let me tell you, there can be no 'I' in this team Sarah."

She crumpled deeper into her seat and began fingering another raindrop.

Dolby inched past the other diners towards her table. Lundy, walking two steps behind. *He* was firmly back on the scene. He'd just turned up one night and Dolby had greeted him as if nothing had happened. Petrified, she'd grabbed the billowing bottom of her princess dress and ran into the night. Sitting on the back seat of the night bus, a rose between a dead drunk and a spitting skinhead. He'd apologised the day after. It would never happen again, he said. But it had happened again, it had happened tonight. The sight of him mockingly raising his glass to her like a punch to the stomach. Tonight though, she had stayed seated. Taking one for the team.

"I'm going to the casino with the boys. I've booked us a room for the night, so you might as well stay here. We won't be too late."

"Do you want me to come?"

"I'm sorry?"

"Shall I come with you?"

"Oh fucking come on …Can't I have a night out with the boys for once? I don't want you to come, not in the mood you're in. I need some fucking fun, some excitement for once. I don't want you bringing everyone down. Here's the key, Room 246. And when I come back, I hope you've straightened your face because I'm close to walking away, for good."

"Right, okay."

"No, I mean it this time. You're dragging me down. You're like a bloody stone round my neck."

She'd finished her drink and retreated to their room; laying in darkness on the large double bed, obliterating herself in the city's fabric – the beating drum of its nocturnal culture.

She wished that she had never met him. She wished that more

than anything else in the whole world. Now that she had though, she couldn't live without him. Through good and bad, in health and now sickness.

What can I do? Will it ever end?

Voices came from the corridor.

"Shush old boy. Keep it down. This is the Midland."

"Oh the Midland, Mr Dolby …Mustn't play up in the Midland. What would the papers say?"

"Shut up, I'm trying to find the right room—"

"Yeah, get the right fucking room. We don't want to goose the wrong bird although there was some fucking talent in there tonight."

"Two forty-six, here we are sir, welcome to paradise …"

The doorknob twisted to the left. A street-lit silhouette magnified a long, bony arm stretching for the light switch, its monochromic reach like a twisted forest branch from the folk tales of her youth. Two dark figures moved into sight: The Brothers Grimm. She knew what was coming.

14TH APRIL 1975

L undy stood in the wooded expanse of his antique shop and began metronomically combing his quiff over his eyes before with stilted fingers positioning it sideways right. *Beautiful, like bloody Samson.* He buttoned then unbuttoned his red polo neck and flicked a piece of fluff from his sleeve. Not the slightest blemish. For the finishing touch, he sucked on his index fingers and ran them over his golden eyebrows. *Perfection personified, old boy.*

Things were finally falling into place: his business was coming along nicely now Tanner had "agreed" to close his shop and today he was seeing Jessica. It was at least five years since they'd last met. Her contact wasn't a surprise though; her "fresh start" with Derek was always doomed to failure – the forced smiles, the formally staged nights out, pretending to be in heaven when they're really languishing in hell. He was amazed she'd lasted this long.

They were rendezvousing at a café in the picturesque hamlet of Battle – an unnecessary diversion in his mind. They both knew why they were meeting and it wasn't to eat scones.

He rode into town like a returning sheriff, the sunlight flickering off the blackened lenses of his aviator shades, the southeasterly wind tousling his blond hair. On reaching his destination, he vaulted from his laser blue Triumph TR6 soft top and stood motionless. *See Jessica, this is the mark of the man. A real man. With a brand-new sports car.* At least that was his plan. In real time, as with most things in England, the rain scuppered that particular vision; the heavens opening midway towards his destination, forcing him to pull over and drag his roof back on.

The things he could get up to in that nice little hotel he passed on the edge of town eased his disappointment. That will do. That will do very nicely indeed.

He pressed his face between the open shutters on the cafe's bay window.

Jesus, is this the last stop to the crematorium? There she is. Fuck, her arse is practically hanging over that chair. She's still blond from the bottle though and that can hide a multitude of sins. No slap-on though.

The bell above the door announced his arrival, customers turning in unison.

"Hello ladies, lovely day for it. You're all looking very smart. Now, I must say, I love that broach. Very nice. Here, take my card. Let me know if you've got any more like that."

He strutted towards Jessica sat in the far corner of the room.

"Jessica."

"Gordon. How are you?"

He pulled a chair from under the table and sat down.

"Okay thanks, you?"

"Yes, okay."

"You look well."

"No I don't, I look like shit."

He reached for her hands, his mouth shaping into a leer.

"Still fuckable though."

She tore them from his reach.

"For God's sake, keep your voice down."

"What?"

"You're still a low-life I see."

"A low-life eh? You keep coming back for more though don't you? How is Derek by the way, how's the husband?"

"We're not together anymore …Not that it's any of your business."

"Oh dear. Nothing I did I hope."

"You're a fucking shit, you really are."

"Maybe, but I have talents in other areas. I'm sure you'd be the first to agree …"

"You're deluded. You're such a prat."

"C'mon Jess, I'm only kidding. Let's not argue, let's not fall out. Look, finish your drink and let's get out of here. I saw a hotel, driving in. Let's reacquaint ourselves there—"

"No! Trust me, that's not why I wanted to see you. That would be the *last* reason why I would want to see you …There's something I need to tell you. You need to know something. You've got a right to know."

"What are you going on about?"

"Look, this isn't easy."

"Well can't we talk about this later?"

"No. You don't understand, this is important."

"What's more important than sex? C'mon Jess, let's get out of here. Let's cut the bullshit."

"Are you deaf? I didn't call you for that. Trust me, you're the last person I'd want to share a bed with."

"Right, if you're going to be like that you can fuck off."

He jumped from his chair and rammed it under the table. The crockery rattling like smashing cymbals, the silver-hairs raising their lined eyebrows.

"Gordon sit down. I'm sorry, I am just nervous. Please don't make a scene. Please let's just talk …Look, you're right in a way. The reason Derek and me split up was because of you, because of us. I left suddenly because I was …God, I can't believe I'm saying this to you. I've practised this conversation so many times."

"Because of what?"

"Gordon, sit down please. You're making a scene."

"Tell me, because of what?"

"Oh, God."

"No, on second thoughts, don't answer that. I'll see you around. What a complete waste of time this turned out to be."

He walked away.

"Because I was pregnant with your child, Gordon."

He sat back down.

"What?

"I'm so sorry Gordon. I did not want it to come out like that."

"Pregnant?"

"Well, I'm a bit past that stage now. June is nearly six."

"June?"

"Yes, that's her name. Your daughter's name is June. Look, I'm really sorry to drop this on you but I couldn't think of any other way to tell you other than, well … to tell you … and it's not the easiest thing to tell someone."

"You're lying."

"No, I'm not."

"Yes you are."

"Believe me, I wish I was but trust me, I'm not. I have had your child. You are a father."

"No. It can't be."

"Why not?"

"It just can't be mine. It's not mine."

"Gordon, I know that this has come as a shock."

"How can you be sure? It could be Derek's kid. How are you so sure it's mine? This is all about money, isn't it? That's what this is all about."

"It isn't Derek's child. We hadn't slept together since Jack was born, it's not Derek's kid … That's why our marriage ended. You're the only other person I've slept with."

"Prove it. Fucking prove it … You're full of shit, it all makes sense. You want my money. Well let me tell you, you are not fucking getting it. Go to your husband for that, not me."

"This is not about money. Absolutely not … Gordon, June is a special little girl, she's not the same as other children. I just need some support with her, not money just support. Please Gordon, I need some help."

"How do you mean special? Special in what way?"

"Special … not like other children. Different."

"What, like super intelligent or good at sports? What do you mean by special?"

"Er … not really, Gordon."

"Well I don't know, you said she was special."

"That's because she is."

"What do you mean then by fucking special?"

A knock on the window interrupted them.

"Oh shit, it's my mum."

"Who?"

"My mum. June must be playing up."

Jessica approached the window.

"Come in Mum, bring her in with you."

"That's all I need, your fucking mother coming in. Who's that with her?"

"That's June."

"Who?"

"Your daughter."

"Now wait just a fucking minute—"

The doorbell now introduced Jessica's mum with a reluctant child in tow.

"She was becoming upset love. She had a tantrum in the library."

Jessica stood to greet them and after delivering a sharp kick to his ankle, Lundy followed suit.

"It's okay Mum. It's fine, just leave her with us. It's fine, go on. I'll ring you later."

"Are you sure? Do you not want me to stay?"

"No, it's fine. I'll speak to you later."

"Are you sure?"

"Yes mum, it's fine."

She's beautiful. She's incredible. The spitting image of me. Her eyes, her nose … She's got her mother's hair colour but everything else is pure Lundy. She's even got my dimple in the middle of her chin. Why isn't she looking at me though? What's with the blank expression? And what the fuck are those noises she's making?

"C'mon June, sit down … sit down for mummy. No, don't go that way … that nice lady is trying to eat her lunch. No June, this way please."

"Never a dull moment today, eh ladies? Can I just say again

how much I love that broach—"

"That's it June, sit down … sit down here with your daddy. Good girl … Look, your daddy's here … Say 'hello daddy.'"

June finally settled in the chair.

"Why won't she stop making that noise? What's wrong with her?"

"That's what I wanted to tell you about. June's a special girl."

"You keep saying that. She doesn't sound very special. Can't you shut her up?"

"Gordon, June is mentally handicapped. She cannot help making noises, she makes these noises all the time. Trust me – she never stops making those noises."

"How do you mean, 'mentally handicapped?'"

"Well, she doesn't talk, or understand things like you and me. Like I say, she's special."

"Stop saying that fucking word."

"I'm sorry. I know it's a lot to take in."

"Shush, be a good girl. There's a good girl."

"Gordon, she's not a dog."

"No, sorry, I'm just a bit—"

"I know, you're in shock."

He slowly extended his hand towards her.

"Nice to meet you June …"

How the fuck did it ever come to this?

He first met Jessica when she was working in the bar of a restaurant that he and Dolby frequented, *The Royal George* in Knutsford. She was a mature student –Dolby said that explained a lot – and worked there part-time to supplement her grant. Seemingly impervious to his muscular bravado, she intrigued him. Dolby disdained her as one of the "hairy armpit mob" but this only made him want her more. He had no idea she was married and had a kid until her husband picked her up one night. He couldn't believe it. One of the ugliest creatures he had even seen: his hairline not so much receding as evacuating and a face so red and blotchy it looked like his skin had been turned inside out. It made him happy and angry at the same time. Happy because she obviously set her bar very low and angry as their marriage disrupted the natural order of attraction – attractive people mate with other attractive people. If attractive people started mating with ugly people, then where was his advantage? What was his point?

"It must be your fault that she's like this."

"I beg your pardon, Gordon?"

"It must be on your side of the family. There's none of that on my side."

"What the fuck are you talking about?"

"There's nothing like that on my side of the family …"

"Like what?"

"You know … I don't want to say it."

"Say what?"

"Well, deaf and dumbness."

"You're fucking unbelievable, you really are."

"I'm just saying that's all."

"Gordon, she's certainly not deaf or dumb, she's your daughter."

"Like I say, I'm just making it clear."

"Gordon, no one knows why she's like she is. For the record, none of my family is mentally handicapped – not that it would make any difference … No one is to blame, she is who —"

Shit, she's got that other kid though and he's not a spastic… Maybe, it's me. No, it can't be. But if it's not her…

"No, you're right Jessica. I'm sorry. It's no one's fault, no one at all. No one is to blame."

"Yeah that's right Gordon, no one is to blame."

"No one. No one at all. We're both completely blameless."

"Yes Gordon."

"Yes, absolutely …Anyway, why are you just telling me about this now?"

"I thought about telling you before but I just didn't know how you would react. Trust me, the amount of times I sat with her outside your house—"

"Whoa, hang on …Don't go near my house. What if Rose saw you?"

"I couldn't give a shit whether Rose saw me or not. Aside from my mum, I've no one else. I need help."

"Right. Yes, I mean, you must do."

"Look, I don't expect you to be dad of the year or anything like that. Just, if you could, I don't know, be there in some capacity for us."

"Right."

"I mean, I wouldn't bother you all the time …Just when I need something."

"Of course, no that's fine."

"Yeah?"

"Yes, of course."

"Ooh lady, put that flippin' doll down and say hello to Daddy …June, say hello …This is your daddy, this man here, yes he is. Say hello to Daddy. Look, here's Daddy. Yes, Daddy …Gordon, she's smiling at you! She's giving you her hand. Clap it. Clap her hand, she loves it. Gordon, clap her hand. Quick … go on

Daddy, clap ..."

Lundy lifted his arm but froze halfway.

"I'm sorry, I can't do this."

"What?"

"This, it's not me. I'm sorry I'll have to go."

Lundy jumped from his chair and ran.

"Gordon ..."

"Never contact me again Jessica."

"Gordon, where are you going?"

"Goodbye Jessica."

10TH JANUARY 1997

Unlike Mat, Tat and Gat, Adam had consistently declined Flames' invitation to join him on the pipe. Given that he had spent the majority of his time in the warehouse rhapsodising about the lifestyle benefits of crack cocaine – even giving the odd rock away – Adam knew this was a risky strategy. Bitter experience had endowed him with a sharp instinct for threats of physical harm and his Spidey-sense was tingling. Walking home with Flames one morning, taking a short cut down the railway line into the bitter on-coming rain, the subject again reared its head.

"Why won't you have a toot with us? Everyone else is doing it, why do you have to be different?"

"I just don't fancy it, that's all mate."

"Nah, it's not that. You think that you're better than us. I've seen the expression on your face when the lads and me come back from having a toot. Like you're the king of fucking England."

"What? No that's not true."

"Yeah it is. You think you're cut from a different cloth. You think you're so fucking superior."

"You keep saying that and it's not true. If anything it's the fucking opposite."

"Bollocks. Fucking bollocks. Why won't you have a toot with us then?"

"It's just not my thing."

"'It's just not my thing...' See, you think you're better than us. Always have done."

"Not at all. If you remember, I tried it at Smithy's party. You sold it to me. I spent all night throwing up in the bog."

"That happens to everyone on their first toke. Your second one is nothing like that, it's miles different. It's fucking great. Trust me. Have I ever lied to you before?"

He can't seriously expect me to answer that.

"No, of course I trust you mate. It's just that ...No, I'll leave it, if it's all the same mate?"

"Don't wind me up Grimes, you're fucking winding me up."

"No, I'm not mate."

"Have a toot now then ...A little livener."

"Flames it's eight in the morning, I don't want a livener. I want to go to bed."

"Shut up you pussy. You're having one. You're going to prove to me that you're one of the lads."

"C'mon mate. There's no need for this."

"There's every fucking need. You need to stop fucking around and step up to the mark."

He reached into his bum bag and pulled out his works.

"No, please Flames—"

"You'll thank me one day for this."

He's actually going to force me. I'm going to be forced to smoke crack. I'm going to be drug-raped. Just look at the fucking state of that. I'll catch fucking diphtheria from that thing.

"Right, I'm going to light it and then pass it to you ...Take a good long toke. Trust me, they're mellow these rocks. It will have worn off by the time you get home. Right, hold this lighter for me ..."

I'm going to have to tell him. There's no other way. This will finish me.

"No mate, please I can't. No honestly, I'm ill see. I'm really poorly."

"What?"

"I'm ill. I can't have a toot."

"I've told you, this shit sorts you out. Harley Street and all them are clocking it. It's got like miracle fucking properties. They're sworn to secrecy of course, by the government and that ...Fucking new world order, innit."

"No, I don't mean physically like. I mean more ... well, mentally."

"Mentally?"

"Yeah, mentally."

"You're mental?"

"Well, I have a mental illness."

"You're mental?"

"Depression, Flames. That's my diagnosis. It's like living under a black cloud. Everything's darker. Things that people brush off in a second really get to me. I'm on tablets like, from the doc. I'll probably be on them for the rest of my life – just like a diabetic would be. Don't think I'm being funny or owt. I just don't think commencing a career in crack would be conducive to my mental health."

"What, do you hear things and see mad shit like faces in walls and vampire mice and that?"

"What...? No, that's psychosis. I'm not psychotic."

"If you say so mate. All makes sense though."

"What do you mean?"

"Well, we always thought you were … you know, a bit weird like. Something not quite right. Smithy thought you were gay – well, we all did to be honest."

"Gay? What's that got to do with depression?"

"Well, put it this way, if I was a bandit I'd be heading straight for the motorway bridge."

"What?"

"If I was bent, I'd commit hari-kari, mate. No fucking doubt about it. Imagine no pussy …"

"Fucking unbelievable. Absolutely. Unbelievable. I've always wondered what this moment would be like, when I finally confide in someone about the biggest problem in my life …My killer illness. In my wildest dreams I couldn't have imagined it would be like this."

"Oi White Coat, chill out on those wild dreams. And if you think you're having any of this pipe, you really are fucking nuts. I ain't taking the blame for no fucking massacre."

"What?"

"Michael Ryan mate, think about it. No, on second thoughts, don't think about it. Get home and get your fucking head down."

"What?"

"Fuck off home."

The thought that his secret was out, to Flames of all people, meant he didn't close his eyes that day. It would only be a matter of time until the gutter press would come calling and he needed to plan his response. Which essentially was to butch it out -sticks and stones – a strategy that was tested minutes into his shift when Flames beckoned him outside for a word behind the blue bins.

"C'mon Grimes, I've not got all day."

"Yeah, coming. You alright mate? I mean we've forgotten about yesterday haven't we? You said you wouldn't say anything. You know, about the illness and that."

"Yeah yeah, calm down White Coat, your little secret's safe with me. But yeah, I did want a word with you about yesterday."

"Yeah?"

"Yeah. I mean I got home, sat down, and put my tunes on and I started to feel fucking sorry for you."

"Really?"

"Yeah man. Imagine a life without Class A. Fucking nightmare. That's just not fair."

"Er, yeah, it's just one of the sacrifices my illness forces me to make, I'm afraid."

"Be afraid no longer, mate. I've got the answer to all your problems."

"Yeah...?"

"Oh yeah. You can't have crack coz it'll turn into a fucking massacre ..."

"Well, I wouldn't—"

"Exactly. But weed won't ...Weed will sort your head out. Weed's fucking top and you've always been partial. What with your documentaries and weird fucking music ...Now you'll be able to join in with the rest of us."

"Yeah, at different speeds ..."

"Will you stop being so fucking negative Grimes."

"No you're right, it's a good idea. I'm sure I've got a couple of spliffs-worth at home."

"You've no need mate, I've already sorted ya."

"Really?

"Oh yeah. Check this fucking pipe out mate. Pure Red Indian. Like a fucking Comanche."

"The colours of the Jamaican flag. Nice touch."

"I thought you'd like that mate. And that's not even the best bit. What good is a pipe if you've nothing to put in it? I've also got you a quarter of Gold Seal, mate. And just like your pipe, it's all the way from fucking Jamaica. "

"Brilliant, cheers mate."

"No probs White Coat. I've got your back, you know that. Smoke well and chill brother."

"Like I say, I really appreciate it.

"Don't mention it. You can pay me for it next pay day."

John, the other new starter at NDC, was influencing the work-force in a more salubrious way. A keep-fit enthusiast in his mid-fifties who ran seven miles, four times a week, he was a picture of rude health – his lantern jaw and undulating ruby-brown hair more redolent of California than Manchester. He was also a dedicated exponent of positive thinking. On his first night, oblivious of street law, he spent the majority of his shift lecturing Flames on how he needed to find his "inner leader" in order to destroy his "inner victim." And he escaped without a scratch to his bodywork. Furthermore, it was no-ticeable the following night that Flames had washed his uni-form for the first time – or at least given it a good scrub with a damp cloth.

Given their very different attitudes to good living, Adam had worried that John could pull the plug on his catatonic col-leagues but his fears were unwarranted. Like most doctrinar-ians, his theories consumed him to the extent that he paid no mind to the other stuff that was going on in the real world of the warehouse. He genuinely seemed oblivious to the fact that his work mates were perennially wasted; that random figures would often wander in the warehouse looking for Flames and his magic stones, and that he and Bailey were the only ones working.

Bailey though had not been so myopic: smoking crack was one thing but Flames had begun bolstering the profits from his burgeoning drug empire by systematically disassembling the warehouse stock. Suspicions raised by Flames leaving work on a bike he did not arrive on, he completed an impromptu stock check and found that many things were terribly amiss. He immediately informed Mr Tanner and the first thing he did was call the Big White Chief.

16TH MAY 1975

His attic had become her special place, a repository of both comfort and devastation. (For some reason Dolby never went up there. He never said why; he just never did.) She would sit for hours at the brilliant-white dressing table, staring out of the small, leaded window like a princess awaiting rescue from a mythical beast. A hero on horseback to take her away for evermore.

It also doubled as her listening post. On the nights that Dolby wished her gone, which were becoming increasingly regular, she would pretend to leave then taking advantage of the vastness of his abode, sneak back in through the kitchen door. She would sit for hours listening to the choruses of perfidy belting out downstairs. A ritual motivated by masochism as much as curiosity: what she heard was horrible but she felt she deserved such a kicking for being so pathetic.

Tonight's cacophony though was on a whole new level. Sounds of defiance and vitriol rapidly replaced by more frantic noises: they were screaming now because this was no longer role-play. This was real life. This was real terror.

She placed her hands over her ears and rocked her head back and forth.

Please stop. Please leave them alone.

"You fucking bastard! You'll pay for this."

A half-naked woman sprinted across the green.

Where are the neighbours? Why is no one helping?

She had asked herself this question numerous times before and always got the same answer.

"An Englishman's home is his fucking castle."

She crept onto the landing and peered over the bannister. She identified two female voices and at least three male – one was Dolby's, whooping for joy, reveling in the wreckage he had created; the others she didn't recognise. Lundy's voice was conspicuously absent.

"Let me go, I promise I won't tell anyone. Please, you don't have to hurt me. You don't have to—"

"Stop fucking whingeing, we're paying you enough …I thought you said this lot was resilient, Taffy."

"I thought they were boss. Listen love, he's only playing but if you don't play nice back, he's going to get angry. And trust me, none of us want that."

"No, please. I'll play, just don't hurt me."

"Glad to hear it. Now put these on."

"Why? I don't need them. I'll stay."

"Because I fucking said so. You're getting on my fucking tits now …Give her a fucking crack, Taffy."

In the past weeks and months, he had taken her to the bottom. To states and places that she could never have known existed, that the vast majority of people would never visit. Her esteem, her sanity, had been systematically torn from her. Piece by piece. A person made base.

"No, don't hurt me, please … I have a little boy, see."

In that instant it became too much. Just too much to bear.

She stopped inches from the distressed-wood door; her body

refusing to go any further, a poolside child periled by deep water. The voices becoming shriller by the second.

"No, please don't. Please no …"

"I said shut the fuck up."

"Please, just let me go."

No choice.

She opened the door. A living picture unfurled, three wild dogs standing frenzied and salivating over a helpless prey. His bear-skin rug compounding the scene's savagery.

"That's enough now. That's it, no more."

Dolby's face fell; its redness drained to white.

"Sarah. You've come back."

A fat bald mound of perspiration motioned toward her, thrusting his crotch back and forth.

"Taffy, leave her."

"Wahey, join the party! She must want some …Do you want some? Come here. John, help me."

Sarah grabbed a vase from the Victorian hearth and threw it at them, just missing Taffy's head.

"You fucking mad bitch."

Dolby stepped forward.

"Sarah calm down. Let's talk about this."

"Talk? Everything you've put me through and you want to talk …No, okay you're right, let's talk. Let's talk about her beat up and chained to the chair leg. Does she want to talk? Do you want to talk love? How are you feeling?"

The girl, bloodied and broken, didn't answer; her eyes focused on the handcuff keys lying near her chair.

"Sarah, whatever you're thinking it's wrong. This is all an act. We're acting, just acting. Fake blood and tears."

"Is that the best you can come up with? You can't even admit it."

"No, you've got it wrong. Honestly, we're acting. Isn't that right Taffy?"

"Oh yeah, our own little film and you've just got a walk-on part. So why don't you take that pretty little top off…"

The prone girl fumbled with the key before liberating her wrist from the handcuff's embrace. She made it onto her knees, rocking as if awaiting a starting pistol. As her captors moved closer to Sarah, she burst to her feet and sprinted towards the door, crashing past Taffy in the process.

"Oi, come back you fucking slag. You're paid up for the night. Come back bitch, I know your face. No one runs out on Taffy. No one."

He turned and faced Sarah.

"That's fucking your fault that is."

"C'mon then. Do your worst. Hit me. Go on, hit me."

"Taffy leave her. Taffy, I said leave her. Taffy that's an order—"

"Come on Taffy, you fat bastard. Do what you've got to do. Hit me. Go on."

"Sarah don't be silly. Calm down …Taffy, stay where you are."

He looked left and then right, a fat dog torn between his master's demands and his instinct. Violence won. He attacked, his left arm protruding forwards, a lance of pure corned beef. Sarah jumped sideways and grabbed a goblet of whisky from the top of the drinks cabinet. This time she didn't miss, hitting him full in the face; sending him to the floor, bawling like a baby.

"Sarah, please calm down. John get her arm."

"Fuck that, she's like a fucking banshee. Calm down love."

"I'm calm. I'm calm. It's you lot. You're not calm. You're evil.

You're sick."

"She doesn't know what she's saying."

"I know what I'm saying. I—"

Blue flashing lights lit up the room.

"Fuck, Dolby it's the police."

"Don't worry about them."

She moved towards the beaded window and inspected the cavalry. *I could tell them everything, I'll never get a better chance. Look at them though …Fat swines, puffing and wheezing. They look like they belong in here. They look like fucking men.*

She ran through the door clashing shoulders with the coppers as they ambled up the garden path.

"Hey you …Shall we go after her?"

"Nah, fuck that, we'll never catch her. It's just another night at Dolby's place."

They gradually stepped through the open door and entered the front room. Taffy had pulled himself onto the sofa, bloodied, dazed and still in tears. The other two stood stunned, soaked and silent.

"Jesus, what have you been up to this time Dolby? You look like you've won a Grand Prix. But not in a good way.

"Fuck off back to the station Jakes. There's nothing for you to see here."

16TH MAY 1975

He stepped backwards onto her crazily paved path and scoured her bedroom window, the veins in his neck ribbed and cable-like. She was definitely in. He'd seen her shadow behind the net curtain.

"I know you're there, Jessica. You can't kid me. We need to talk …If you don't open the door, I'll say what I have to say out here …I will you know. I'll say it."

Yeah, let's see what the neighbours say. Miss Perfect's dirty little secret.

A blurred figure emerged from behind the door's frosted glass.

"What are you doing here?"

"We need to talk Jessica. Open the door."

"No, we don't. You made your intentions pretty clear the last time we met."

"Please, just give me ten minutes then I'll go, I promise."

"Look, just go away. Leave me alone."

"Jessica, please can I just come in? I was in shock – you just sprung it on me. You admitted that yourself. I just want to talk. Please, just for ten minutes."

"What, so you can blow your daughter out again?"

"That was the shock, honestly the shock. I've come to terms with it now. Just give me a chance. Please. For June's sake."

The door latch clanked and rattled.

"For June and June only. Ten minutes."

"Right. Okay."

He strode into the living room; its light, airy vibe and coffee-cream fittings flooding his mind with warm thoughts. He could have been very happy here. Indeed, at one point in their affair, he had seriously considered leaving Rose for her, until she informed him she would never leave Derek for him.

"Where's the kid?"

"Do you mean June? That's her name you know. She's at the day centre."

"Oh right ...God, it's been a while since I've been in here. Do you remember the last time, eh? When Derek came home and I had to run out of the back door...?"

"Why would you bring that up? Why would you think that at this juncture that is the right thing to say? You know your problem, Gordon – you're thick, thick as two short planks. Your brains are all in your dick."

"Okay Jessica, there's no need for that."

"I think there's every need for it. Well sit down then. The clock's ticking."

He moved her magazines off the wicker sofa onto the glass coffee table and sat down; rubbing his hands together as if scrubbing them under a tap.

"Right, well obviously we need to talk about the other week ... Straighten things out so to speak—"

"'Straighten things out!' Jesus, you're unreal ...Go on then."

"What?"

"Straighten away. I'm all ears."

"Well ...I'm sorry for walking out on you for a start. Like I said, I was in shock."

"'This is not me' you said."

"Well it's not."

"What does that even mean?"

"It means that I'm not used to this kind of thing. Especially, well … you know … with her being handicapped and all that. It's not my bag. It's not what I am used to."

"And you think this is what *I'm* used to? A toddler *and* a handicapped girl with only my mum to support me while you play happy families with Rose, is that what you think?"

"No, of course not, and I feel bad about that …"

"You don't feel bad about anything. You must be fucking joking."

"No, I do. I mean you're right, and I'm as surprised as you are. It's definitely not like me but I do. I feel … bothered about the whole thing."

"'Bothered.' You feel 'bothered about the whole thing…'"

"Yes."

"Gordon, this isn't losing a rugby match or pranging your car, this is life. This is your daughter."

"I know that. Of course, I know that. I've thought of nothing else since you've told me. I am human you know."

"Ha, who told you that?"

"Yeah, yeah. Look, will you just tell me what you want me to do?"

"You shouldn't have to be bloody told."

"What?"

"You shouldn't have to be told. You should know what to do."

"Well I don't, okay? Like I say, this is not my bag."

"For God's sake, share some of the burden. Take some responsibility for your actions for once."

"Is that how you see her – as a 'burden'?"

"Oh, that's really rich that is. Mr Absent Father is lecturing me on my morals …Jesus, are you for real?"

"Tell me what you want me to do. Give me some specifics."

"I don't know. Like I said in the café, be there for us."

"In what way?"

"Well, I would say money but I know what your response would be to that."

"I'll give you some money. How much do you want?"

He pulled his wallet from his trousers like a cowboy drawing his weapon.

"I don't know, ten pound a week for her clothes, stuff like that …Kids do not come cheap; especially when this one has effect-ively ruled me out of the job market for the foreseeable."

"No problem."

Lundy handed over a wad of cash.

"Thank you, but don't think that you're getting away with it that easy. It's more than money; it's a lot more than money."

"How do you mean? What else do you want?"

"She needs a father. I need you to be a father to her. A kid *needs* a father …It's like the other afternoon, the day centre had a party, all the kids and their parents were invited – nice game of musical chairs, a dancing competition for the kids and then one later for the parents …Do you know, June was the only one there without her daddy? Every other kid had their mummy and daddy there, even those that are not together anymore. I mean it was embarrassing …The caretaker had to partner me for the slow dance at the end."

"Right …"

"It's not fucking funny."

"I heard he's quite a mover."

"Compared to you Gordon, he probably is."

"Cheeky. Look, I'll do all those things."

"Bollocks. You're so full of crap."

"No, I will."

"Gordon, I would like to believe you, I really would. But as you keep saying it's not your bag, it's not fair to June for you to come in and out of her life. We need a commitment."

"I can commit. Honestly, I can. I promise you. Like I said, I'm as surprised as you about this but she's really got to me. I want to be her father. You were always telling me that I needed to change and I think this is my catalyst. How can I change though, if you won't give me a chance?"

She twirled her hair between her fingers.

"I suppose you've got a point."

"But you also have to promise me something."

"What?"

"Well, two things actually."

"Don't push it."

"Firstly, Rose must never find out about this and secondly, you can't give me access and then just take it away because as you said, that's not fair."

Jessica paused.

"Okay. If Rose finds out, I can assure you it won't be from me and I'll only take her away if you ever hurt us, okay?"

"Yeah, that sounds reasonable. Right, where do you want me to start?"

13TH JANUARY 1997

The shift had broken him. A two-hour long lecture from John on the benefits of occasional fasting was compounded by Flames playing his gabba techno at full blast again. He'd sought asylum in the crumbling toilet next to the building's main entrance. A formidable stench of piss preferable to the pieces of shit in the warehouse. It was from here that he spotted him; a bony, bedraggled man dressed in matching black drain-pipe trousers and jacket. He looked a bit older than Flames' usual clientele but he'd presumed him a Benzedrine conquistador from the beatnik Fifties. A cool cat degenerated into an incorrigible beast.

Flames also spotted him; his incongruity begetting a wide smile. He was a bit under the weather tonight and a beached vulnerable a long way from home was just what the doctor ordered.

"Here's another stone head ...Do you want a couple of stones? Do you need a rush?"

"I beg your pardon, are you addressing me?"

"Yeah, I'm addressing you. Who do you think you're talking to dickhead?"

"Who do I think I'm talking to? You don't have the slightest idea who I am, do you?"

"You what?"

"You haven't the slightest idea of who I am and the consequences for you lot, have you?"

"What the fuck are you talking about?"

Adam approached from the rear.

Fuck! Someone with a body that frail and balls that big could only be one thing: The fucking law and I've got a quarter of Moroccan black hiding in my rucksack. I need to shut this down.

He moved behind the man; mouthing at Flames from over his shoulder.

"He's the law."

"What the fuck are you talking about Grimes?"

The man turned and faced Adam.

"And who might you be then?"

"Me officer? I just work here."

"Shit, the filth."

"Officer? You think I work for the police? No, I don't work for the police."

"Who the fuck are you then?"

The man spun back around and answered Flames in superior tones.

"I'm over you. I stand over you all. I am the manager of NDC and I can see that you are in no fit state to work. Look at your eyes …So, as well as a horde of thieves, we have a bloody opium den on our hands. Taylor, you had better get in here."

The sound of chafing thighs and laboured breaths introduced a vast slab of a man wearing a long ginger beard and white boiler suit.

"You'll have a field day with this lot, Taylor. So come on, who is it? Which one of you is stealing from me? Someone is, and the only thing Taylor hates more than a thief is a liar. Isn't that right Taylor?"

Taylor solemnly nodded his head.

"Yes, things like this really upset Taylor. Despite his love of inflicting pain on people, he is, in his own way, a man of deep principle. Are you not, Taylor?"

Taylor again nodded.

Why has no one mentioned the law? I'd take a caution over what that daft big cunt has got up his sleeve any day. Just look at fucking Flames. He's got that stupid look in his eyes. Please God don't do anything dumb.

From a far corridor, John waltzed into the picture, pushing a trolley full of coffee-making machines, talking to no one in particular.

"I mean, I read in *Perfect 10* NASA is interested in looking into fasting to improve the performance of their astronauts. Well, if it's good enough for them—"

"Who the bloody hell are you?"

"John, and you?"

"I own this place. I'm James Dolby, the CEO of New Direction."

"Pleased to meet you Mr Dolby. It's always nice to meet a motivated man."

John extended the hand of friendship. Dolby's brow furrowed as if the gesture was alien to him, before finally touching palms. To their left, Flames rocked on his heels. His eyes darting left then right.

"Fuck off!"

He bolted forward like a debauched greyhound, Taylor's full-length lunge no match for his dancing feet.

"See ya wankers ..."

Amidst the confusion, in a hail of squeaking trainers, Tat and Mat also made a run for it. Gat too moved into position before eventually thinking better of it – marooned in sports equipment, too far from the arch of freedom.

130

"The fucking bastards. Leave them Taylor. Leave them! We'll get their names. We'll get them, don't worry."

John spoke.

"Look, could someone please tell me what's going on."

"Taylor, take them out back."

"Hey, I said what's going on?"

"You say your name is John?"

"Yes."

"Well John, I suggest you shut up, or I'll get Taylor to break your back. Taylor, take them outside please."

28TH MAY 1975

No one needed to tell her that she should quit NDC and go to the police. She wasn't stupid. She wasn't weak. But she hadn't done either of these things. And she wasn't sure why.

After foiling his attack on the girls, she staggered home and collapsed on her bed. Her mind, body and soul dragged through a brutal hurricane. In the middle of this turmoil though there were other emotions, largely unformed but hinting towards a final relief. That it was becoming a horrible memory instead of a living nightmare. The next morning though she awoke more desperate than ever to call him, to receive his explanations and promises, to begin another chapter of the same old story.

She launched herself into her work. Although Dolby was ruthlessly efficient outside of the office, inside he was a complete shambles – the dark recesses of his filling cabinets full of unpaid invoices, unsigned contracts and outdated insurance documentation. She didn't know where to start but she started anyway. It took her days before she finally began to get on top of things. It was supposed to be therapeutic but it wasn't. Despite not darkening the door, he still dominated the atmosphere. Through the static hum of the room, she swore she could hear his warped threats and put-downs.

The office morning had passed like all the others. No one

visited her. No one spoke to her. No one called her. She could've cracked open his Scotch and put her tapes on and no one would've been any the wiser. Instead, she made a start on the sandwiches that her dad had made her. If only he knew that hunger was the least of her problems.

The phone rang.

"Hello, New Direction Catalogues, Mr Dolby's receptionist speaking."

"You still there then? God, you've got some fucking front, haven't you?"

"What do you mean?"

"I'd thought that would have been obvious."

"Well it's not. Where have you been?"

"Never mind that. That's none of your business. I cannot believe you're still there, in my office …You embarrass me in front of my friends, make me look a right fool and you have the temerity to presume you're still under my employment."

"You were attacking those girls. Those girls were pleading for you to stop. She was handcuffed to a chair for God's sake. What kind of monster are you?"

"That, my dear, was role play. Drop the act Sarah, it's getting tedious."

"What act, what do you mean?"

"That you're all naïve and innocent, when we all know what type of girl you are."

"Do not change the subject. What you were doing with those girls was real."

"Oh, fuck off Sarah. Stop acting so bloody innocent. It's a grown-up world and this is what grown-ups do. I don't know why you didn't join in …To be honest I was surprised that you didn't."

"You're sick."

"And you're a fucking headace. And what's more, get out of my office. I'm coming in this afternoon and I expect you not to be there, okay?"

"I'll have you know that I've sorted this office, this company out, while you've been wherever you've been. It was a right mess. This place would have gone under without me."

"Ha, oh my, that's a good one that is …Delusions of grandeur my dear. There is nothing in that office, in that place, that I don't know about. Nothing moves without my say so."

"That's rubbish. This place was in a right mess—"

"You don't get it, do you? You have served your purpose. You're over. Clear your desk and get out."

"Sorry?"

"You're over. Finished. Kaput. Thank you and fuck off."

"You're sacking me?"

"My, you catch on quick."

"I've done nothing wrong. I've worked so hard."

"God, you're pathetic. 'I've done nothing wrong.' Listen carefully, coz I won't say it again …Pack your stuff and fuck off."

"You can't treat me like this."

"That's just it Sarah, I can treat you anyway I wish. You're nothing to me."

"I'm going to the police—"

"And say what …Go on, what will you say? 'I'm a tart who sleeps with two men at the same time.' They'll laugh in your face. Ask for Sergeant Jakes, he's a good friend of mine. He'll sort you out. Slander darling, look up what it means before you go shouting your mouth off. You have two hours to get out and then I do not want to see any trace of you ever again."

"I'll tell the union—"

"Two hours!"

He negotiated the mountains of paperwork covering the entrance to the garage as if he was on a tire-drill.

"What the fuck is going on? This is a bloody disgrace."

Inside, things were even worse. His personal effects scattered all over the floor – his Crombie, his favourite cup, his pictures drenched in shards of glass and wood.

He faced his workforce who to a man stared open-mouthed at his office window.

"Who's done this? What the fucking hell …Look at the state of the place …Which of you fuckers has done this? C'mon, fucking tell me. Tell me! Was this you? I'll fucking murder whoever's done this."

"Don't know Dolby. We're more interested in who's done that."

"Done what? What are you fucking talking about?"

"That over there …"

Dolby looked up towards his office window.

"The fucking bitch. What has she done?"

In scandalous red capitals, still wet and dripping, was the word,

RAPIST.

"Where she's gone Jackson?"

"I don't know boss, maybe the police with a bit of luck because if she doesn't, we will."

"Jackson, you're fucking sacked."

"Fuck off Dolby; you're nothing but a sex case."

Clive spat his chewing gum at him, hitting him full in the face. The crowd cheered and applauded.

He vowed to up his game.

13TH MARCH 1947

He inched deeper into his bed. Consumed by woollen waves, twenty-thousand leagues under the sea. From the surface came a familiar cacophony of late-night music and rambunctious laughter, a reminder that he could run but never hide.

"James … James."

Please Father, stop this. Please save me.

"James! Don't be insolent now. You know what night it is. Don't disobey me."

It was her but it didn't sound like her. Or at least the 'her' he cared to remember. Whisky and bitterness had long since captured her voice and they weren't negotiating.

"Yes mother. Coming mother."

He unbuttoned his pyjama top and brushed away his tears with the back of his hand.

Remember what Father said. We cannot falter in the face of fear nor succumb to evil. I must be brave. Like he was.

She was waiting at the bottom of the stairs, her orange hair whipped like an ice cream. Warpaint by Coco the Clown. She held her cigarette holder like an Olympic torch (which was apt, as that too never went out), its fallen ash staining her blue floral frock.

"You better not show me up tonight, lad. Not like last time.

You're going to fight like a man, not a bloody Aunt Sally. And don't forget, if you give up, I'll finish the job myself."

Mr Turnpike, owner of the cavernous hotel on the corner and Mr Thompson, the retired sports teacher, had taken their positions on the Queen Ann sofa like a pair of elephant seals awaiting thrown fish.

"We need an improved performance don't we James?"

"Yes, Mr Thompson sir."

"None of that blubbing and whining like the last time."

"Yes sir. Absolutely sir."

Across the living room stood his brother, George, his bare chest glazed with perspiration. His black hair cropped to the bone. He was a year and a half younger and a couple of inches shorter than James. These disparities though conferred only advantages: his torso more powerful, his mentality free from the pressure of victory. He banged his battered gloves together, never taking his eyes off his target.

"That's the spirit George. Get stuck in. Mr Turnpike and I want to see a good, competitive fight. Now we know the rules don't we? You fight until one of you is knocked out or submits—"

"I've told him, if he gives up again, I'll finish him myself…"

"Quite, Mrs Dolby. Okay boys, on the count of three. One … two … fight!"

George barnstormed forward, snorting like a bull, his right hand cocked. James ducked right, barely suppressing a scream, his reflexes honed by pure terror. A left hook hit him flush on the nose; waves of nausea overcoming him, his brain spinning like a rouge waltzer.

Please Father … please

A left jab contorted his jaw. He stumbled backwards, propped up by the window ledge. *Pain. Too much pain.* He glanced towards the living room door but she had it covered.

"Don't even think about it. Not this time."

A left hook slammed into his gut. His diaphragm spasmed; his lungs emptying of air.

I'm suffocating.

Mr Turnpike and Mr Thompson were by now on their feet.

"Finish him George. Finish him."

George did as Mr Turnpike told him; pulling his right hand back like an archer's arrow before ...CRACK. A fountain of blood burst from James' eyebrow. He dropped to his knees, swaying like a Weeble. His whole world turned upside down. A hand gripped his shoulder, steadying his motion. Was this too much even for her?

"Don't you give up like last time – fight like a man. Like your father did. Don't you dare soil his memory."

She pulled him up and pushed him back into the centre of the room. For the first time, George's face betrayed a wince.

"Shall we stop, Mother?"

"If you stop, George, I'll hit you myself. Is that what you want?"

"No Mother."

"Then win the fight."

The end was nigh, time slowing to a standstill. The rabid anticipation on the faces of Mr Turnpike and Mr Thompson, his mother's scowl, his on-coming brother, all demonically enhanced by a red film of blood.

Finish me. Finish me for good.

11TH JUNE 1975

The park was emptying at a rate of knots. The only thing not calling it a day were the squadrons of gnats that had terrorised the picnic and swing areas and were now, despite Lundy's best efforts, moving onto the graveled car park.

"Fuck off. Leave me alone."

He threw down his rolled-up newspaper and escaped to the opposite side of the Triumph.

"Tell me, what is the point of those little bastards?"

He pulled a fag from his top pocket and sparked it. To his right, Jessica and the other diaphanously dressed mums marched their cherry-faced children towards the changing rooms.

"Try not to work too hard, Lundy."

"I'll try my best. I'm pacing myself. Don't take ages."

"I'll take as long as it takes ...Unless you want to take over?"

"No, no, you're doing a great job."

He took a deep drag of his burn and blew its smoke towards the ruddy sky.

I'm not the man I was. I'm shedding skins. I'm weakening. I'm weakening.

She'd fallen over in the sack race; her face marked by confusion and discomfort. Jessica stood yards in front of her, putting the world to rights with the other mums. He had waited for her to pick June up, but she had other ideas.

"C'mon June, you can do it. Get up and carry on for Mummy. C'mon June ..."

Hessian entangled her from top to bottom. A big fish in a small net. A feeling of intense sickness, a terrible delirium, began smashing up his feelings box.

"I'm coming kid, don't worry, I'm coming ..."

He ducked under the string separating the parents from the grassy track and ran towards her.

"Okay kid? Okay June? Do you want to carry on?"

"Gordon, what are you doing?"

"Nothing Jessica. Just picking her up that's all ...Okay June? C'mon June, up you get."

"She can get up herself. Piss off over there, you're making a scene."

He skulked back under the rope, his face pure crimson, desperate to disappear within the cloak of spectators. As he negotiated his way past puzzled looks and picnic blankets, he thought this conclusive proof of something Dolby had always said. Virtue is a fatal vice.

His snakeskin boot rubbed his ash into the gravel. "Tut, look at that. Where's that come from?" He leant over the Triumph and fingered a mark away from its bonnet. This was another change: he'd become a clean freak.

"You got a light, pal?"

"What?"

"A light, my bloody lighter has run out."

"Er ... yeah, hang on."

Buy some fucking matches then you speccy bastard.

"There you go."

"Cheers pal. You must be very proud of your daughter; she's a real fighter. I presume it was your daughter, the girl in the sack race."

"Yeah."

Who the fuck are you?

"Mine's over there. See the blonde-haired girl, just jumping into the sand pit? Oh my God, look at the state of her trousers, her mum's just changed her."

Who's that then, fucking Yoko Ono?

"Right."

"It's Charles by the way."

The man extended his hand.

"Gordon."

"Nice to meet you Gordon. I've not seen you here before, is this your first time?"

"Yeah."

"I thought it was when I saw you duck under the rope there. Don't be ashamed of letting your emotions get the better of you. These are emotional events."

"I bet."

"Listen to me though like I'm some kind of old timer, this is only my third time here. My excuse was I was working too bloody hard …Anyway, got my priorities right now. Once you've been, you can't wait for the next one."

"I'm sure."

"Yes, it's Miss Hughes, the woman just stood there in blue jeans that does most of the work. She's a real hero."

"Right."

"Yeah, she is. Well, anyway, I better be going and stop my wife from having a nervous breakdown. Nice to have met you, I hope to see you again sometime."

"Hmm."

"See you then. Oh, my goodness, what on earth is she doing now?"

"Wait."

"Yes?"

"Does yours speak?"

"Sorry?"

"Does your kid speak?"

"Well, she communicates more than she speaks."

"What do you mean?"

"She shouts when she's excited and she makes it known when she's not happy."

"June's like that."

"That's a lovely name."

"I didn't name her."

"Oh okay, it's still a nice name. My girl's called Vanessa."

"Right. I've only known her a couple of months."

"Who, June?"

"Yeah."

"Really, goodness me. This must have really come as a shock."

"It has, I had no idea I had a kid, let alone a …"

"Special child?"

"Yeah, a special child. Her mum was a bit of a fling really."

"I see, easy done I bet. We are all red-blooded men after all."

"Have you been caught out too?"

"Well, no but I remember watching a programme on that sort of thing."

"Right. Yes, she just asked me to meet her one day and introduced me to her."

"My God, no wonder you're a bit, well, affected by the whole thing."

Lundy moved closer and lowered his voice.

"How do you cope?"

"Sorry?"

"How do you live with it?"

"How do you mean?"

"That she isn't normal."

"Erm … what's normal?"

"They're not normal. We're not normal."

"I don't quite follow."

"They're never going to talk. They're never going to grow up or get married or have kids."

"Yes, that's true."

"Doesn't that bother you?"

"Well, yes—"

"And it doesn't bother you that we're failures as men?"

"What?"

"We're wrong inside, we're shooting junk."

"Jesus man, who told you that?"

"It stands to reason, doesn't it? We're not real men. The one thing that we're put on this earth to do, we can't do it."

"You really believe that?"

"Don't you?"

"No. I'm not a scientist but I think that I'm on safe ground saying there are numerous reasons that can cause a child to be handicapped, not just deficiencies in the male er ... well, sperm."

"Really?"

"Yes."

"That's fucking brilliant. What a relief that is. Fantastic."

"Well, if you say so."

"I knew it was her mum. I knew it. She tried to imply it was me but I knew it was her."

"Quite. But tell me, if it was down to us and by your logic we were defective and not real men, then how would you view June, as broken, as abnormal, as less than human?"

"No, of course not."

"I'm afraid that's what your logic is implying."

"No it's not. You're putting words into my mouth."

"I don't think I am."

"You fucking are."

"I think you'll find I'm not."

"Yeah, you are."

"No, I'm definitely not."

Lundy moved menacingly towards him.

"Listen you fucking poof, you're skating on thin ice here. Just because you wear a fucking kaftan and throw words like 'logic' around does not make you better than me."

"Hang on, let me make one thing very clear and I really cannot stress this enough ...I've never, ever, worn a kaftan in my life."

"Very fucking clever. You better fuck off pal before I do you."

"Okay, if only to reaffirm your manliness for the second time today, I will humbly retreat."

"Good decision."

"Bye then and don't be too hard on yourself."

"Yeah, walk away dickhead."

Yeah, I needed that. Lundy 1, John Lennon 0. Why do I feel like shit then? Hang on, he's fucking winning. He's walking away the better man.

"Hey, what do you mean reaffirm my manliness?"

The man stopped and wearily turned around.

"Look, I don't want to argue with you. I should be more sensitive to the fact that you are still new to this and it must have been such a trauma for you. It's just that I'm sensitive to any inference that my daughter is any less of a child, any less of a human. Because she's not and I wouldn't change Vanessa one little bit."

"Now I know you must be on fucking drugs. You wouldn't change her? Fuck off ..."

"No, I wouldn't, not one bit. She is who she is and I love her for who she is and I will always love her. And do you know why?"

"Go on."

"Because she's my daughter and I am her fucking father, okay?"

Fuck, look at him, he means it. Despite everything, all the looks and snide comments, he loves her ...What shall I do now? I'll kick him in the balls.

"I'm sorry."

"Don't bother yourself Gordon, it's fine."

"No, really I'm sorry. I'm sorry for threatening you. You're right. You're right about everything. It's just, I can't explain it. I think I'm ..."

"Gordon, it's fine, there's no offence taken. Listen, I hope you don't mind me saying this but with everything you've been through, have you thought about seeing your doctor?"

"She knows my wife. My wife can't find out about June."

"Oh right, I see."

"I can feel myself being overpowered. I look at June and I see so many other faces, so many different things. Everything's moving too fast."

26TH MARCH 1983

With trembling fingers, he slowly pulled ajar the door. His father was in his usual position, sat at the large wooden table in their large wooden kitchen; his bald plate almost halo-like under the flourescent ceiling lights; his moustache twitching as he examined the blueprints that were rapidly becoming default tablecloths. Dave checked the undercarriage of his Spitfire MkVb Messerschmitt. It felt precarious, the adhesive flaky and forlorn.

Oh no, it's collapsing. I can't give him this. I'll never hear the end of it.

He turned and made for his room, climbing the red Axminstered stairs two at a time. His mum was coming the other way, a grey face pack covering her elfin features.

"I thought you were showing that to your dad, love?"

"The glue's not sticking Mum. It's falling apart."

"Give it here."

"I can't Mum. I need to re-glue the bottom."

"Let me have a look. You don't want to cake it in glue. You'll spoil it."

"No, Mum ..."

"Give it here, David."

"No, it's loose, you'll break it."

"David!"

"Okay, here you are, but it's going to collapse. Thanks very much for that."

She held the model to the light.

"There's nothing wrong with it."

"The undercarriage is wobbly. He'll notice. You know what he's like."

She put her hand on his shoulder.

"Love, it's fine. Honestly, it's perfect. I know how hard you've worked on this, go and show him. He'll be pleased you're taking an interest in his work."

He didn't move.

"Go on, show him."

He gradually turned around and shuffled back down the stairs before stopping on the penultimate step and turning towards his mum.

"Go on love. I'm proud of you, we're proud of you."

He knocked on the door, a nervous child entering the headmaster's office. There was no reply. He knocked again and received the same response.

"Go in love. He'll be lost in his work."

He inched the door open.

"Dad, have you got a sec?"

"Sorry?"

"I want to show you something."

"What do you want?"

"I want to show you something I've made, Dad."

"What's the matter?"

"Nothing Dad, I just want to show you this that I've made."

"I'm busy David. I'll look at it later."

He turned towards his mum, standing arms folded in the doorway.

"Gerry just look at it, the poor bugger has been working on it for weeks."

He threw his pen across the table.

"Right, give it here then. I mean, it's not like I've not got any proper work to do."

Dave placed the model in his dad's hands as if it were an injured bird. He lifted it to eye level and studied its wings and cockpit. He fingered its fuselage and checked its horizontal stabilisers. He examined its nose and insignia. He even moved it through the air, measuring its aerodynamic potential. Then he handed it back to his son.

"Like I say, I'm busy."

7TH JULY 2002

His Guinness stood neglected. He was too preoccupied with the implications of his surroundings. Its mock-Tudor pretentions, ornamental brasses and carvery families confirming his worst fears. This was the last place on earth he'd expect him to frequent.

He ripped open another beer mat, its white innards falling onto the adhesive carpet, his mum's words replaying loop-like in his mind.

I kept a lot from you David. I didn't want to upset you, see. Didn't want you to think bad of your father. This isn't the first. He's had many others. He's always stayed with me though. He's never left me before. I just want him to come home. I just want things back the way they were.

"Hello, Son. Great to see you."

"Right, yes."

"Good choice of seat this."

"Is it?"

"Yeah, you get a real panoramic view of the place from here. Must be your copper's instinct …"

"Must be."

"Got a pint, have you?"

"Er … yes. I've got one, thanks."

"Right, I'll just get myself one then."

"Okay."

"You sure I can't get you a top-up."

"No, I'm fine thanks."

He sauntered towards the bar, aiming a dig into the ribs of a man standing next to a luminous fruit machine. He returned the favour and a jocular sparring session broke out.

What the fuck is he doing? Why is he trying to act like a normal bloke? With his Pringle and fucking turtleneck ...He's not a normal bloke; he's my father. My father is not normal.

He returned with a pint of bitter and a packet of crisps.

"Nice place this isn't it David?"

"Er, I suppose so."

"Good crowd too."

"Yeah, seems it."

"Had a cracking night in here last week. A band played, *Taylor's Dummy* they were called. Bloody good. Better than all that rubbish in the charts."

"'The charts.' Since when have you known what's in the charts?"

"Well, I don't. Not really anyway but I bet a pound to a penny that they were better than anything in the charts. The singer had a beautiful falsetto on her."

"Dad, what the fuck is going on?"

"What do you mean?"

"This pub, that *Pringle* jumper, the fucking affair you've been having that has left Mum in pieces ..."

"Right, that's why you wanted to see me."

"Why else would I fucking want to see you?"

"Well, I thought you may want a pint with the old man."

"Dad, it may have escaped your attention but we don't have that kind of relationship. I mean, throughout my childhood you barely said a friendly word to me. The first time I saw you smile was when *You've Been Framed* started on the telly and by that point I was fucking eleven years of age. And now it's all pints and toy fighting with guys in pubs … and shagging other women."

"David, I won't have you using that language in front of me."

"Oh, I'm sorry if my language offends you but it's just that the way you've treated Mum really fucking offends *me*."

"I'm just saying that you can make your point without swearing that's all."

"You've lost any right to lecture me."

"I'm not lecturing you; I'm just saying."

"Who is she then? Who is your bit on the side?"

"She's not my bit on the side. Her name is Jayne and I love her."

"Are you serious? You can't be serious?"

"I'm absolutely serious. One hundred and ten percent. You know when you know."

"And what about Mum in all this?"

"Well, yes, I'm very sorry about that. Trust me, if there was any other way—"

"She said you've confessed to numerous affairs. Is that true?"

"Well, yes. I suppose it is."

"How many?"

"Numbers aren't important, David."

"'Numbers aren't important.' Shit, were you that prolific? Are we talking single or double figures here?"

"Don't twist my words David. What I meant is that by the very fact that I sought solace elsewhere tells you that your mother and I were over a long time ago. No one regrets that more than I do but that's the reality of the situation. That said, I've given you both a good standard of living – I mean, you could not have had a better start in life, David – and now I just need to be happy. Don't worry about your mother, she'll be fine, she'll find someone else. She's still a good-looking woman."

"You've gone fucking nuts. You're having a mental break-down."

"Oh, don't be so overdramatic."

"You know, I was thinking before while you were rough-housing with your mate over there—"

"Who Barry? He's a great lad. He's invited me to Silverstone for the Grand Prix."

"Fucking hell …Anyway, as I was saying, even though you were never much of a father to me, there was one thing about you I always respected – you always knew where you stood. You had principles. I didn't appreciate it at the time but … for example, do you remember when I was a kid and we were watching the news and that politician was at the war remembrance with a scruffy jacket on—"

"Michael Foot, bloody Communist scumbag."

"Yeah him. Well you probably don't remember this but I made a comment about not understanding the fuss, that it was only a jacket. Mum didn't say anything and neither did you. I forgot I even said it. You left the room and we just presumed that you're back at your table. You're gone for about ten minutes and then you return with a big sheet of paper and stick it on the wall. You never said a word, you just stuck it on there. Can you remember what it said?"

"Vaguely, it was such a long time ago."

"There was two headings. One of them said *Us* and the other *Them.* Under *Us,* you put *Maggie, God Save the Queen, The*

Wrench's and for some reason the fucking *SAS*. Under *Them* you put something like *Michael Foot and his mates Scargill & Benn,* I remember *CND* being on there ...Oh yeah, and with your finger firmly on the pulse, *The Rolling Stones.* I mean, don't get me wrong it was weird. Very weird. But at least you stood for something. What do you stand for now?"

"I still stand for all those things. I was in the RAF for forty bloody years."

"Do you really though?"

"Yes, really."

"Bollocks."

"Absolutely, I do David. Look, as I said, I was unhappy with your mother for years. Very unhappy. I wanted to leave – like him next door but one to us. Do you remember? He left his wife for another woman ...Two young kids they had – but I couldn't do it. I couldn't leave you without a father. I stayed for you, David. I mean, in many ways and I'm not saying that I expect this or anything, you should be thanking me."

"What the fuck are you talking about?"

"I was desperate to go but I didn't and that was because of you. I delayed happiness and contentment for you."

"Oh, thank you so very much. Where's the phone? I've got to ring *Modern Parenting* magazine, we've got a late entry into their 'Dad of the Year' competition."

"There's no need to be sarcastic David."

"I mean, maybe you should stand on the table and inform everybody about your sacrifices. Tell them all what a wonderful, principled man you are."

"He who casts the first stone, David ..."

"And what's that supposed to mean?"

"It means we've all done things we regret."

"I'm sorry?"

"Nothing, forget I said it."

"Whoa, hang on, if you've got something to say big man let it rip. Don't spare my feelings, it's never stopped you before."

"I said forget it."

"Go on; get it off your chest. Show some balls."

"Alright, seeing as you've pushed me, I will. I was simply pointing out you've got a bit of form yourself in this regard."

"Oh, it's all coming out now isn't it …That's the icing on the cake that is."

"I'm sorry if it's a low blow, I'm just pointing out we are all human. We are all fallible."

"Really."

"Yes, really."

"You fucking bastard. I cannot believe you've brought that up. You know what she meant to me. I fucking loved her."

"Yes, like I love Jayne, David."

"Janis was very different to your tawdry setup."

"Yes, she was married."

"To some jerk who didn't deserve her."

"Two kids, if I remember rightly."

"So?"

"So you split the marriage up."

"The marriage was already split up."

"And what about that other girl you were seeing? She was bloody engaged. You got a punch in the eye that time."

"Again, Angela was unhappy. She was trapped with a thug, a bully."

"That's not what you told me. When I asked you why don't

you find someone unattached you said something like … well, you implied it was a strategy."

"That's crap and you know it."

"'Birds in long-term relationships fixate on what they hate rather than love about their men and you just need to do the opposite,' you said. I was shocked. And your mother—"

"I said that the night me and Angela broke up. I was pissed. Pissed up bravado that was. You knew I wasn't serious."

"Fine …Look David, I was merely pointing out that affairs of the heart are tricky. Morality tends to go out of the window."

"No, you're right. Maybe I'm a chip off the old block. Monkey see, monkey fucking do. But at least I feel bad for some of the things I've done. You couldn't give a shit."

"That's not true David. I feel very sorry for you and your mother, truly I do, but I just can't fight my feelings any longer."

"It's all about you isn't it?"

"Look Son. I don't expect you to forgive me instantly but I'm sure that over time you'll appreciate my point of view. And I'm also sure that once you've met Jayne, had a chat, got to know her, you'll feel differently. She'll be here soon. You'll see."

"What … you've invited her to our meeting? One of the most important conversations that we've ever had and you've invited your bit on the side?"

"I've not invited her David."

"You're unbelievable. What are you after, my blessing?"

"I didn't invite her David. She works here; this is where I met her. She's working the evening shift."

"She's a fucking barmaid!"

"And what's wrong with that?"

"You're taking the piss. Could you actually be any more midlife crisis?"

"If you like …Look, I love her. She's fifteen years my junior and she's bloody gorgeous."

"You're unbelievable."

"David, I'm happy. Is that not important? For the first time in years, I'm happy. Does that not make *you* feel happy? Or would you be happier to see me sticking to my principles but continue to be miserable. Is that what you want?"

"I want you to go back to Mum and work it out. She's in bits."

"And like I say, I am sorry for that David, truly I am. But I cannot go back."

"There must be some love still left between you …"

"There isn't David. I wish there was – it would make things a lot easier but there isn't."

"Well, as long as you're happy eh Dad? Enjoy the rest of your life."

Dave stood up, slammed his chair under the table and walked away.

"I am happy David, and I am simply not willing to compromise my feelings any longer."

16TH JANUARY 1997

His letterbox accepted today's missives of doom as if it were a hunger striker being force-fed. Its screeching madness though was music to Adam's ears. That his shithole still merited something as formal as an address evidence of his worth. In reality, his house was a house in the respect that it had four walls; none of the other accoutrements of a property were either present or correct – a floor bereft of craters, a functioning kitchen, glass windows. The housing association had given him a final warning but this was almost five years ago and he'd heard nothing since. He'd figured, like most people, they just couldn't be bothered dealing with him. His letterbox burst into a cacophony again. It couldn't be the postman this time.

Oh shit, he knows where I live. He's come for me. He's not finished.

It didn't stop. It got worse. Louder. Enhanced by the bang of an unknown boot.

"Grimes, it's me. Open the fucking door."

A new sensation overcame him: A feeling of relief at the sound of Flames' voice.

"C'mon Grimes, it's fucking brass out here."

"Coming mate. Just a sec."

His thigh collided with one of the plastic garden tables strewn across his living room.

"Ow you bastard."

"What?"

"No, not you Flames. I banged my leg."

"Hurry up!"

He limped towards his front door – a wave of mail carrying him the final few yards, and yanked it open.

"Fucking finally. Jesus Christ, have you seen the state of your face?"

"Of course I've seen it. It's pretty hard to fucking miss."

Oh fuck, here we go. Go on then, hit an unmarked spot.

"Don't push it Dickhead."

That he issued a yellow card for what would normally be a headbuttable offence was for Adam confirmation he accepted culpability for this mess. And what a mess he was. His face resembled a battered street football with bulges of rubber bursting through its decaying leather.

"Can I come in or what? It's fucking freezing out here."

"Yeah, of course, it's freezing in here too though, my electric's run out."

He pimp-rolled into the hallway, colliding his fibreglass shoulder with Adam's midriff.

"For fuck's sake, it's colder in here than out there!"

"I know, sorry, come and sit in here, if you can find a space."

"Fucking hell Grimes, you need to get a fucking grip. What a shithole."

"That's ironic that is because this is your shit. Your fucking garden furniture that's been sat here for over a year now."

There was to be no more second chances. Flames moved towards him as if a crocodile stalking a labouring prey.

"No please don't. I am sorry; I'm just in a lot of pain that's all."

"Listen you cunt, I'll only make so many allowances for your injuries. Don't take advantage of my good nature."

"No, you're right, I'm sorry mate. I'm just a bit shook up. I'm sorry."

"Okay, but you need to sort your fucking head out."

"I will. Listen mate, you sit on the chair, I'll take this plastic one. Make yourself comfortable, put your feet up. Do you want a drink?"

"Not from your skanky fucking cups I don't."

"That's probably wise."

Adam lowered himself into the chair.

"Fuck!"

They say in a fight, adrenaline inoculates pain. However, to use the word "fight" to describe what went on in the bowels of that warehouse would be a misnomer. He was not in a fight; he was subject to a beating. A fact of which his hip had just reminded him.

"What's up?"

"Nothing, my hip is really sore."

"Who did that then, the fucking law?"

"No, he did it."

"Who?"

"The guy from the warehouse, the owner."

"Who, that old bastard?"

"Yeah, well his henchman that big ginger guy did most of it."

"He didn't call the law?"

"No, I wish he would have done."

"Thank fuck for that …I cannot believe he fucked you up though. He looked super straight to me. His henchman looked toy as fuck as well. What happened, did he just do you?"

"Well he took me, John, Gat and the old guy, Bailey, into the bogs, right? The boss, Dolby he said his name was, takes Bailey outside. Then it goes quiet. The big fucker guarding us isn't saying a word and we're too busy shitting ourselves to say anything. Every now and then though you can hear like shouts and screams. Dolby comes back in after about five minutes, flushed as fuck, and there's no sign of Bailey. But I can see blood on his knuckles, so he must have given him a good slap. Then he asks John and me to get our bags because he wants to search them."

"Fuck, did you have owt on you?"

"Yeah, my fucking pipe and at least a quarter of weed, nothing stolen though ...Gat has fuck all on him and as for John, 'course he's got nowt on him. I mean it was like the fucking *Generation Game,* I could have told you what he had in there before he got it out: a bag of pumpkin seeds, some mad vitamins and the fucking Dali Lama's autobiography. Straight up!"

"Ha, did he ask about me?"

"Yeah, he wanted to know your address."

"Cheeky bastard. You didn't give it him did you?"

"No, of course not but John told him we were mates, so he lets him go and then it's just me, Gat and the two of them."

"He's a fucking cunt that John. I never trusted him. What did they do?"

"They ask Gat, does he know you or any of the other runners and he says 'no' and because he had nothing in his bag, they let him go. By this time, I am feeling pretty uneasy about the whole thing."

"Fucking Gat, the stuffy bastard."

"Tell me about it. Next right, he tells me straight off the bat that he's not going to call the police and says something about being in the army and how they deal with things differently there."

"Fuck off."

"No, seriously ...He pulls his chair right up close to me. He's saying, 'who nicked my stuff, was it you?' And I keep telling him that it's not me, that I've never been into robbing and then he says it's to feed my drug habit and I'm telling him I don't have a drug habit, I just smoke a bit of draw that's all. And he just keeps getting closer and closer into my face, just repeating, 'tell me who's stolen my stock, give me a name.' Then he says like, 'Taylor, give him a reminder,' something like that and that's when he cracks me for the first time."

"Fucking hell, it's like a proper gangster film."

"Then he starts going on about serving in Belfast and how he's got information from a lot better than me and that big fucker just keeps hitting me. Grabbing my throat with one hand and hitting me with the other."

"And you never said owt, you stayed schtum?"

"Yeah, after a while they presumed I didn't know anything so they let me go."

That he'd delivered his account with an air of nonchalance was an attempt at conjuring some street kudos from the affair. In reality, he had kept his mouth shut insofar as he didn't tell them who had pilfered their stock. (Whatever savagery Dolby and his porridge-box droog meted out would be nothing compared to his fate if he had grassed Flames up.) In every other sense though, his mouth was wide open, begging them for mercy, pleading his innocence, screaming like a teething child. The only reason they let him go was that they could no longer stand his caterwauling.

"You're a proper fucking soldier. I never knew you had it in you."

"Well, I'm tougher than I look."

"Too fucking right you are. I don't want you to worry about it though mate, we'll get the bastard back."

"Yeah?"

"Oh yeah, I've got the perfect plan."

"Right."

"He won't know what's hit him."

"Good ...Listen mate, I appreciate that but to be honest I'd rather leave it."

"Leave it. After what he's done to you, no chance mate. Fucking no way are we doing that."

"Cheers man, I mean I appreciate the support and all that but like I said the other day, fighting isn't my bag. Don't get me wrong, I can look after myself; I just don't see the point of it. If it's all the same to you, I'd rather leave it."

"Whoa, hang on, who said anything about fighting? I'm not suggesting that we fight him; I'm talking about robbing the bastard. Proper fucking payback. I know where he lives, see."

16TH JUNE 1975

T he hallway was dead. A ten-storey pendulum clock the only challenge to this formidable quiet. He sat on the bottom stair, his head cradled in his hands. How much further does he want to go? What depths are there left to trawl? Where will this end? No one needed to tell him. It would end in cold blood and that wasn't him. At one time maybe, but not now.

He had never said no to him before – his excuse for not attending his last party was a phantom flu bug and doing so felt like the end of the fucking world.

He picked up the phone then put it down before picking it up again.

"Hello pal."

"Is that you Gordon?

"It certainly is Mr Dolby."

"How's things Gord?"

"Not bad, you?"

"Good. Very good in fact. I'm just putting the finishing touches to our next little soirée"

"Right, good."

"Yeah, I've been assured these brasses are, how can I put it … a little bit more resilient than the last lot, if you know what I mean. John's bringing a new piece and some of her friends as well. Barely out of school uniform he reckons."

"Have you heard from Sarah?"

"What the fuck do you care?"

"Nothing. No, I don't care. I'm just wondering, that's all."

"Trust me, that fucking bitch is not going to ruin this party."

"Absolutely."

"Did you hear what she did?"

"Yeah, Taffy rang me the other day."

"Ungrateful bitch, after all we've done for her. No mate, this party will be fucking perfect, trust me."

"I bet. To be honest pal, it's the party I want to speak to you about."

"Yeah."

"I can't make it."

"What, again?"

"I'm sorry pal."

"No, you've got to be there. You're already accounted for."

"I know. I'm sorry to let you down, something's come up."

"Cancel it."

"I can't James. I really can't."

"No, you need to."

"I'm sorry mate, I can't."

"Is it Rose? We can come up with a cover story. C'mon man, we've done it plenty of times before. I need you at this party. Listen, these brasses are fresh meat we can do what we want to them."

"No, it's not Rose."

"Well it must be pretty important for you to sell-out your

best friend for."

"No, it's not like that James."

"What is it like then?"

"If I'm being honest old boy, I need a bit of a break. It's not making me happy anymore."

"What the fuck has happiness got to do with it?"

"I've just got other things on my mind that's all."

"What other things? C'mon Gord, you can't break up the old partnership, the old team."

"I'm not breaking it up James, just giving it a rest for a bit."

"Fine. Just come on Saturday then."

"No, like I say I can't."

"Okay, I'll expect to see you Saturday then."

"No, James I can't."

"Listen you selfish bastard, you're coming to this party on Saturday whether you want to or not. Because if you don't ... well you'll see. You're getting me angry now Lundy."

"Do you remember that married woman I was seeing, Jessica? Lived just off Hastings' main road, on Algeron Street?"

"Yes, so? What's that got to do with the price of fucking fish?"

"She's had my daughter."

"What?"

"I'm a father. Jessica's invited me round for the first time on Saturday for a night in with her and June ...That's her name, June."

"You stupid bastard. You stupid, stupid bastard."

"C'mon old boy, I thought at least congratulations would be in order."

"How do you know it's yours? If my memory serves, wasn't her husband a loser? Worked on the fucking parks or something like that? This is a money thing you know."

"No, she's definitely mine. She looks like me and everything."

"Does Rose know?"

"God no."

"I can't believe it. A kid. You stupid bastard."

"No, it's not like that. I'm really fond of her."

"Oh Jesus, have you heard yourself, you stupid bastard."

"You'll know when you've had one. You'll know then what I mean."

"Don't patronise me you idiot. I'm a colt son, a wild horse. I don't need anybody weighing me down. Just deny it's yours … Listen to me Gordon, you're being very weak here and you'll end up regretting it. Say it's not yours, and if she starts getting uppity threaten her."

"No, it's mine; I want it to be mine."

"Where's her husband in all this?"

"That's just it, he's gone. There's no one to help bring the kid up."

"Right, that's very noble of you."

"Thanks James."

"I was being sarcastic you fucking idiot."

"Now come on James, don't be like that."

"I'll be exactly how I want to be and no two-bit woodworm seller is going to tell me any different. Okay?"

"Okay."

"I always knew you were fucking soft. I always knew you had a tendency towards this kind of thing—"

"What kind of thing?"

"This fucking nonsense - 'I've got a fucking kid and I'm such a good family man. No, I can't go to the pub tonight because I've got a date to walk around fucking *Mothercare* with, some fucking gold-digger.' You're making a mockery of everything we stand for."

"To be honest James, I'm not sure we stand for anything."

"But that's where you're wrong, Gordon. Don't tell me that you thought this was just about the sex?"

"Well, yes."

"C'mon James, I shouldn't need to explain this to you. Yes, the sex is part of it but it's what it symbolises that's important. We do what we want, you see. We're not straightjacketed by the mores of the damned and the fucking ignorant. We're beyond that ...Take the Romans, conquerors of the world; their attitude to sex was all about unleashing the animal inside, servicing female slaves whenever they wanted ... Fighting, conquering and fucking themselves raw in brass houses. Anything went, incest, the fucking lot, whatever they felt like ... because they made their own rules, see. Remind you of anybody mate?"

"Leeds United?"

"Oh, so it's a big fucking joke—"

"No I'm sorry. Us, definitely us."

"Yes Gordon, us. Strong decadent men. Doing what nature intended, raping and pillaging"

"I know mate, but like I say I can't."

"Cancel."

"No mate. I can't."

"One last chance Gordon. Tell me you're coming or I swear we're finished."

"C'mon James, don't overreact. Let's not fall out. You're my best mate …"

"If I am your best mate, say you're coming."

"I can't."

"Then you're fucking dead to me."

21ST JUNE 1975

B it by bit, day-by-day numbness had enveloped him. A kingdom of moss devastating his mind, body and soul. The stupefaction of sadism his only reprieve. (And he wasn't even feeling that anymore.) On route to Jessica's though he could barely drive for all his hand-rubbing and fist-pumps, he was like a kid on Christmas morn. A gift-wrapped brand new family his reward for being a complete bastard.

In a further testament to his new mentality, he'd come bearing gifts of his own. It had taken him an age to set it up on her dining room table. And he was beginning to wish he hadn't bothered.

"What is it?"

"Jessica, it's state of the art this you know."

"I'm sure."

"I thought you'd be impressed."

"Gordon, how can I be impressed? I don't know what it is."

"It's a projector."

"A projector?"

"Yes, a projector."

"Right."

"It's state of the art."

"It's going to scratch my dining table."

"No, it's not."

"It better not. Whose is it?"

"I got it from a mate of mine."

"Does it work?"

"'Course it works ...You can get a cracking picture from one of these."

"Really?"

"Yes, really."

"What are we watching then? I hope it's not one of your home videos; I've just had my tea."

"Actually, it's a Disney film, *Fantasia.*"

"Disney?"

"Yes Disney. You know, Goofy, Tom and Jerry ..."

"I'm a bit past that. It's hardly *Jaws* is it?"

"That's because it's for June. I got it for June."

"I know, I'm only kidding. No, it's a lovely thought, it really is. Although I don't know how much you'll get from her. She's been a right sod today."

"Nonsense, everyone loves a bit of Disney."

Jessica laughed.

"What's so funny?"

"Nothing."

"Well, you're laughing at something ..."

"Nothing I said."

"Tell me!"

"No, it's just that last sentence that you said."

"What about it?"

"'Everyone loves a bit of Disney' is pretty much the most incongruous thing I could ever imagine you saying."

And that's why I said it. I'm a new man. A new man who wants to get back into your knickers.

"I don't know what you're talking about. June, c'mon and sit down love …"

"I told you, you'll be lucky."

He tiptoed towards her.

"Nonsense, I'm her dad."

"Okay Daddy but you've been warned, she'll have you."

He grabbed her hand as if fetching a ball from a nettle bush.

"C'mon June …That's it; nice and easy …Are you sitting here, no? C'mon June, sit down. June …"

"Let her stand if she doesn't want to sit."

"Okay. Right, okay, shut the curtains then. C'mon, Jessica!"

"Alright, I'm sorry. I'm new to the movie business."

He strode over to the table and fiddled with his machine.

"Here we go, it's clicking, it's starting …Look June, it's starting …See, I told you it was a good picture. Look at that, June, look at those ponies …"

"Sorry to burst your bubble Uncle Walt but those are baby Pegasuses."

"Are they? Okay then …June, look at the Pegasuses – whatever the fuck they are – and this little fella playing the trumpet."

"Actually darling, it's Beethoven's Sixth. And this isn't the start of the film."

"It's a forty-five-minute reel Jessica. You just get the highlights, the good bits. Gets rid of all the boring stuff that nobody is interested in."

"Hark at Orson Wells."

"Right, if you are just going to belittle me—"

"No, honestly I'm only kidding. It's a lovely thought, it really is …We're touched aren't we June? June? Oh my God Gordon, look at June!"

Her metronomic rocking had slowed to barely a stop. Her head moving from side to side, her face unravelling like a loosened knot.

"I've never seen her like this before."

"I told you she'd like it."

"Look at her Gordon; the music is soothing her."

Jessica burst into tears.

"Hey, what's up? Why are you upset?"

"No, I'm not, it's beautiful. It is really beautiful. I mean I never know what she's thinking, whether her brain can process any meaning or not. She just looks so confused and anxious all the time. But I know what she's thinking now. She's thinking what I'm thinking – the music is beautiful. This is beautiful."

The mother Pegasus began teaching her young to fly.

"I know, yeah."

"Gordon she's calming. Look."

"I am. I am."

"It's amazing, isn't it?"

"Yes it is."

"You don't seem very amazed, Gordon."

"No, it's the opposite … it's just I'm no good at expressing myself. It is beautiful. It's the most beautiful thing I've seen. More beautiful than when my nana first took me up to North Hill to see the stars. I'm just not really used to this. I see only shit and misery. I don't know what to say."

Jessica sidled beside him and draped her arm across his shoulder.

"Don't say anything then."

"It's like when—"

"Shush. Savour it. Savour the moment."

"Yes, okay."

The sound of squeaking hinges interrupted their vision.

"Isn't that your front gate?"

"Yeah. Who's this now? What a bloody time to come."

"Who will it be?"

"I'm not expecting anybody. My mum said she wouldn't be back with Jack until past ten."

"Whoever it is, tell them to fuck off."

They waited for a knock at the door but it never came. Other noises did though: shuffling feet on gravel, an order to "do it," and a brick bursting through her window.

"Oh my God Gordon. June. June!"

It landed in slow motion, missing her by a foot or so. The shards of glass had more luck, covering her like thrown water. She staggered back towards her chair. Her face tightly re-wound again.

12TH FEBRUARY 1997

The NDC debacle had coincided with a gradation in Flames' criminal activity. Rather than simply setting fire to things, he began pursuing rewards more tangible. To steal what he never could own, to sell more than he could ever keep. He started small, perfecting his craft on the vast swathes of sheds littering the estate before quickly advancing onto houses. Robbing from his fellow residents on the estate though was problematic, as they had nothing worthwhile to steal. Consequently, he sought targets further afield, to the more salubrious enclave of Worsley village to be precise. It was on one of his first reconnaissance missions that he spotted the saurian figure of Dolby emerging from his mock-Tudor castle. All his Christmases came at once.

Adam wanted no part of this revenge mission. Aside from a brief foray into protest graffiti, he had never broken the law and wanted to keep it that way. He just wouldn't be any good at it. He wasn't of the right stuff, or rather its wrong equivalent.

Flames was initially surprisingly sympathetic to his concerns but soon reverted to type, telling him that he had "no fucking choice in the matter. So, shut the fuck up and get on with it."

Sitting on his plastic chair, brushing the dust off the gloves and balaclava combo that he'd somehow found at the bottom of his distressed wardrobe, he recalled the documentary he'd watched the other night on the history of democracy. He would regularly watch such programmes not because he enjoyed them, he would count the minutes to their end, but the fact he could understand them reinforced his belief he was different to the rest. This programme though, with its conclusion of the need to protect this sacred institution from mad Mullahs and dog-lead anarchists, angered him to the extent he nearly threw one of Flames' gnomes through the TV set. He knew nothing of this civil society. Where he lived words like freedom, tolerance and democracy were just that – words, floating in the sky like cotton clouds, while back on terra firma the strong and psychopathic ruled at the point of a jackboot.

The house shook.

"C'mon Dickweed, open up."

"Alright, I'm coming."

If I had a coronary, I wouldn't have to go. Nice warm hospital bed too.

He limped to the door and wrenched it open.

"You're not wearing that."

"Why, you said wear a balaclava."

"Are you fucking stupid? It's the one you used to wear for school."

"So what?"

"It's got your fucking name on it in big white letters, you prick."

"Is that a problem?"

"'Is that a problem,' he says ...No, 'course it's not. Why don't you just write your address on the back of your coat ...Get a fucking grip. Here, wear this bobble hat."

"That'll be too small."

"No it'll be fine. You'll look the part."

"It's too small."

"It covers that big fucking carrot top, so it'll do."

"I look a dick."

"You are a dick. Right, you ready?"

"Not really."

"Good, let's go."

They stood in the deep woods in front of the tall wooden fence that shadowed the length of Cherry Tree Grove. According to Flames, they were standing directly in front of Dolby's place and it was sure to be empty, as he always went out on Wednesday evenings and didn't return until the early hours.

"Right, screwdriver, torch, crowbar, hammer, okay good. Now listen Grimes, you're going to help me over this fence and I'm going to force my way in. I don't want us in there longer than ten minutes. In and out."

"What about the alarm?"

"What?"

"The alarm. What happens if the alarm goes off?"

"Look at the alarm."

"What?"

"Flash the torch on the alarm. Notice anything?"

"No, it's just an alarm."

"Look closer."

"No, I can't see anything."

"Exactly, there are no lights on it. It isn't flashing. The tight bastard's got a dummy."

"I don't follow?"

"It's a blag Grimes. It's bullshit."

"Oh right, a dummy. I see."

Maybe this isn't such a bad idea. He's got all the gear with him. Could be an earner too. I mean, I've not a prayer of getting the fifty-fifty he said but I could get a few bob out of it. And imagine the bastard's face when he sees what we've done.

"Right, cup your hands Grimes."

"Why?"

"To give me a foot up."

"Okay, right."

"Cup them then."

"They are cupped."

"Make sure there's no give."

"Okay."

"Right, you ready?"

"Yeah, ready."

"Go."

He lifted him barely a few feet; Flames nearly going over his shoulder, Adam swaying like a sliced tree.

"Right, keep me steady. Keep me steady you fucking dick."

"I'm trying."

"Right, now lift. C'mon lift, lift!"

Adam's elbows shook.

Jesus, there's nothing there. I'm like a newborn baby.

"Lift, lift you soft bastard."

"I'm trying, I'm trying."

"You're moving away from it. Get closer. Straighten up for fuck's sake."

Adam careered into the fence allowing Flames' left hand to

grip its peak.

"Okay I've got it, now hold it steady, hold it for fuck's sake ... Right, one big push. With everything that you've got. Right ... now!"

He lifted from his knees, a surge of anger at having to live this way propelling Flames up the fence, enabling him to swing over his right leg.

"Fucking made it. Jesus, you've got the muscles of a fucking gnat Grimes."

"I got you up didn't I?"

"I got myself up you dick."

"Yeah, yeah. Now how do I get up?"

"What?"

"How do I get up?"

"How the fuck do I know Grimes? Climb that tree and jump over."

"I can't do that. I can't climb a tree."

"Just climb the fucking thing you soft bastard."

"It's fucking huge."

"Climb it you fucking freak."

"I'll break my neck."

"And I'll break it for you if you don't."

"Why couldn't you lift me up and then you climb the tree? You know I'm no good at this kind of thing."

"Well it's a good time to learn, Mr Fingers And Fucking Thumbs."

"What if I can't? You'll have to do it alone."

"No, I won't because I'll get back over there and beat the shit out of you if you don't. Now fucking climb the tree!"

He contemplated his adversary from bottom to top like a mountaineer at the foot of Kilimanjaro. After a farrago of slips and false starts, a shit monkey in a farcical jungle, he clambered onto a protruding branch.

Flames slow-clapped him.

"Well done Mr fucking Spiderman. Now walk on that branch, it leads right into the garden."

"It won't take my weight."

"'Course it will, stand on it, move along and then jump."

"No way will that take my weight."

"You're about three fucking stones, just fucking stand on it Grimes."

"I don't like heights."

"I swear, I'll fucking swing for you. Stand on it now!"

"It's slippery."

"If you don't, I won't be responsible for my actions."

"You're never responsible for your actions."

"Right that's it, I'm coming up there."

"Okay, okay, I'm doing it."

He inched across the branch.

"Fucking hurry up."

"This branch is creaking. It's like I'm walking a fucking plank here ..."

"Is it fuck creaking, stop being such a drama queen."

"It is creaking ... I'm fucking going here. Shit, I'm falling. Shit ..."

He landed face-first into a lake of mud.

"What a fucking prick. Get the fuck up."

"I'm fucking sodden ... and I think I've busted my ankle."

"Have you fuck."

"Just look at the state of me, soaked from top to bottom. I'll catch my fucking death."

"Grimes, shut up and sort your fucking head out."

"I'm going to have to go home and change."

"It's not the *Talk of the North* you prick. You can grab a towel in there …Right, now stop fucking around and listen. You need to focus. I want you to stand over there near that gate. You'll be able to see everything coming in. If anybody is approaching, I want you to blow this whistle as loud as you can, okay?"

"Right."

"Yeah?"

"Yeah."

"Good, let's do it."

Flames made towards the kitchen window, torch on, crowbar poised, while Adam took his position beside the iron gate. He surveyed his surroundings. All was quiet. The Mercs and Five Series convertibles had stood down for the evening and bedroom lights shone behind heavy winter curtains. The place was familiar. He had come here carol singing one year as a kid. It was an unforgettable venture: not for profit or humiliation accrued but for the glimpses of hallway snatched from those unlucky enough to open the door to him. Antique clocks, varnished coat stands and Sunday mums were painful reminders of the wretchedness of his life.

"Grimes, fucking come here."

"What? I can't. I'm keeping watch."

"Fuck that, you've got to see this. Quick, come on!"

Scared yet intrigued by Flames' fluster, he moved towards his voice.

"I can't see you."

"In here."

He stumbled through the rear door and turned left into some kind of extension.

"I can't see shit. What's up, Flames?"

"This room is fucking mad. The door was locked but I booted it and a key fell from its frame. Look at this ..."

He shone his torch towards the left of the room.

"What is it?"

"It's one of those fucking mannequins."

"It looks like fucking Bet Lynch. Look at that frock ...What's that on it?"

Flames moved the torchlight closer.

"He's slit the dress so the tits point out. Sick fuck. Urgh, there's fucking teeth marks all over them. It's like she's been breast-feeding an Alsatian ...Fucking evil."

"I don't like this room Flames. Let's get out."

"Fuck off you girl. There's fuck all to be scared of, just some sick bastard."

"I'm going to get back and keep watch."

"No, you stay here."

"I've got to keep watch though, what if someone comes?"

"No one is going to come."

"I'll go back just in case."

"I said you're fucking staying here, Grimes."

"Why, I thought there was nothing to be scared of?"

"Don't get lippy. Make yourself useful and check that out over there."

"Where?"

"Over there. The big fuck-off thing in the corner."

Adam crept towards a dark mass.

"Shine the light on it. It's like an old dresser or something."

"Check inside it, Grimes."

He pulled and rattled the dresser doors.

"It's locked."

"For fuck's sake, you soft bastard."

Flames strode over, pulled his crowbar, roughly inserted it into the front end of the draw, and pushed down.

"Fuck …It's stuck fast. Help me then Grimes. Put your hand on here and push with me."

"Right."

"Put your hand here, right, push …Push man."

"I'm pushing."

The drawer burst open.

"Got it, you fucker."

Flames pushed him out of the way and dived in.

"Fucking tat most of this …Old rings and women's chains. There's fuck all here."

"What's that?"

"Just some fucking book."

Flames picked up a leather-bound binder and threw it across the desk.

"Let me have a look at that."

"Leave it, it's fuck all."

"It's a scrapbook or something."

"I said leave it. Help me sort through this shit."

"Pass me your torch Flames."

"No, I'm looking at this."

"Just give it here for a sec."

"For fuck's sake, if I would have wanted to rob second-hand books, I'd have done fucking *Scope*."

Adam opened the book and shone Flames' torch over the first page.

"Oh my God, that's fucking horrible. I'm going to be sick."

"What?"

"Look at the pictures."

"What?"

"The pictures, look at the fucking pictures …"

"Alright, calm down. Let's have a look then …Shit, is that what I think it is?"

"It's a dead body. Look at the face, it's been fucking mutilated. Come on Flames, let's get out of here."

"I've told you he's not coming back tonight. Right, I see it now. That's his face, or what's left of it. Fucking hell, look at those fucking holes in his neck …Look at this one, his chest is like Swiss cheese. He's a fucking butcher this guy. Look, there's a bird in this one …"

"That's sick."

"Tell me about it."

"Fuck this, I'm off."

"You're not going anywhere Grimes. Don't you see what we've got here?"

"Yeah, a fucking psychopath. We need to go to the police."

"And say what, 'Oh, you'll never guess what we found when we were out burgling the other night …' No, we need to be smart here. We'll take the book and blackmail the fucker. We could make a fucking fortune."

"And what makes you think he won't do to us what he's done

to that poor bastard. The fucking size of him and he's savaged him. He'll do the same to us …Okay, going to the police may be a bad idea – we'll send them an anonymous letter or something. Or even just forget we've seen anything."

"Give me the torch. Give it here …Fucking hell; he's abusing some bird in this one."

"Oh my God, that's fucking sick. We need to leave."

Flames flipped through the pages.

"That's that dress Grimes."

"What dress?"

"The bird in this newspaper cutting, that's her dress on that mannequin."

"It's pretty jaundiced. I can't tell. "

"Look man. It definitely is."

"Yeah, you're right, it is as well."

God, she's beautiful. Kind eyes and a midsummer smile.

"Read it out Grimes."

"What?"

"The article. Read it out."

"Flames we haven't got time."

"Just fucking read it."

"You read it."

"Are you trying to be funny?"

"No, no, sorry mate, I forgot …Alright. But if we get caught it's your fucking fault."

He squinted and lowered his torch.

"A 22-year-old woman committed suicide by drowning in Worsley Lake, a coroner ruled today. The body of Sarah Gregory, of 12 Hartington Road in Manchester, was found by dog walkers on the banks of the popular beauty spot on November 21st last year.

Her father, Mr Ian Gregory, told the coroner how she had left home a couple of months prior to the tragedy and this was something out of character for his daughter.

'She just left home. It was completely unexpected and out of character. She told me she was staying with friends but she would never tell me the address or who these friends were exactly. She said things were happening to her but she couldn't tell me what. I'm devastated by this. I miss her so much I ache all over. My life is over.'

Her manager at New Direction Catalogue Company, Mr James Dolby, also told the coroner that Miss Gregory had left work in usual circumstances weeks before her death.

'I had just promoted Sarah as my personal secretary. I felt that she had a lot of potential and she was a ray of sunshine around the place. Unfortunately, I feel this may had contributed to this terrible incident. In hindsight, it was too much too soon. I noticed her becoming increasingly withdrawn. Next thing I know she had trashed the office while I was away on business. I never saw her after that.'

In closing, Coroner Catherine Moore-Clarke said 'this is one of the saddest cases I've ever ruled on. Sarah was a young girl with her whole life in front of her. Her career was just taking off. Based on the evidence, I'm forced to conclude that Sarah was suffering from an undiagnosed mental illness and this contributed to her taking her own life.'"

Adam manically flipped the pages of the book backwards.

"Flames that's her. Look, the girl in these pictures being abused is the same girl that's in the article. That's her. The only thing contributing 'to this terrible incident' was that fucker."

"Let's have a look …Yeah, it fucking is as well. No wonder she went loopy with all the shit that was being done to her. Having said that, she's fucking comatose in most of them."

"I don't care what you say I'm taking these to the police."

"Alright but you're on your fucking own."

A sound piqued Adam's attention.

"What was that? Did you hear it?"

"Will you stop getting fucking paranoid …For the millionth time, he's out until the early hours on a—"

"Shush, there it is again, a car door banging. There's someone fucking coming."

"It's a street you dick, of course there's going to be bangs. It's probably next door."

"It's too close. Listen."

They froze as if baby wildebeest identifying shadows upon the plain. A cough straight from the Devil's pit reverberated around the room, then a voice emitting a shiver of relief at hitting warm air. A light switching on in a distant corridor confirmed their fate.

"Oh shit."

"'Out all night.' You fucking idiot."

"Grimes, move, quick, and don't forget that fucking book."

They sprinted towards the exit.

"Oh fucking hell, it's him."

Through the frosted-glass door, the blurred but unmistakable bulk of Taylor approached at speed.

"Don't stop. Keep going."

Taylor pushed open the door and switched on the light; smiling at the pair, almost as if he'd been expecting them.

"Charge the cunt Grimes."

British Bulldog.

"Take that you fucker."

Flames flung his torch at Taylor, hitting him on the shoulder. It made no difference; he advanced, a grizzled prop forward about to break a couple of callow wingers. They hit him head on, rebounding backwards like kids on a bouncy castle. Taylor slammed the door shut and turned the key. Lights out.

"Please, we're sorry. We didn't steal anything. Please let us go. It's all a mistake. It's all a mistake. Tell him Flames …"

20TH APRIL 1975

They were back at his old offices again. It's where every debauched night in town ended. A semi-derelict, bird-shit stained, gothically tinged monument to a dying past. Dolby had convinced the top brass to retain the building after they'd upscaled to Trafford Park. It would appreciate in value, he said. His true motivation though was its proximity to Manchester's red-light area; and that once up the iron stair-case no one could hear their screams.

Tonight was a perfect case in point and as Dolby pushed a flabby middle-aged woman with ginger candy-floss hair over a rubbish-strewn desk – the orange glow of an outside street lamp dazzling her eyes – he did so from a position of complete impunity.

"I told you to be careful …"

"And I told you that I'm not paying you to talk. Gordon, c'mon man."

"Kinky stuff's extra you know?"

"Just put it on the bill and shut up. Gordon, pass me the bag. Gordon!"

"Sorry, I was miles away."

"What's up with you tonight?"

"Nothing, I'm tired but I'm fine. I—"

"Fucking tired, are you kidding me?"

"I've had a busy week and … I've got a bit of a headache."

"A headache? You're beginning to sound like Rose."

"Fuck off."

"Get a grip and get a swig of this down you."

Dolby passed him a bottle of Scotch. He unscrewed the top and imbibed a basic gulp.

"Are you going to have a proper drink then?"

"Alright, get off my back will you."

He returned the bottle to his mouth; his Adam's apple throbbing as the liquor gushed down his gullet.

"Satisfied?"

"Yeah, feel better?"

"Yeah, I suppose so."

"Good. Right you old fucker, pass me the rope then."

Lundy reached for the black holdall before pausing.

"Shall we leave that for tonight mate? I'm not in the mood."

"Pass me the rope you soft bastard."

"No, c'mon, let's just fuck her."

"Where's the fun in that Gordon? Get the rope and the gag."

"Woah, now hang on a fucking minute lads."

She shrugged of Dolby's shoulder-hold and turned towards them, her face war-torn yet stoic.

"Listen gentlemen. I don't know what you are planning tonight but before you do anything, let me show you something …"

She walked them past the broken chairs and boxes towards the window.

"See him there?"

"Who? What the fuck are you on about?

"Him, over there, look he's staring straight at us."

"So?"

"Well gentleman, he's … how can I put it … my manager. Marvin's his name, Marvin the manager. He's six feet six and a black belt in karate."

"Looks nothing more than a big daft coon to me … how about you Gordo?"

"Too right, James."

"Oh dear … now he hates that kind of language. I mean, he really loses his temper and you cannot blame him can you? Now, if I were to tell him what you have just said and what you were planning to do with me, he would get really mad. I've seen him beat a man near to death for calling him that. Plus, he's very protective over me. He says I'm his favourite girl."

"He's just your fucking pimp, you're just a piece of meat to him."

"Now whatever you do, do not let him hear you say that either. He hates when people call him a pimp …I've told, you he's my manager."

"Come on Dolby, let's call it a night. This is going nowhere."

"No fucking way. Look, I hope you're not stupid enough to be threatening us …"

"Now you see, that's exactly what I am doing. If you so much as hurt a hair on my head, he'll make fucking mincemeat out of the two of you and remember, there's only one way out of here and he'll be waiting at the bottom of the stairs."

"Now that sounds like a challenge to me, eh Gordo?"

"No, let's leave it mate. I'm not in the mood."

"Get a fucking grip of yourself, man. I'm not bothered whether you are in the mood or not, I am and we're not giving in to this fucking slag, okay?"

"Right, I am sorry. I've just got a headache that's all."

"Shut up about your fucking headache."

"Sorry to break up your lovers' tiff but you've got two choices …Either you can shag me with a tiny bit of rough stuff … on second thoughts, what you consider rough stuff and what I do is probably very different, so I think we'll leave that for today …Okay, you either shag me and pay up, or you're wasting my time and I'll fuck off."

"Let's just fuck her Dolby and get out of her."

"Okay, then you can go first Blondie as you sound like the romantic type."

She took his hand and walked him back towards the table. Dolby was blood red, banging his fist into his forehead.

"Bitch. Fucking bitch."

"Pipe down dickhead. You know as well as I do that without Blondie onside you couldn't batter me, never mind fucking Marvin."

She assumed the position while Lundy dropped his trousers in the perfunctory manner of a constant porn star.

I have had your child. You are a father. I have had your child. You are a father. A father. A father. A father like you never had. A special girl. Be a man. Be a father. A girl to love. A life to live.

"What's up lover, not feeling it?"

"Shut up, stop fucking talking."

"Just relax and try not to think of England."

"I said fucking shut up."

What's happening to me?

"At this stage boys, I think it wise to tell you that there's no refunds for non-performance."

He spun around and began tugging on his cock like a jackhammer.

"Not much of a turn-on for a girl that you know …"

"Gordon? Don't tell me you've … oh, for God sake man."

"It's nothing Dolby. It's just taking a little time to start that's all."

"Poor love, you really must have a headache."

"Fuck off, bitch."

"Charming."

"Gordon, what's the matter? This is fucking embarrassing."

"If it's any consolation, it happens more than you think. Rarely with anyone under sixty though."

"Gordon, this is not how we take care of business. Stop being pathetic and get on with it."

"Shush, you're putting the poor love off."

He flew around and faced his tormentors.

"My God, look at that! It looks like a popped balloon hanging from a wall."

"Just all fuck off and leave me alone. Fuck the lot of you."

"Not with that you won't, lover. "

"That's it; I'm not taking anymore of this."

He wrestled his trousers up and ran towards the iron staircase.

"Gordon, where the fuck are you going man? Don't leave me here. Gordon!"

2ND JULY 1975

The orange phone went off like a siren. Each ring mining new depths of pathos. Mr Gregory was sitting in the back yard, spinning the rear wheel of an upturned bike. Over and over again.

"Wait, wait, don't ring off."

He ran through the kitchen and collided with the clothes maiden before diving for the receiver like a catcher in the slips.

"Hello?"

"Dad it's me."

"Sarah, thank Christ for that. Are you okay love?"

"I'm okay. Are you Dad?"

"I was just outside, love. I had to run for the phone."

"Get your breath Dad."

"It's fine, I'm fine. Where've you been love? I've been going crazy; it's been weeks since I last heard from you."

"I know, I'm sorry—"

"Don't be sorry …As long as you're okay, that's all that matters."

"I'm fine. Honestly, I'm fine."

"You sure?"

"Yes fine, I'm okay Dad. Stop worrying."

"How can I stop worrying, sweet? You leave without so much as a goodbye. I don't know where you're living, or who you're living with."

"I'm fine Dad. I've told you I'm living with friends in Rochdale. I'm enjoying a bit of independence."

"Where though?"

"In Rochdale, Dad."

"I know that but what's your address?"

"I don't know it off the top of my head."

"Oh, come on Sarah, you said that last time, you must know it by now."

"No, honestly I don't."

"Who are you living with then?"

"I'm living with friends."

"What friends? Do I know them?"

"No Dad. You don't know them. They're friends from work."

"What I still can't understand is why you had to leave so quickly."

"Like I said before Dad, a flat came up at short notice and I had to move on it or someone would have taken my place."

"Sarah stop lying to me."

"I'm not lying Dad."

"He came around here. That boss of yours."

"Who?"

"Your boss, Mr Dolby."

"Oh my God. What did he say?"

"It's alright sweet. It's okay. You've done nothing wrong."

"How do you know? What did he say?"

"Nothing. He did say though that you don't work for him anymore. Sarah? …Sarah?"

"I'm still here Dad. It's not a good line."

"I know. Sarah, please listen now, you need to know that I love you …And you can tell me anything. And I mean anything. You know that I will never judge you."

"I know that Dad."

"Sweet, are you poorly? I mean, in yourself?"

"What has he said? Don't believe a word that he says. He's a liar."

"He's not said anything bad; he just said he was worried about you. And, that …"

"What? Dad what did he say?"

"Nothing really. Rubbish I bet."

"Dad, please, what did he say?"

"He said that you smashed his garage up. I told him that you'd never do that. I told him straight, sweetheart."

"Right."

"Sarah?"

"Yes."

"Did you do it?"

"Yes, I did Dad."

"Why Sarah? That's not like you love."

"Dad there's been a lot of things happening to me. Things I can't tell you about."

"You can tell me, sweet."

"No Dad, I can't. Not this. I can't talk about this."

"What. Why?"

"Because you're my dad and I'm your daughter."

"What does that mean?"

"Nothing ...It meant nothing."

"Well, it should mean everything. It means everything to me."

"No, I didn't mean it like that Dad. Of course you mean everything to me."

"I just need you to tell me what's going on and I can help you."

"I can't Dad."

"Of course you can. I promise I will make it better for you."

"No Dad. Stop it."

"Please Sarah."

"I said stop it!"

"Okay sweet. I'm sorry. It's just that this is my worst nightmare, I feel like you're slipping away from me."

"I know Dad, please don't worry. Look Dad, the pips are going to go in a second—"

"No love. Please don't go. Please sweetheart, I just want to make things better for you. Please ..."

"I'll speak to you soon Dad. I love you."

"Sarah, please don't go."

"The pips are sounding now. Bye Dad. I love you. I love you."

5TH JULY 1975

In normal circumstances, Lundy would not touch The Hastings Town and Country Show with a shitty stick. Livestock trading, craft marquees and children's entertainment tended not to be his bag. That was before Jessica asked him to accompany them to this year's event and although risky – despite Rose being safely ensconced at her mums for the weekend, some of her friends could be there – as they strode down the oak tree-lined path, Jessica pushing June in her chair, he wouldn't have wanted to be anywhere else in the world.

Look at all these people, laughing, having fun and without anyone getting fucked.

"I mean it's like that officer said, although it's completely out of character for Derek, he's got the greatest motive. It's just so unlike him. I mean the damage that could have been done … That's not Derek. He must be having some kind of breakdown. Gordon … Gordon!"

"What? Er … yeah, absolutely."

"You're not listening are you Gordon?"

"Yes, I am. I'm just taking it all in. It's packed isn't it?"

"Have you never been here before?"

"Never."

"What, not even when you were a kid?"

"No, never."

"You must have."

"Jessica, I haven't. I have never come here before, ever."

"You must be the only person who hasn't."

"No, I think there's still a few of us holding out."

"If you say so. The main thing is that you're here now. I mean, he could be anywhere, he could be in this crowd. They released him without charge, you know."

"Yeah, you said."

"If he has lost his mind, he could be capable of anything."

He draped an arm around her shoulder.

"But you don't need to worry about that do you because I'm here."

"I know you are Gordon ..."

Yeah, I'm your muscle. Your big love muscle.

"I was only saying to my mum yesterday that I've seen a completely different side of you. The old Gordon would have been straight round there to sort him out—"

Sort him out? I'd shake him by the hand if I could.

"... But you've dealt with it so responsibly, so maturely."

"Well you've got this little lady to thank for that."

Their eyes joined. Soul gazing on heaven's doorstep.

She shook free her shoulder and pushed forward.

"Right, c'mon then, we're going to miss the band. June says that she doesn't want to miss the band. Look, they're starting —"

"What band?"

"*Incantation* they're called. They're a folk band. They played here last year. They're great."

Although he maintained a steady succession of comic grimaces throughout their set, their primal sounds made quite an impression on him. So much so that as they left the field, he vowed to have a go at that acoustic guitar that had stood in the corner of his shop for as long as he could remember.

"I've gone cold all of a sudden. What time is it Gordon?"

"Quarter to seven. I'll give it to those folkies, they've got some stamina."

"I know, they did drag on a bit. What's left to see?"

"Just this field here, I think."

"I'm freezing, feel my hand."

He grabbed her palm.

"Hmm, yeah, they are cold. I'm fine. I'm just right."

"I'm cold-blooded you see."

"There's nothing cold-blooded about you Jessica. You're good from top to bottom. "

"Thank you Gordon … that's lovely … that's really nice."

He squeezed her hand. Their gaze collided again. A couple of seconds as though a couple of years.

She blinked first.

"Is that what I think it is?"

"What?"

"It is as well. Look Gordon, game stalls! I used to love these as a kid. My dad was a dead shot at them. The amount of times he won …Can we have a go Gordon?"

"No chance, they're a right bloody catchpenny."

"Oh go on, please. You could win June something."

"How much is it?"

"Look, it's only fifteen pence …"

"Only fifteen pence. You've no chance."

"Oh, come on Gordon, don't be tight. Tell him June …See, June's telling you."

"No she's not."

"She is. She makes that noise when she wants something."

"She makes that noise all the time."

"No she doesn't, trust me, I'm her mum."

"And I'm her dad."

"I know – that's why you're going to win something for her at the game stalls."

"Okay, okay, if it will stop you nagging."

Jessica addressed the lanky, tarred-hair teen manning the stall.

"How many goes do I get for fifteen pence?"

"Three, miss."

Gordon jumped in.

"Four?

"No sir, three."

"I could've sworn you said four."

"Okay sir, just because you're playing on behalf of your lovely girl, or should I say two lovely girls, I'll let you have four."

"Good man. Right, what do I have to do?"

"Okay, throw these rings around the head of these ducks. You only need one for a prize but if you get more than one, you'll get two prizes."

"Okay. Right, let's go …"

"Look June, Daddy's going to win you a present."

Lundy steadied himself and threw the ring. It wobbled on the duck's head, before falling onto the floor.

"Unlucky sir."

"God, that was nearly on ..."

"Keep your eye on the duck, sir."

"Yes, keep your eye on the duck Gordon."

"I'm trying. It's bloody hard."

"Concentrate sir. Clear your mind."

"Yes, clear your mind Gordon."

"I would do if you two would shut up."

His second attempt sailed over the duck's head.

"Oh, unlucky again sir. Third time lucky, I've got a good feeling about this one."

"Go on Gordon. I won't put you off this time."

"That would be helpful. I've just got to get my eye in. Just got to—"

"Lundy, you fucking bastard."

"GORDON!"

Two men leapt from behind a cluster of trees, one was fat and the other thin. The fat one was old, bald and wearing shorts; the thin one younger, trousered and with a mane of black hair flowing over his blue-collared shirt. The fat man swung a lead pipe into Lundy's face, provoking a burst of blood from his nose.

"Not so big now. Take that you bastard. Take fucking that. You don't do that to me. No one does that to me. Fucking no one."

The man in the stall leapt from behind the counter and ran away.

"No, don't go. Help us. Stop them. Help!"

"Jim, deal with her."

The thin man grabbed Jessica and forced his hand over her mouth.

"Tanner leave it. Tanner you bastard, I'm with my kid."

"I couldn't care less Lundy. Why would I care after what you did to me? Not so big now. I'll fucking kill you. God forgive me, I'll kill you …"

He curled into the foetal position covering his head with his hands. It made little difference. The lead pipe just moved onto his rib cage and kidneys.

Jessica broke free from the thin man's grip.

"Gordon! Please leave him alone. Please, I beg you. His daughter's here. Look, she's poorly. Oh, my God."

"Jim, shut her up will you."

"Right …Shut it love. Or when he's finished on him, he'll start on you."

Tanner continued his attack, slamming the pipe onto Lundy's hands, driving for his temple, before pausing and furrowing his brow.

"Look I'm sorry about this love, he lost me my business, see. He ruined me. Got me pissed in a pub, pretended to be my mate, and then beat the shit out of me. He even threatened my kid for fuck's sake. Two hundred yards apart we were and he couldn't handle it. Fucking bully. He deserves this. I'm only sorry you and the girl had to witness it."

"Okay, you've made your point now. He's hurt. Leave him now, please."

"After the state he left me in? Scaring my kid to death? You must be joking love. I suggest that you and the girl get out of here. You don't want to see this."

"No please. Please don't. He's learnt his lesson …"

"Ha, that's a good one. You obviously don't know him like I do. No love, the only way to stop him doing anything like that again is to paralyse the fucker."

I'm going to do it. There's no choice. It's too late. I'm going to do it. She'll forgive me. She'll understand.

He opened his mouth and lunged towards his fleshy calf.

"Argh fucking hell! He's biting me, Jim he's biting me …Get of me—"

I am a Shark. Bite harder and deeper. Rip the skin. Gnaw the bone.

"Get off me Lundy, you sick fuck. Jim, get him off me."

Jim moved forward before stopping dead in his tracks.

"Jim fucking help me!"

"I will. I will …"

"Lundy you dirty bastard. Get off me. Jim what are you waiting for?"

"I know, I'm doing it. I'm doing it."

"Look he's breaking the skin! Jim help me …Lundy stop. Argh shit …"

Riven by currents of pain, he dropped the lead pipe.

"Jim, get the pipe. The pipe … get it and hit him. Hit him."

Jim pushed Jessica aside and picked up the implement.

"Right, let go of his leg now mate. Let him go and we'll forget all about it. This never happened."

"Don't negotiate with him, fucking hit him. Hit him!"

"Fuck off Tanner, you said I wouldn't be involved. You said that he was a paper tiger. He doesn't look like a fucking paper tiger now does he? He looks like the real fucking thing. And where's he coming after he's done with you? For what, my beer money paid for a week? Fuck that."

"No Jim, please don't go. I beg of you. I'll pay you double, whatever you want. Just get him off me."

"Fuck that."

He turned on his heels and sprinted away nearly colliding with the group of Women's Institute and fairground labouring types that had surrounded the scene.

"Jim no, no, no. Please come back …Lundy you bastard, you fucking bastard, let go."

Jessica addressed the gathered throng.

"Please, will someone ring the police? They came out of nowhere. They attacked him."

"Don't worry, they're on their way dear. Oh my God, is he biting him?"

"Lundy, you bastard, you fucking bastard, let go …"

"No, he's not like that, it's self defence. He's just protecting himself and his family."

Tanner put his hand into Lundy's mouth, attempting to prize his teeth apart. An understandable but critical mistake. The same one that mammoth Scouser in Newquay and the mouthy bouncer in *Suggestions* made. Tried and tested.

"No, God no, don't … argh, fuck, fuck. He's got my finger, he's got my finger! Okay you win. I submit. Please, I submit."

"Gordon, you can let go of him. Gordon let go of him please. Gordon, he's given up and the police are on the way—"

Gnaw the bone. Decent meat. Animal, animal.

"Gordon. Please stop now. You've won. Let go now. For me and June let him go now."

"Help me!"

"Oh my God, he's biting his finger. That man, he's biting that other man's finger."

"Gordon, you must stop now. You've gone too far."

A grizzled snap, an almost otherworldly sound, turned the air red. Tanner stepped backward, holding aloft what remained of his butchered digit.

"My finger, it's missing. He's eaten my finger. He's eaten my finger. It's gone. My finger … gone."

Lundy stood up, his mouth and shirt sopping with blood, and spat the rest of the finger back towards him, as if used chewing gum. "Fucking yeah." He turned towards Jessica and flashed her a smile; his blood-drenched teeth on full unexpurgated display. Coliseum cool from the baddest cat in the jungle.

"Gordon, what have you done…"

Two worlds had collided.

6TH JULY 1975

Situated in a leafy suburb of Manchester called Chorlton, Oakdene Womens' Refuge was a four-storey, twelve-bedroomed Victorian terrace, standing in an endless line of other four-storey, twelve-bedroomed Victorian terraces. She was lucky to get a room here, as it was filled to bursting with domestic refugees. From her top-floor window, she counted multitudes of them sent back down the cobbled path. No room at the inn.

A fellow lost soul had given Sarah their number after they'd spent the night together in the marbled cubicles of an all-night toilet in Piccadilly Gardens. Her name was Kelly. They had a lot in common, swapping tales of travesty and woe into the early hours. In the morning, Sarah found a scribbled number pushed under her door. She was there within the hour.

A month later and she was going nowhere. Her room was nice and the older residents mothered her like crazy. The only negative was the daily meeting – a circle of truth and recrimination that could last for hours. It was a different story when Tracey was there. Sarah liked her. She made it interesting. At first, her mugshot eyes and blonde crew-cut scared her witless but that was merely cosmetic and she now hung off her every word. This morning was no exception.

"I've got friends that are addicts. All they care about is fixing. They beg and rob and some of 'em even sell themselves, for sex and that. And I'll see them; beaten up, embarrassed, crying because of the things they've done for a fix. And that just makes them want it even more. And that's us. We do that. Our fix though is them. And the worst they are to us, the more we're drawn to them. We're not victims: we're addicts."

Mary, the oldest resident in Oakdene shook her head; her grey mane sashaying as if in an awful shampoo ad.

"Tracey, why the fuck are you talking about drugs and fixing? Listen love, I lived longer than you. I've seen a lot more life and let me tell you there's one issue and one issue only … all men are bastards. They should all be shot. God forgive me for saying it."

Sameena, Oakdene's social worker, rubbed her milky brown cheeks and sighed. Mary was on the top of her game today.

"Now, Mary, what have I told you about comments like these …They don't help the situation. Today is about discussing why women stay with abusive men. It's complex. It's a—"

"Because they're scared of what the bastards will do to them. Let me show you this—"

"Oh please Mary, not again."

Mary lifted her green sweater and exposed a discoloured v-shaped scar underneath her ribcage.

"Do you know who did that? A man with a red-hot iron. Branded me like I was fucking cattle."

"I know Mary, we've seen it. I can't imagine what you've been through. And you know I'm here for you whenever you need me. But today, it's important that we discuss this specific issue. It's vital we explore this. Tracey, I'm interested in your point, please continue."

"I'm just saying it as I see it. I've been in more drying-out clinics than I care to remember. Sat in circles just like this one. I'd always split the patients into three groups. Group A, B and C. Group A know their condition, why they booze and what it does to them – mind, body and soul. They've got the best chance of staying on the wagon. Now Group B kinda get it, but some days they fall back into … y'know, 'why can't I just have one drink? I like a drink. I can handle it.' And then there's Group C, well they've just got one hand back on the fucking bottle."

"Very interesting Tracey, I never heard it put that way before and I'm not sure everyone will agree but … yes it's interesting. Sarah what's your view on it?"

Not again. She's knows I hate speaking. Stop looking at me. Speak to someone else.

"No? Okay, don't worry Sarah. You don't have to speak if you don't want to. Anybody else?"

The meeting finally passed; likewise the afternoon craft session and early evening assertiveness course. In lieu of nothing to do, Sarah and her roommate Susan had retired to bed. They would usually talk into the night. Susan fantasising about how things could be different if only her man could get the help he so desperately needed – her uniquely busted nose and constant disguise of blonde wig and shades failing to temper her vision. Tonight though, they'd had words. Sarah had admitted to being a Group B girl but Susan refused to commit and terminated further enquiries by switching off her bedside light and pulling her eiderdown over her head.

Hours later, as dawn broke, a creaking floorboard settled the matter.

"Susan?"

"Shit, Sarah you scared me."

"Where are you going?"

"Nowhere, to the shop."

"You've got your case."

"No, I've not."

"Susan it's in your hand. You're going back to him, aren't you?"

"Yes."

"No Susan. Why?"

"I don't know. I've just got to."

"Susan, I know it's hard but those feelings to go back, they come in waves. I've found that myself. It's like an urge. Just fight that urge and it eventually goes away."

"I love him."

"It's not love Susan."

"It is, you said that you loved your fella."

"It's not love; I know that now. It's fear. It's because they've broken you."

"It may be for you lot but it's not for me. I should never have come here in the first place. I need to go back home."

"What are you talking about? Out of all the people who should be here, it's you. What about the injuries you've had. When you told the group, they were shocked. Even Sameena was shocked."

"There are worst things than someone hitting you, you know. He's a good provider."

"Susan, he won't even let you leave the house."

"So, he's possessive, at least he cares. He's just old-fashioned."

"Jesus Susan. Please just go back to bed and think about it."

"I've thought about it. Yesterday when we were in that meeting and Mary was going on about how she hates men and they're all the same and … well, you know what she's like and I just thought I need to go home. And yeah maybe that makes me a "Group C-er", so what? I love him. For all his faults, I love him."

"Susan, look in the mirror. Look at your nose. Is that love?"

"That was an accident."

"An accident? So, his fist accidently hit you in the nose, just landed there by mistake. C'mon Susan ..."

"I'll make sure he gets help. It will be a fresh new start for us. This place makes you look at everything negatively. Well, I'm looking at things positively. This will have been his wake-up call. He nearly lost me and he will lose me if he doesn't get help. He'll change, I know he'll change."

"He won't."

"I'd rather have a man who you can change than having no man in the first place."

"Susan that's rubbish and you know it."

"No, it's not. They all make it sound so easy in here. But even if I stayed, we can't live here for the rest of our lives. We're going to have to leave eventually and what happens then? It's okay for you; you've got a family and have had jobs. I've got no one and have done nothing. He's my only option."

"They'll help you here with all that. They prepare you for it all."

"What, they're going to give me a ready-made family and fancy qualifications ..."

"No, but—"

"Exactly."

"They'll give you support though. They'll keep in touch."

"I want a normal life. I don't want to be looked after by this lot. I want to be looked after by my man."

"He's not a man."

"Yeah, well he is the closest I'm going to get."

"Susan, please don't go."

"I've got to Sarah."

She moved towards the bedroom door and opened it.

"Are you going to wish me luck then, or not?"

"No, because this is crazy."

"Goodbye then."

She inched out of the room.

"Susan. Susan!"

"Keep your voice down. What?"

"Stay safe."

"Yeah, you too Sarah."

13TH FEBRUARY 1997

They sat side by side on oak dining-room chairs, their legs and arms tightly bound. Screaming had achieved nothing but the wrath of Taylor's baseball bat, which he was now spinning Samurai-like from his position just outside the extension. Another one of Dolby's cronies stood beside him. He was smaller than Taylor but equally unsettling: his youthful garb of a West Ham football top, cargo half and halfs and pristine white trainers in outright conflict with his face, which was so full of lines and crevices it resembled a rotting pumpkin.

Flames had lapsed into unconsciousness. Taylor had been ruthless with him. The suspicion on the street was that Flames, like most bullies, would crumble in the face of a superior foe but he resisted his onslaught like a demonic kangaroo and although this made no difference – Taylor brushed his punches off like crumbs from his sweater – he definitely wasn't a bully, at least not a flat-track one. Other descriptions though were still very much on the table.

"You brain-dead fucking moron. You stupid fucking idiot."

"Are you talking to me Grimes?"

"Sorry, I thought you were unconscious …No, hang on, yes, I am talking to you. Everything was going fine until you started in the warehouse and now look at us. Sat tied to a chair waiting to die. You know your problem?"

"Shut the fuck up Grimes."

"No, I won't shut the fuck up. I'm going to tell you what your problem is. Your problem is that you're fucking stupid. Dumb. As thick as two short planks. And no one has had the cock and balls to tell you before."

"I said shut up."

"No, this is the least you fucking deserve. You couldn't resist it could you. You're just such a fucking criminal. You get a job and you're not content with earning a few bob, you have to start selling crack and fucking bleeding the place dry. Then when you get caught and I take the beating for you, you decide to rob the only person in the known fucking universe who is a bigger psycho than you. But it's okay because Mr Pass-Me-The-Matches-Big-Time-Fucking-Criminal has done his homework. Dolby goes out on a Wednesday and doesn't come back until the early hours. Except he does, doesn't he?"

"I'm fucking sorry, alright."

"It's too fucking late for that."

"What the fuck else can I do?"

"Nothing, you've done e-fucking-nough already. You're responsible for my death. Congratulations."

"I said I'm sorry."

"Oh well, that's okay then. You said you were sorry, that makes it all alright then doesn't it. You're such a stupid bastard."

"Don't push me too far Grimes."

"Or fucking what? Go on, or what? What the fuck are you going to do that them two over there are not going to do to me? You don't get it, do you? You're playing with the big boys here. This is the big leagues son and you're nothing but a second division psycho."

"Fuck off."

"No, you fuck off."

This paroxysm of rancor drained their final resources of energy. They sank deeper into their chairs, bowing their heads in silent supplication like monkish prizefighters. The approaching balm of unconsciousness a blessed relief.

"Heads up."

West Ham launched the tennis ball into the air with an Olympian grunt. Taylor watched it drop before volleying it straight into Flames' mouth. His head bolted backwards, splashes of claret flying in all directions. They'd been out for about twenty minutes.

"What the fuck was that? Grimes …Adam, what the fuck was that?"

"What?"

"Something hit me."

"Yeah, him over there, Babe fuckin' Ruth."

"Thank fuck …I just had the worst fucking nightmare. I dreamt I was in hell and it was just how you'd imagine it. Loads of fire and gargoyles and that."

"You don't need to dream you dick, you're fucking in it."

"Yeah, I know, I know. Too right …Do you believe in hell Grimes?"

"Shut up."

"No seriously, do you?"

"Do you?"

"I've never really thought about it until that dream."

"And are you scared that's where you're going to end up?"

"Well, yeah."

"Yeah, fucking right you are. Unfortunately, you're in luck, there's no such thing. It's all bullshit."

"I fucking hope so, I'd be gutted if I was you though."

"How do you mean?"

"Well, all that fucking do-gooding you've done, all for fuck all."

"What the fuck are you talking about? I'm not a do-gooder. I'm just not a twat like you."

"I'm not a twat."

"Are you fucking serious? You're the biggest twat in the world."

"You're lucky we're tied up."

"Oh yeah. I can hardly believe my luck. How lucky I am to be tied up, waiting to die."

"You know what I mean."

"Just shut up you dick."

Flames spat out a gob-full of blood as if it were used mouth-wash.

"Are you sure? I mean there must be something there like—"

"Stop concentrating on things that are not real. This is real. Concentrate on getting us out of here."

"What the fuck can I do?"

"Nothing, like I say, you've done just about enough already. You know, when I got that job I genuinely thought I was going to turn my life around. That this was a brand-new start for me. That maybe, in a couple of years, I'd be able to get off the estate and you never know ... get a girl, settle down. But little did I know that my daydream was about to be gatecrashed by a big fuck-off black cloud."

"I'm sorry, okay."

"Stop fucking saying that. Just because you're saying sorry and you've never said sorry before does not absolve you of any responsibility. What about saying sorry for all the other bad things you've done. Like when you mugged me for a tenner the other month; or when you battered Smithy in front of his new girlfriend after watching *Rocky III* – he's still got the scar on his forehead; or when that girl you were seeing in the fifth year dumped you and you decided to beat someone up every day for a month like it was our fault. You would announce the victim's name from the back of the school bus."

"I'm sorry, alright. I'm sorry for the lot of it."

"Yeah, I fucking bet."

"No, if we get out of this, I'll change. Honest I will."

"Bollocks."

"No, Grimes, I will. I defo will."

"Why are you such a twat, anyway? What's your fucking problem?"

"What?"

"Why are you such a bastard?"

"Fucking embarrassment, I suppose."

"What?"

"Nothing, change the subject."

"Tell me."

"No, fuck off."

"Go on. Treat it like a death-bed confession, a final shot at redemption. You never know, if I am wrong, this could be your only chance of getting into heaven."

"Fuck off. I'm no soft cunt."

"You're something else you know that don't you ...You're beyond fucking parody."

"What does that mean?"

"It means that even now, on your fucking last, you cannot be a decent human being. You cannot begin to make up for all the hell you've put people through. At the point when your own stupid selfish actions result in me, a person who purposely has never hurt so much as a fly, getting wiped out, you still maintain this ... this ...You know what, words fail me. You're nothing but the scum of the earth."

"Alright, I'll fucking tell you then. You want to know? You want me to open up?"

"To be honest, I'm not bothered. Do what you like."

Flames spat out another mouthful of blood.

"Right ... remember at primary school—"

"I told you I don't want to hear it."

"No, please listen. Remember at primary school, we had some right brainy fuckers in our school, some right posh cunts, you know what I mean?"

"So?"

"Do you remember Peter Murray-Jones?"

"Kind of."

"Do you remember that talk he did on fucking rocks or summat like that?"

"No, I can't say I do."

"Well, anyway, he did a talk in assembly and I remember watching him and thinking 'he is so much better than me.' His school uniform was like fucking immaculate and I looked down and I had my *Six-Million-Dollar Man* t-shirt on, full of stains and that, and then I looked around at everyone and they were so much better than me. You know, they all looked better and they were defo brainer than me and I felt like nothing, just fucking nothing. And I was only a fucking kid – a kid should never feel like that should he? Anyway, he comes off the assembly stage and gets a round of applause and I can feel the, like, anger building up inside of me. I've never felt anything like that before or since. So, at afternoon break I ask him to show me some of his rocks. I take him behind the prefabs near the canteen to 'get a bit of peace and quiet' and he's starts dead carefully getting the rocks out of his bag. And just as he's about to show me the first one, I punch him and his nose just fucking bursts and I go on to beat the fucking shit out of him. And when I stood over him, and he's moaning and whimpering, I felt better than him. A bit like when some mongrel batters like a champion pedigree dog. Who's better? The mongrel's fucking better coz it's beat the champion dog. Well, I felt better than all of them. I was stronger, tougher, harder than them. I couldn't talk their language but they couldn't talk mine, do you know what I mean? I could never do what they did, but they could never dream of doing what I did. I made sure of that."

"But we were all in the same boat. You picked on your own."

"I picked on everyone because everyone was fucking better than me."

"That's bollocks."

"Is it though? My dad never worked a day in his life, spent most of his time in the boozer; my mum's a fucking slag. My old man used to say that she was a 'lady of the night who shags like a rabbit in the day too.' Fancy saying that to a kid about his mum. I never had a chance. I had no choice."

"We've all got a choice. It's just that some of us have more choices than others."

"You really believe that?"

"Not really, but if you didn't you may as well lay down and die."

"I laid down and died fucking years ago."

That a man of such strength and sadism was breaking in front of his eyes hit him harder than Taylor ever could. It was like when he watched rank underdog Buster Douglas pummeling

Mike Tyson, "the baddest man on the planet" in their world heavyweight bout. Smithy found it hilarious watching Tyson crawling on the floor searching for his gum-shield like a paralytic bear. Adam though was of another mind; although no fan of Tyson, the sight of him being humiliated brought tears to his eyes. What does the one-trick pony do when his trick has deserted him?

"Flames, there's just one question I want to know."

"What's that?"

"Did you give him the rocks back?"

"What?"

"Did you give Murray-Jones his rocks back?"

"Did I fuck, that night I used them to smash the assembly windows."

"Ha, ha."

"Laughing in the face of death, would you believe it, the spirit of these people. True Northern grit, you have to admire them."

Dolby entered the building, pulled a chair from the corner of the room and sat down directly in front of them; bouncing his clasped hands against his bottom lip.

"Look Mr Dolby, we've made a terrible mistake and we are so sorry, aren't we Flames?"

"Yes, we are."

"So, if you let us go we won't tell anybody about anything we've seen."

"And what have you seen – it's Adam isn't it?"

"Yes. Er ... nothing, nothing at all."

"Oh, I think you've seen a little bit more than that, haven't you?"

"No, honest."

"Taylor tells me he caught you with my scrapbook. Could you pass it to me, Taylor."

"We just looked at the opening pages and then put it down. It's nothing to do with us, sir. Nothing to do with us at all, we were just after money not books."

"Thank you Taylor. Well you're right about one thing, it is nothing to do with you and you've made a very grave mistake opening it."

"We know, don't we Flames?"

"Yeah."

"And as you've seen the contents of the book, I would presume you've worked out your fate already."

"No, you don't need to do that."

"I think we both know different, don't we Adam."

"No, honestly Mr Dolby, you don't need to do that, we promise we won't say anything, will we Flames?"

"No, we won't say a word."

"I'm really angry at you boys for putting me in a situation like this—"

"We're sorry—"

"I'm talking now Adam. You don't talk when I talk. I'm a man of principle you see, a good man. Now of course looking in my book you may think differently, what with all those pictures, but you see those people crossed me. If you cross me, you pay the ultimate penalty and I'm afraid that is that. Now you boys have crossed me not once but twice. You've only got yourself to blame. What other option do I have? I'll tell you, I've got no other option."

"You're a proper tin-pot cunt, aren't you?"

"I'm sorry, what did you say?"

"Flames, shut the fuck up."

"What's the point Adam, he's going to kill us. Don't give the fucker the satisfaction."

"See what I mean Taylor about the Northern spirit. Remarkable."

"Look at you; you're like a shit Bond villain …You and that big brain-dead fucker over there. And as for that other fucking weirdo, fuck knows what circus you found him in."

"Fucking weirdo, you say."

"Yeah that's right. A proper fucking weirdo. Big deal you've killed a bloke and some bird and now you've captured the two of us. Hardly makes you Al Capone does it? No mate, you're fucking tin pot. Just do what you've got to do and stop fucking around."

"He doesn't mean that Mr Dolby."

"I mean every fucking word. You're a sad bastard. I mean, I'm no oil painting but I'll tell you something, I've never had to drug a bird to get some. You dirty fucking pervert."

Taylor moved towards Flames.

"Oh, here he is Mr Special Needs. Where did you pick this cunt up from Dolby, Barnardo's? Look Grimes, he's fuming, has someone stole your Tonker truck mate?"

"He's just scared Mr Dolby, that's all it is bravado. That's all just bravado."

Half a smile spread across Dolby's face.

"Leave him Taylor, we'll stick to the plan."

"Fuck your plan Dolby. Here's my plan. See what you think of this – you can do anything to me but let Grimes go. None of this is his fault. I had to force him to come today and he had nothing to do with stealing your stock. That was all me. The kid's no thief. He's a good lad who shouldn't be caught up in all

MARK NEILD

this. He's a civilian."

"So, let me get this straight, you're now bartering with me."

"Yeah, if you like."

"So, we can do whatever we want to you if we let this guy go."

"Yeah, that's about it."

"Anything at all."

"Are you deaf? That's what I said."

Dolby turned and faced his droogs, stroking his chin in exaggerated contemplation.

"I mean it seems like a fair deal. Presumably you think it's a fair deal Adam?"

"Er ...I'd rather you let us both go but he's right I had nothing to do with any of this."

"There's just one problem, are you thinking the same as me, Taylor and John?"

They nodded in unison.

"Why should we let him go so we can do anything we like to you when we can do anything we like to you anyway?"

"No, what—"

"I'm speaking now Mr Flames. This is what we're going to do. John here is an absolute genius with poisons and he's been working on a cocktail of drugs so potent that your head will literally spin round on its axis. So, we're going to give you a blast of his latest concoction and then we're going to dump you in the woods, so that when you're found everybody will presume that you're just two more poorly little soldiers from the estate that couldn't handle their medicine. And there'll be a few tears shed and a few hands wrung but deep down no one will really care because at the end of the day it's two less thieving bastards on the planet."

"No, please no Mr Dolby."

224

"Taylor, the tubes please. John, the medicine if you will."

"No, Mr Dolby, please don't."

"Don't cry Adam, it will be over soon. I'm not the bad guy here. You and your friend brought all this on yourselves."

"Fuck you Dolby. You'll get yours."

"Mr Dolby please, we'll do anything, I'll do anything. Please, I'm begging you."

"Do your fucking worst Dolby but I'll tell you one thing, we'll fucking haunt you. You have my word on that. We'll haunt you!"

9TH JULY 1975

Jessica's mum stood in her daughter's Habitat-endorsed living room dragging a brush through June's black mop of hair. In an adjacent mirror, Jessica was putting her face on. She had an interview this morning for a temping job at a local office. Her bank balance and psyche demanded success but she was struggling to focus and her mother wasn't helping.

"I mean, what kind of man bites another man's finger off?"

"Leave it Mother."

"Just answer me that question."

"I've told you, he was protecting us. They'd already smashed my window, don't forget."

"Protecting you! If it weren't for him, you wouldn't be at risk."

"Those men had a grudge against him, they were jealous of his business."

"Tell me, in all the years that you were with Derek, did anything like that ever happen."

"C'mon Mum, you know the answer to that. Derek would have run a mile."

"He may well have run a mile, but he wouldn't have bloody needed to because nobody ever wanted to kick the life out of him."

"Can we not talk about this now please?"

"It was the biggest mistake you ever made leaving that poor

man."

"He left me Mum."

"The poor sod didn't have much choice."

Stop talking you demented old bat. Go marry Saint Derek yourself if he's so fucking perfect. She's right as ever though. What type of man bites off the finger of another man? What kind of father?

"You better get her dressed Mum; the bus will be coming soon."

"Right, come on then love …That's the best I can do with that."

Jessica's mum led her granddaughter up the stairs.

"Make sure you give her teeth a good brush, her breath was shocking yesterday."

"Don't worry about us. Have you made her sandwiches?"

"Yes, they're on the side."

"What time is Jack back?"

"Around half seven."

"Will you be in?"

"Yes, of course I'll be in."

"Good. Now get out of that bloody mirror. You'll be late, you know."

"I know, I know. I'm going now."

"Okay. Good luck."

"Thanks Mum. See you later. See you June. Love you."

Jessica pulled her coat from its stand and checked her watch. She was cutting it fine. A barrage of envelopes crashed through her letterbox. She picked them up and threw them on her coffee table. A distinctly unofficial one, her address written in large slanted handwriting, piqued her attention. The second stage of Gordon's charm offensive? Despite herself, she tore it open. *This better be good.* A single sheet of white paper and a mass of pictures fell to the floor. She bent down and scooped them up.

Dear Jessica,

Is this really the man you want to bring up your child with?

"Oh my God."

The flushed features of an unconscious girl lying upon a lake of pillows, his engorged penis resting on her left cheek.

A blonde girl unconscious on a bed, his legs wrapped in hers, an evil smile stretching across his face.

The money shot, too brutal to bear.

She threw the pictures on the floor as though handling them for a second longer would lead to her catching the same disease as him.

"Mum!"

14TH JULY 1975

In his alpine-blue bathroom suite, jammed between the sink and toilet, Scotch waterfalling down his chin, he thrust his head backwards against the wall, his every thud smearing the tiles in blood.

It's better to have loved and lost than never to have loved at all.

It's better to have loved and lost than never to have loved at all.

It's better to have loved and lost than never to have loved at all.

It's better to have loved and lost than never to have loved at all.

"Stop saying that, it's fucking bullshit. It's not true."

Another phrase began jockeying for position in the debris-strewn thoroughfare of his mind. One that was much more appropriate.

Whatever a man sows he will also reap.

Whatever a man sows he will also reap.

Whatever a man sows he will also reap.

A new pinball alley had opened on the outskirts of town. A perfect destination: he could showcase his power and dexterity and its noise and lights would no doubt provoke June into spasms of joy.

He bounded down her path, a comically large teddy bear in one hand, an explosion of flowers in the other. Jessica was waiting for him on the doorstep – a distraught sentry with clenched fists and blood-red eyes. She didn't say much, save for the fact that he was the sickest bastard on God's earth and would never see his daughter again. Something's not right here, he thought. It became clear exactly what when she reached into her coat pocket and threw an envelope towards him. Before it hit the ground, it spilled what he initially thought were business cards – and in a way, they were. This was the business he was in, the business of depravity.

"What are these?"

Scurrying to pick them up, he soon found out.

Oh no. How did she get hold of them? Who gave them to her? Is that me? Yeah, it's me. It's all me. The real me. In the fucking flesh.

"Did you touch her?"

"What?"

"Did you do this to June?"

"God no. I would never do that to her."

"Did you take her picture, you sick bastard?"

"Please no. You've got to believe me."

"If I ever find out that you've done anything like this to her, I'll kill you. I swear, I'll kill you."

"No, of course I haven't."

How could she say that? Oh yeah, the pictures. The fucking pictures.

"If you ever dare darken this door again, I swear I'm calling the police. That's if I haven't already."

He sprinted back to his car. Before he wheelspinned into oblivion, he snatched a final glimpse of her staring blankly through leaded windows. This would be the last time he would ever see her. He knew this.

He crawled into the bedroom. Everything was dark apart from Rose's Gideon Bible, which shone like a beacon. She had once told him that there was a copy in every hotel bedroom in the Western world. Despite being in more hotel rooms than he cared to remember, he'd never noticed one. Now it was his only hope. He had nothing to lose because what he cherished most had already gone. He fell onto his knees. Surely, God wouldn't want to see a child without a father. Or a mother cast alone without mannish support. He would just want evidence of the genuineness of his contrition and that would not be a problem, as he had never been so penitent.

He tore off his clothes – in every sense he wanted nakedness – and lifted the Bible high in the air.

"God. I'm so sorry for the things I have done. You must believe me when I say this. I am so sorry. I've never prayed before, never prayed once in my whole life. However God, I am praying now. I have done some terrible things. To women, and men. I know this must have angered you. But I am changing; I can feel myself changing. Every day I am changing. You know what has changed me? My daughter has changed me. Please don't take her away. Please, I beg of you. I'll be the best Christian in the world. I promise. Rose always said that you're a merciful God; please show me some mercy now. I don't want her to go. Please don't take her away …"

"Gordon, what on earth are you doing?"

"I'm praying Rose."

"I can see that but you're naked and … goodness me, you smell like a brewery."

"I need help Rose. I need God."

"I know you do Gordon."

"Hold me Rose. Please hold me. Help me find him Rose. Help

me find God."

"I will Gordon. Shush, don't cry Gordon."

"I've betrayed you Rose."

"I know Gordon, I heard you."

13TH FEBRUARY 1997

Adam slumped deeper into the orange plastic chair, tears coursing down his ruddy face. Another day. Another hospital visit.

"I just want to see her."

The kindly nurse, Irish and old school, rubbed his shoulder

"Adam, your mum isn't very well at the moment."

"I know that."

"Well you wouldn't want to see your mum poorly would you?"

"I don't know, probably not. I'm not sure."

"No, of course you wouldn't."

"I can see her when she gets better though can't I?"

"Er ... yes, of course you can."

"Can I just see her for a minute then? Just to say hello. Please, just a quick two minutes."

The nurse blew out her cheeks.

"Okay, I'll go and have a word with her."

"Thank you."

He turned towards his dad.

"You need to stop mithering Adam and let them get on with their job."

"I just want to see her Dad."

He shook his head and patted his trouser pocket.

"I'm going for a cig."

Adam rocked back and forth on his chair. His body terribly alive. His senses turned all the way up to ten. From his position of vantage on the marbled wall, the boy in the *Measles is Misery* poster gave his standard response of wide-eyed bewilderment.

"You and me both, pal."

The nurse left his mum's room, straightened her pinafore, and slow marched towards him.

"Right Adam, I've just had a chat with your mum and she says that she's worried that you could catch the heavy cold she's got. Remember, I told you that on top of everything else she's got a cold, the poor love."

He did not remember having this conversation and as this is something that he would have remembered, he knew she was lying. He wasn't angry though; this episode had taught him there were different types of lies, the good and the bad kind.

"So, we've agreed that you can go around the back and wave to her through her room window, is that okay?"

"Why can't I stand here in the corridor and see her?"

"What, and catch all those germs? No, you can see her perfectly well from outside."

She took his hand and pulled him through the hospital car park onto a gravel verge marked by angry weeds and fading crisp packets.

"Why can't I see her in the hospital though?"

"You're going to see her now, Adam."

"No I'm not, not properly. I've got rights you know. You can't stop me from seeing her."

"There she is, now give her your biggest wave."

"I can't see her; I'm too far away."

"Nonsense, now give her a big wave."

He did as he was told and she returned the gesture, limply though, like a puppet on a string. Even from this distance he could see how thin she had become.

He just wanted to be close to her. An urge so strong, his head throbbed like a jet engine.

I'm going to do it, burst through the doors and hold her, hug it all away.

He rocked on his heels but at the moment of lift-off his dad emerged outside the main entrance. A dry slap was the last thing he needed. He turned back towards her room but she had stopped waving.

His eyes blinked open. A battalion of ants passed by his nose, transporting a leaf back to their colony. Were they real? Their automation seemed cartoonish, like the multitudes of brooms in the *Sorcerer's Apprentice.* Regardless, their simplicity of purpose, their uniformity, appealed to him.

With all our brains and all our problems …

His particular brain felt torn and incomplete. He imagined it as a severed orange, a mass of shredded vesicles the only indication of its previous totality. He ran his hands over his head. It was all there … just.

Voices broke through the trees: rays of sound carrying gruffly spoken words.

"You got everything you need Geoff?"

"Yeah, you can load him for me; I've got everything I need."

"Scrubs?"

"Yeah, I'm done."

"Where are you leaning on this?"

"Well the Methadone and Diazepam bottles in his pocket, could point to an overdose."

"What about the bruises, he seems pretty beaten up. Could be suspicious."

"Nah, occupational hazard for these scrotes. You know, I'm sure he's the bastard who nicked my golf clubs. He looks the spitting image of him. Anyway, let's see what the post-mortem says."

"Okay boys, he's all yours."

Adam pulled the foliage apart like a net curtain. *Oh my good God, no. Shit, shit.* Two doughty men carried a shrouded body towards the pathway leading out of the woods. *What the fuck happened? What's gone wrong?* A series of images promptly reminded him: How he had got here. What he had been through. It ended with Taylor forcing a tube into his mouth and Flames headbutting a tree. Could this be dream fiction? (Unlike that raw documentary footage of the final time he saw his mother.) The two empty medicine bottles in his pockets said not.

The men placed Flames in a white minivan and slammed its doors shut.

It should have been me. It should have been me. A mercy killing.

"John, you and Pete mark the outer parameter near that fence and bring it round to there. I don't want anyone getting in who shouldn't be here."

"Right Sarge."

A couple of fresh-faced coppers carrying incident rope approached, shadowed by a phalanx of men in bunny-white overalls and latex gloves. He dropped back onto his knees; dragging his battered body through the mud, his pale white fingers digging into the moist black dirt. He looked back; they were getting closer.

"Pete, check this out …"

"What is it?"

"It's his wallet, I think."

He had a wallet.

Their discovery gave him some breathing space. He inched forward, pulling himself to within sight of a sodden path. *Keep going. Through hell and high water.* A young couple wrapped in bubble coats and woollen hats, walking two mud-caked spaniels, came from the rear.

Thank God, rescuers. People. Good people.

"Please hel …Help."

They stood rigid and unbelieving. The girl looking around as if waiting for someone to shout "cut." The man moved towards him, proffering a supportive arm, before thinking better of it.

"C'mon let's go. C'mon!"

"Please, mate. Help me. Don't leave me."

No room at the inn.

With a final lunge, he hit the path. All he needed to do now was stand on it. He reached for the fence as if a broken boxer desperate to beat the count. His nails digging into its nobbled summit *C'mon you bastard. C'mon you fucking bastard. C'mon. Lift me Mum. Lift me.* With a bloodied scream, he finally made it. Forward motion though was another matter and it was at least an hour before he left the wooden rail. A virgin skater at a municipal ice rink.

Although snails were overtaking him, sweat gushed from his every pore. A workout from hell. He wiped his brow with the back of his hand. From nowhere, a trace of turquoise shadowed his motion. *What the fuck was that?* He repeated the action and the same thing happened. He moved both arms simultaneously and again this line of colour mirrored his movements. From the dark of the bushes, beams of purple, deep red and laser green stretched towards him, as if introducing themselves as his own personal rainbow.

Oh my Lord, I'm seeing the colours, man. I've developed a third eye.

He had no idea what Dolby's stooge had put in his potion but he began to think he had done him a favour. He wheeled around, arms lofted in the air. Finally free from all the conditions of which he had no control, dancing between the lines, lost within nirvana.

Shit, man. I could be an urban mystic, with a velvet cloak and big cane. Delivering salvation amongst the shit and concrete. A street Dali Lama. Or maybe a superhero, Radiation Man! Defending the beaten with my army of colours. Think of all the good I could do. A Nobel Prize here and there. And the women. Think of the women ... Jesus, I feel fucking rough. I feel as sick as a dog. Shit, no, I'm going to throw up. Oh my God, my stomach. It's bursting open. Please, no. Oh shit, I'm going. I'm dying ...

The coloured beams, at first ordered and distinct, now moved at manic speed, blending into each other and then violently separating. A series of convulsions began ripping through his body; cascades of vomit erupting from his mouth like errant lava. His knees hit the floor. The sound of breaking bracken a cap-gun salute. The colours sped towards him. He opened his mouth and attempted a scream but nothing came out.

10TH NOVEMBER 1975

She never asked him about June. His reasons for seeking redemption were not important; that she was getting a man reborn in Christ was all that mattered. Lundy wasn't sure. The most noticeable thing about God's guiding hand was that he couldn't feel a thing. What if he had washed his hands of him? What if there was a waiting list? What if his dark force returned?

"Nothing's happening Rose. I've studied the Bible, sung the hymns but there's nothing there. There's nothing there at all."

"Old Nick's not letting you go without a fight, love. Putting all these doubts and temptations in your mind. We've got a real battle on our hands here ...I know what we'll do."

"What?"

"We need to roll our sleeves up; get on our knees and we'll pray together. Through me, he will reach you. Why didn't I think of this before?"

"Okay."

It didn't work. Praying with her was even worse than making love to her – although the bottle and a half of Jim Beam he sank just to get his knees on the carpet didn't help matters.

"Maybe Gord, the Lord wants some proof of your commitment to change. That you're willing to get your hands dirty for him."

"What do you mean? What should I do?"

"Well ..."

He began trawling the dark places of Hastings; searching for the decaying and desperate, offering them food and even money, while she gave the thumbs-up from the Triumph.

He sat in strip-lighted motorway service cafés, proselytising to bearded and baffled truckers about the redemptive power of Christ, sounding like an Eastern Bloc newsreader reciting another day's propaganda.

In sepia-toned parlours, he apologised to street girls for his barbarous past – even settling his bill in two establishments. "You can change. Just like I have. Accept Christ as your saviour and begin the road to paradise. What have you got to lose?"

Unbeknown to Rose, he even visited his local parish priest for private counsel. He vowed to tell him everything, leave no muck-ridden stone unturned. And he mostly did – aside from some of the more graphic details – emptying his soul to such an extent that on journeying home he would have to pull over and similarly expel the contents of his stomach.

None of this worked. God and June remained as distant as stars in the sky.

Aside from biblical duties he mostly stayed at home, wearing out the Wilton like a caged bear. He figured swapping dissoluteness for domesticity could rejuvenate his relationship with Rose. It did the opposite: that they would spend the evening in almost complete silence, evidence of how terminal their marriage had become.

Television became both a distraction from, and an excuse for, this invincible quiet. On rare occasions, such as tonight, it even prompted conversation. She was keen to watch the Monday night film. He wasn't.

"What's this film called, Rose?"

"*Quatermass and the Pit.*"

"What's it about then?"

"The paper says 'When Dr Matthew Roney and his assistant Barbara Judd are called in to investigate some unusual simian remains unearthed by building work on a London Underground extension, they uncover the wreckage of a UFO and there begins a strange story involving evil visitors from the unknown.' I've heard Joyce from the choir talk about this. It's about this place near a tube station that's really spooky and haunted."

"Sounds like a load of old crap to me. What else is on?"

"There's a documentary on the life of someone called Balzac on two, and on three … oh, that dreadful show, *The Sweeney*."

"I forgot that was on, put that on."

"No dear, I don't want to, it's terribly violent."

"Life's violent Rose, it's realistic."

"Even more reason not to have it on. This house is a refuge from all that. No, let's watch this film. Joyce said it was really good."

Celluloid was not his thing – his interest generally lasting as long as it took to determine whether there was any nudity on the cards. This film though had him gripped from the start.

"So, who is doing the haunting then Rose, the ghosts or the aliens?"

"Those insect things they found in the spaceship in the underground station, they're the aliens and—"

"I know that but who's causing the hauntings? That's what ghosts do. Aliens don't do that. It's like that vicar just said "'spiritual evil.'"

"Kind of both."

"I don't get it."

"Right, the aliens implanted themselves into those funny looking ape-men, because they'd destroyed their own planet and they couldn't live here for some reason. So they kidnapped those apes and … well, altered them in some way."

"But what's causing the ghosts?"

"If you think about it Gordon, they've copied this idea from what we were talking about the other night; you know, original sin."

"How do you mean?"

"Well like I said, original sin means that all people are born evil and only by pledging our souls to the Lord can we save ourselves. Now we know that Adam and Eve caused sin by disobeying God in the Garden of Eden, but what they're saying here is that human sin is caused by aliens implanting their evilness into monkeys and because of these powers, that's how we've developed into humans. It's quite clever, I mean it's rubbish but it's clever."

"But who's causing the hauntings?"

"I'm not sure yet Gordon; let me watch the film and I'll tell you."

His brain had sweated more in the past forty-five minutes than it had in the whole of its previous forty-five years. It was all becoming clear now though. The hauntings were not demonic in their origins but extra-terrestrial and the spaceship buried in the subway was at the centre of it all.

"They're turning on each other. They're killing each other, Gordon."

"'Cause when the spaceship is disturbed it sends out evil energy … a bit like the Pied Piper. A call to those with the most alien inside them to kill those with the least. The ghost powers are just part of their tool-kit."

"Oh my goodness, what's that?"

"It's like a big devil in the sky."

"Oh my, it's horrible. Do you know, I bet Old Nick looks just like that. Yeah, I bet. That's what we're up against, love. But don't worry, he's no match for the Lord. He's defeated him before and he'll do it again. 'I saw Satan fall like lightening from heaven.' What's he doing now Gordon?"

"He's going to use that crane to kill that demon."

"How's he going to do that?"

"God knows."

"Don't blaspheme Gordon"

"Sorry. He's done it though, blew it to smithereens."

"Is that it? Have they killed it?"

"Yep."

"Thank the Lord for that."

"Actually Rose, it's the opposite to original sin."

"Sorry?"

"It's the same principle but turned upside down. God saves us from the evil deep within our soul but that spaceship was the thing that brought it to life for them. Now it's been destroyed, they're back to normal …Like they've awoken from a nightmare. They could only be free by destroying their source; that which made them evil."

"Hark at Barry Norman here. You're a right dark horse. I've never seen you so taken with a film …Are you okay, darling?"

"Yes … fine love …I've just remembered, I've got to go away on business for a couple of days. Is that okay? I should have told you before but it slipped my mind."

14TH FEBRUARY 1997

A brigade of blurred faces floated before him as if in a snuff version of the Bohemian Rhapsody video. He inched up his concrete bed, frozen to the bone. The dawn chorus of rush hour pounding his ears; his heart bursting through his fleece. The concrete soon gave way to mud and gravel. The stones as sharp as sharks' teeth.

"Argh, you bastard."

An older man, dressed in paint-stained overalls, his face ruddy and pot-marked, span around and stopped him in his tracks.

"Just stay here son. You're okay, we'll look after you. The ambulance will be here soon. Give me a lift, love."

With the assistance of a middle-aged miracle in purple Lycra, he propped Adam up against a No Flytipping sign outside the entrance to the woods.

"The ambulance is on its way, love."

"Looks like drugs to me. Why do they get themselves into such states? A lack of hope, I suppose. Tragic, really."

"Well, we don't know that for sure. He may have a medical condition. Now just stay still son, the ambulance will be here soon."

"No, trust me it will be drugs. I mean his pupils are like saucers. Right, I've had enough of this; that ambulance is not coming any time soon. I'm going to take him myself in my car."

"I don't think that's a good idea, mate."

"Of course it is. He's drugged out of his mind. Time is of the essence."

I've seen the colours and morning mist shrouding cold, dank murder. I know that voice, as sharp as broken glass. I know that face.

He flinched like a dog catching sight of its sadistic owner.

"No!"

"Listen friend, I was a medic in the army and if this man doesn't get urgent attention he will begin convulsing again."

"No, please no!"

"Calm down son, you're okay, you're safe."

"Dolby please, leave me alone. Please, someone call the police. Call the police!"

"It's okay son, you're safe. Is he talking to you?"

"I have no idea. I haven't a clue who this 'Dolby' is. It certainly isn't me. I've told you, this will be the drugs."

Adam began crawling backwards on his hands like a schizoid B-Boy.

"He drugged me. Him. Dolby. He killed my friend. Call the police. Keep him away from me. He's a murderer."

"See, the boy's clearly delusional. C'mon help me put him in my car; we can't wait for this ambulance any longer."

"Fuck off you bastard. Call the police. He is going to kill me."

The older man extended his arm across Dolby's path.

"I don't think that's a good idea mate. The lad's petrified of you."

"Did you not hear what I said, he's on drugs, he's clearly delusional and I'm an ex-army medic."

"And I'm a painter and decorator but even I know it's not a good idea for you to take him in your car. I know he's out of his head but that's even more reason to wait for the ambulance. The poor bastard will have a heart attack if you get any closer to him."

The purple goddess stepped in.

"Look, I know you're trying to be helpful but I'm a care assistant and I think we should wait for the ambulance. They have powers you know; they can get him detained, get him the treatment he needs."

"So, everyone is a fucking expert all of a sudden."

"Hang on mate, the lady was only trying to be helpful."

At her funeral, the Vicar said she had "lost her battle against cancer but what a battle she gave." Adam hated him for that. You cannot lose a battle that you could never win in the first place. Years later, the Irish nurse told him: "never had a patient clung so hard to life. We were begging her to let go but she wouldn't. For you, she couldn't quit." A will indomitable. A score draw. *Like Mum, be like Mum. Her arms wrapped around me. Always there.* His legs began to twitch, currents of adrenaline cursing through his body, reviving him, bringing him back to life. A chip off the old block.

"Look friend, if I was you I wouldn't play the hero.... or me and you will have to have a walk in the woods and I'll show you a few other things that I learnt in the army."

"Oh, anytime pal. You're not the only one with a background in the forces."

"Will you two grow up. We've got a person in grave distress here if you hadn't noticed. The ambulance will be here – shit, he's running! He's going. Quick get after him."

Dolby, the painter and decorator and the jogger gave chase. The old man lasted barely a couple of seconds before he pulled up clutching the back of his thigh. Dolby faired little better, combusting into a mess of spittle and rage not ten yards passed. The woman lasted longer but her physical prowess was no match for the inferno in his gut and he pulled clear. He just wanted it more.

13TH NOVEMBER
1975

Lundy knocked hard on the wooden door. There was no turning back – seconds out. He pulled up the sleeve of his sheepskin coat and checked his watch. Just past midnight, the witching hour.

"Gordon. What are you doing here?"

"I need to speak to you James."

"Right. You better come in then."

He followed him down the hallway. Its dark panelling festooned with ornaments of brass and copper. The Dolby clan's coat of arms hung above the living room door complete with ceremonial sword. Once these delusions of grandeur amused him; now their military connotations shuddered him to a halt.

Breathe. Keep breathing. Keep moving. Just stick to the plan. Everything will be fine if you stick to the plan.

"Gordon?"

"Coming, just admiring your ornaments."

"Forget what they look like?"

"No, I always admire them, every time I come."

"Jesus, you really are finished aren't you."

"Sorry?"

"Nothing. Drink?"

"No, thank you James."

"Come on, have a drink with me."

"No, I'm fine."

"C'mon."

"No, honestly."

"For God's sake, live a little."

"Er ... go on then, I'll have a Scotch.

"Good man. Take a seat."

He obeyed his command readjusting the knife in his back trouser pocket to stop it digging into his flesh.

"Ice?"

"Yeah, please."

Dolby stood over him with his drink, a temporary inversion of statures. Pinning him on the ropes.

"Are you not sitting down, James?"

"What?"

"You're making the place look untidy, old boy."

"Sorry, yes. I was just working out the last time we spoke. Three or four months ago if I remember rightly ..."

"Yeah, something like that. I've been really busy with the shop."

"Evidently. I'm surprised you found the place."

"Well, we had words the last time we spoke didn't we. I wasn't sure what reception I'd get."

Dolby sat down next to him.

"That's because you let me down Gord. You betrayed our

friendship."

"No I didn't James. I would never do that."

Dolby leant towards him and whispered into his ear.

"But that's exactly what you did do, Gord. You let me down."

"Well, I don't think I did but that's why I'm here, to clear the air so to speak. We need to get a few things straight."

"Oh, we do, do we."

"Yes James."

"So what do you want to get straight first then?"

"I know it was you."

"I'm sorry, what did you say?"

"I know it was you."

"What are you talking about?"

"You sent the letter to Jessica."

"I've not got the slightest clue what you're going on about."

"The letter, the pictures, it was you that sent them."

Dolby stood up, his jaw gaping, and retreated towards the centre of the ring.

"Look pal, if you've come to throw wild allegations, you can fuck off."

Lundy also stood up; his bulging arms spread wide, his palms upturned.

"No, you don't understand. I'm not angry at you. I can understand why you did it. "

"Did what? I didn't do anything."

"You did it for me, James. You were worried about me and you were right. The letter did the trick, it brought me to my senses. You were right and I'm here to thank you."

He extended his hand.

"Shake on it partner."

Dolby eyed him long and hard before slowly reciprocating the gesture.

"I did it for you Gordon."

"I know you did James and I thank you for that."

"Sod the handshake, come here you old swine, let's bury the hatchet."

Lundy flinched as he moved towards him. Close contact could expose his plan and it was imperative Dolby's guard remained down.

"What, too suave for a bit of brotherly love?"

He engaged in a half-heartedly quick coming together before breaking back towards the sofa.

"I knew it wasn't you Gord, all that stepping up to the mark bullshit. Women can do that to you though. Presumably, you're not still seeing her."

"No, strangely she didn't fancy it after seeing those pictures."

"Ha, her loss old boy. And the kid?"

"Jessica has stopped me from seeing her."

"No bad thing that Gord. You don't need those kinds of responsibilities. Especially with it being a retard. I mean, she won't remember when you've visited her so what's the point. I think it's more humane to get rid of those types of kid at birth."

He dug his nails into the sofa's leather upholstery.

"Yeah, you're right James."

"No, thanks to me you've dodged two very big bullets there old boy and that's why women are so dangerous. When they get their claws into you, it's like a sickness of the mind. I mean, if you could have heard yourself 'it's not making me happy anymore.' That's when I thought he needs a friend to jolt him out of this; and I know what I did could be viewed in bad form but it was the only way to bring you to your senses."

"No, you were right, you did it for me, I know that."

"Good, anyway enough of all this naval gazing. Since you've come to your senses, I've something to show you. To be honest, you couldn't have come to see me at a better time."

"Why's that then?"

"Come with me."

"What for?"

"Come with me and find out."

He followed him up the timber staircase. Could he stab him in the back? He would never get a better opportunity. Dolby though was practically sprinting up the stairs and a clean shot was imperative. He deferred. A wise warrior waits for the moment of greatest opportunity.

Dolby stopped outside his bedroom door.

"You won't believe the surprise I have for you."

"What is it?"

"You'll see old boy, are you ready for this?"

"Yes, go on then."

"An old friend has dropped by."

He slowly opened the door.

"There she is, in all her glory."

Supine on the bed was the unconscious figure of Sarah, arrayed in a brilliant white nightdress.

"Little Miss Sleeping Beauty. We're going to have some night tonight Mr Lundy. She's out for the count. We can do whatever we like to her. She's all ours."

He had regularly reviewed the footage of what they had inflicted on Sarah. Not for gratification but solace. Something to fortify his premise that he too was a victim of Dolby's pain game. The images though were too real and raw and within seconds he would be on the floor. Ergo, the sight of her in familiar pose, live and exclusive, was like a cannonball to his solar plexus.

"Er ... yes, great."

"Let me show you something else as well. Danny England gave me a load of new kit. He's a right dirty bastard you know, makes me and you look like a pair of choirboys."

He led him into a small room decked in white floral wallpaper, his wardrobe of weapons standing in the corner.

"Get a load of this little lot. It's fucking magic. Hang on, where's my fucking keys? I've just had them. Just this second ... Oh, for fuck's sake."

This is it. When he gets his tools. In the back of his neck. Bang. Goodbye demon. Back to the underground.

"You've not seen them have you Gord?"

"Sorry?"

"My keys, I had them in my bloody pocket. I fucking hate losing things."

"You've not left them downstairs?"

"No, I've not left them down fucking stairs. I had them in my pocket ...There they are."

Dolby picked up the keys and opened the wardrobe door. Lundy rubbed his hand on the back of his trousers. He was ready.

"Yes, after tonight, our little Sarah's going to have a bit of trouble sitting down. Look at this little lot."

"Impressive James."

"There's some cracking handcuffs in here, if I can find the bloody things. Police issue these, the real McCoy. Tut, where the fucking hell are they? Finally, we've got a decent set of cuffs and I can't find them. Why am I losing everything?"

Through his pocket, he fingered the contours of his weapon.

I do this in your name Lord. For the glory of Christ.

"Here they are Gord, look at—"

"BASTARDS!"

Both men turned and confronted Sarah, convulsing from the bedroom door, her eyes bloodshot and manic, a knife protruding from her left hand.

"No Sarah. Please no ... no!"

Lundy extended his arms but she ducked below his guard and punched the knife deep into his abdomen.

"Sarah, please listen to me."

He pushed her away, sending her crashing into the Yucca plant standing in the corner of the landing. With almost cartoon-like speed, she jumped back onto her feet and came again, her arms spinning like two Catherine wheels.

"Sarah please, please calm down. I'm on your side!"

"Die you bastards! Die."

This time, she hit the bullseye. Cascades of blood burst from his neck like a live version of a Pollock painting, covering the walls and a paralysed Dolby in vermillion red.

"Sarah stop, please stop."

His hands compressed his injured neck, surrendering the mass of his torso. She tore into it like a feeding shark.

He fell into a prayer pose, beseeching her to cease; however, he possessed neither the strength nor credibility to maintain this stance and he soon bowed his head in readiness of justice. Like every guilty man should. She stopped her attack and surveyed the landing before grabbing a porcelain vase and lifting it above her head. Strangely, he heard the thud as she brought it to bear. Then there was nothing.

13TH NOVEMBER
1975

She gripped her cardigan sleeve and began wiping the window condensation in a slow, circular motion. Through this portal, she studied those below standing mute and moribund like used mannequins. A world away from this travelling circus with its orange façade and performing animals; screaming, shouting, rough-housing, she could ride this bus forever. After all she'd been through, it was the perfect tonic.

A drowned rat wearing paint-decimated black overalls climbed onto the top deck and sat down next to her. *Oh God, here we go.* He tilted his head and ruffled his ginger feather cut, covering her in rain.

"Sorry love. I didn't realise how wet I was."

"That's okay. Don't worry. It's not too bad."

"It's bad enough. Typical me, clumsy as buggery."

"Honestly, it's fine."

"It's this bloody weather."

"Yeah, I know."

He pulled a cigarette from his top pocket and sparked it.

That smell. Dad's smell. I could call him. I'd kill for a hug. Stop. You've exhausted this. You know why not.

"Excuse me, please don't think that I'm being cheeky but

could I pinch a cigarette?"

"A fag?"

"Please."

"Sure love. It's the least I can do after soaking you. They're menthol though."

"That's fine. Thank you."

"You're welcome. I'm trying to go easy on my throat. I'm a singer in a band, see. I tried *Players Mild* but they still battered my voice. What's your normal brand?"

"Er … I haven't really got one to be honest."

"Just smoke what you can get your hands on, eh?"

"No, this is the first cigarette that I've ever smoked in my life."

"Oh, right."

Leaving Oakdene was inevitable, she knew that now. She was a Group C girl through and through. Her exit came without fuss or preamble. The day's meetings had finished and a blanket of torpor covered the building. On waking up from a nap, without thinking – it was as if someone was pulling her strings – she grabbed her suitcase from the wardrobe. Ten minutes later, her bed was neatly re-made with a goodbye letter adorning the pillow. Fifteen minutes thereafter, she stood shivering at the bus stop. Her shin bleeding after it collided with the iron steps of the fire exit.

How will this end? A fresh start or a new beginning? A change of heart? His? Or mine?

"Thanks for the ride."

"It's a pleasure love."

She jumped into the night. As their paths slowly parted, the school kids on the back seats began waving manically and blowing kisses at her. With comparable vigour, she returned the favour. Goodnight and God Bless.

She moved to the edge of the pavement. The headlights of the stacked traffic illuminating the weakening rain. She fastened up her checked trench coat. Her breath shrouded in frozen vapour.

Her reserves of energy were too low for the circular path to his house. Instead, she made for the village green leading straight to the heart of his street. Within minutes, she was standing outside his mock-Tudor castle; partially lit by a solitary street light, bare oak trees obscuring its front.

He opened the door in seconds, almost as if he'd been expecting her.

"Sarah! Thank God you're okay. Come in, please, come in. Sarah darling, it's okay. Come in."

She inched into the hallway, somehow suppressing a scream.

The phone he threw at me. The stairs where I begged him to stop. My crying stair, second from bottom.

"Are you okay darling? My God, what an idiot I've been. Please Sarah, can you ever forgive me?"

"You don't even know what you're asking me to forgive."

"Oh, I do darling."

"Is it the rape, the pimping me out to your sad little friends, the violence? Is that what you're sorry for?"

"Yes, all of that. Listen, Sarah, I have been getting help. Professional help. From a psychiatrist who used to be in the army. I'm changing."

"Why did you go to my mum and dad's house?"

"To see if they knew where you were, to see if you were okay."

"To see if I've gone to the police, more like."

"Sarah please, just listen … like I said, I've been getting help.

Mental help – professional help. I'm a new man. Honestly darling. Please just give me one more chance to prove it."

"You must be joking. After all the pain and hurt you've put me through."

"And I'm sorrier than you could ever imagine. But you must understand I was in turmoil, in such terrible pain. It was the army—"

"Change the record."

"I know, I know, it's an old story. Nevertheless, it's true. I was trained to be an unthinking, unfeeling, killing machine. It became second nature, or in my case, my first nature. I'm changing all that now. That man is no more. But do you know the biggest thing I'm dealing with? My mother ...My horrible, cruel, so-called mother. I'm finally getting her out of my system."

"I thought you said your mother was dead?"

"Physically yes, but she lived on in me. All the anger, the pain, all the fucking *sadism*."

"What are you talking about?"

"She beat me Sarah. She'd make my brother beat me and get people to watch. She would make me do other things in front of her. Things that no mother should ask her son to do. It scarred me Sarah; it is not going to scar me any longer. I'm finally healing."

"So why have you never mentioned this before? Why now?"

"The doctor stated that I needed to make amends; that's why I called around to your parents, to try and find you. I wanted to make amends."

"How often are you seeing your doctor?"

"Every week, religiously. Sarah, this is just the start of you and me. Erase the past, let's look straightforward. Please let's stop looking back. Our life starts now. It would be a crime to waste this opportunity."

"You're so full of crap. You'll never change …You're too bad."

"But can't you see it's not been my fault. I didn't know how to deal with all the hurt and pain I'd suffered. But Sarah … I do now. Sarah, please, I love you more than words can say and I wish I could turn the clock back but I can't. All I can do is promise that starting from now, our lives will be full of love and laughter. Please, just stay tonight. Let's have something nice to eat and then talk some more or maybe just watch a bit of television."

He looks sincere. Can you make yourself cry? I don't know. I just don't know what to do. My heart or my head?

"I'll stay for a bit. I'm not staying the night though."

Her dad's beach. Their beach. A small and sandy cove sheltered between clay-coloured cliffs. They were all here – Mum, Dad, Nana and Uncle Stan, who wasn't really her uncle but ran the battered holiday flats that they resided in every year and had become a family friend.

"Mum, I'm freezing. I can't get warm."

"I don't know why, I'm warm and the sun is out."

"But look at the sky Mum."

"Why, what's the matter with it?"

"It's purple."

"The sky's always purple."

"Is it?"

"Of course it is."

"I've never noticed before."

"That doesn't surprise me Sarah. You're a right dozy sod. I wonder who you get that from …"

"I'm not."

"You bloody are. If you can't eat it, drink it or play it on that record player of yours, you're not interested."

"That's not true."

"Shush, I'm not arguing with you. Have you seen your father?"

"He was over there, fishing with Uncle Stan."

"We'll have to be making tracks soon, get the tea organised. Will you stop shivering—"

"I've told you, I'm freezing."

"Stop being soft."

'I can't help it."

"No, you never can."

"You know what I was thinking Mum?"

"No, but I'm sure you're going to tell me."

"How great it is that you and Dad are getting on so well. It's come from nowhere."

"You know why that is don't you?"

"Why?"

"Because none of this is real."

"What do you mean?"

A barrage of noise began invading the borders of her dream-state. Fevered whispers, the whirling noise of a projector, a woman in the throes of pain or was it pleasure? "That's what I mean. He's done it again - filled you up with bad medicine - and you've fallen for it because you're just like your father – desperate for love."

A succession of people began approaching her. Random fragments from past lives: a substitute Geography teacher, whose name she couldn't remember; a young kid who left her street years ago; Mr Bannister who ran the hardware store near her school. Each one imploring her to escape.

"I can't, I'm paralysed. Mum, where have you gone? Mum, don't leave me. Please come back. Mum!"

Despite the beach being small with oppressive rocks surrounding its margins, a strong wind was developing, filling her eyes with water.

"Mum? Dad? Please, where are you? This isn't funny. Argh …Oh my God. Oh shit, no."

The sea covered her feet, the tide advancing like an invading army. All escape routes blocked. She spun around like a dervish, her body infused with terror. Her first instinct was to swim for it. But to what end? The sea would soon swallow anything to which she could cling. Just like he had. She scanned the rocks, focusing on the coastal path at the top of the cliffs. The one her dad would always insist they walk. He said it was his favourite place in the whole world. With its loose cattle and overfamiliar nettles, she never shared his enthusiasm. Now it was her only option. Taking two steps back, she launched herself towards the cliff face. It permitted her barely a few feet before throwing her to the floor. She shot back up and ran at it again only for the rising tide to drag her back into the maelstrom.

"Help … hel—blughh …

"Are you okay love?"

"Dad, thank God. No, I'm struck. I'm drowning."

"Where is everyone?"

"They've all left me. Where did you go?"

"For a smoke."

"You don't smoke."

"Neither do you – or so I thought.

"What?"

"Never mind …Climb up this cliff."

"No, I keep slipping down."

"Right, give me a second."

"Dad, where are you going? Don't leave me. Please."

"I won't be long."

The waves were now toying with her, lifting her up and throwing her against the rocks.

"Dad, where are you? Dad!"

"I'm here Sarah."

"Dad, I'm dying. I'm drowning."

"No, you are not. Right, grab this rope."

"A rope? Where did you get a rope from?"

"I'm not saying but if you bump into Tarzan, you haven't seen me."

"Dad, don't make me laugh."

"Okay, I want you to keep calm and concentrate. When I throw the rope, I want you to grab it. "

"It won't work Dad."

"Sarah, it will. Trust me, just grab the rope."

He flung the line into the swelling sea; the wind pushing it wide to her left.

"Grab the rope love, with all your strength swim towards the rope."

"Okay Dad."

"Good girl."

She plunged her head underwater and swam for her life.

"Keep going Sarah, you're nearly there. One big push."

"Got it Dad."

"Good girl, now hold on to it as tight as you can. Whatever you do, don't let go of that rope."

"I won't."

Tying his end to a fence stump, he rolled up his sleeves.

"Right, I'm going to start pulling now love."

"Okay Dad. Please hurry."

"Hold on tight."

"I'm moving. I'm moving. Dad, you're doing it."

"Just hold on."

"Keep going Dad."

She had never thought of him as particularly strong but he was pulling the rope with the strength of a thousand horses.

"Not far now love, feel for the rocks with your feet. And hold on."

"I can feel them Dad."

"Right Sarah, you need to climb up the rope now."

"How?"

"I'll keep it tight and just step up the rock face."

"Are you sure?"

"Yes love. Try and find a ledge."

Her foot pawed at the rock until she found a small ridge. On applying her full weight, however, it promptly crumbled sending her crashing back into the sea.

"I can't get a grip. I can't do it."

"You have to Sarah. Try again."

This time her foot found a sturdier ledge and she hoisted herself onto the cliff.

"Good girl, now take one step at a time.

"I'm scared Dad."

"Just concentrate on your steps. I've got you."

"Okay Dad."

"And don't look down whatever you do. Look towards me."

"Okay."

"Just listen to my voice and take one step at a time."

"Okay. I love you Dad."

"I love you too sweet."

"Don't cry Dad."

"Just keep pushing, with all your might keep pushing."

"It's too hard Dad. I can't do it."

"Yes, you can. Fight Sarah, fight with all your heart. With all the love we share."

"I'm doing it Dad. I'm doing it."

"That's it kid. Jesus, you're practically running up it."

"I'm nearly there Dad."

"Yes you are. Yes you are."

"Please stop crying Dad."

"Just one last push."

"It's hard."

"I know but you're so close."

"I've made it."

"Well done sweet. That's my girl."

She opened her eyes but her father was nowhere to be seen.

That sound. It's horrible. Can't someone turn it off? Jesus, what's happened here? How am I at the bottom of the stairs? My night-dress …Why is it covered in blood?

She gripped the banister; a mosaic of blood stains burnishing the fading gloss.

"Oh, shit."

She confronted his Victorian mirror in stages.

"ARGH."

She stumbled backwards. Her face layered in blood, her eyes as round as dinner plates. *What's he done to me? What's he done this time?*

The alarm was still going off; a pneumatic drill straight into her cranium. Desperate to stop it, she began negotiating the stairs. Deep red marks stained the carpet and an upturned house plant dangled from the top step. On reaching the landing, shards of ceramic sent her into a tap dance of pain. Her next sense perception though was infinitely more distressing: the mutilated body of Lundy, punctured yet bloated, a troupe of flies encircling his body.

"Oh my God."

Her two hands automatically covered her face. A burst of pain spasmed from her right palm; she brought it to her eyeline. Tattooed onto her skin was the reddened imprint of a handle.

It was me. I did it.

It all flowed through her: the two of them inspecting his tool-box of sadism; the Swiss army knife on his bedside table; them raping her in the Midland dressed in matching penguin suits; that she stabbed him until her own hand bled.

I am a killer. A killer am I. I've killed him and myself.

Anger began building inside her as if water in a geyser. She fell onto her knees and ripped the knife from his chest before ramming it back in again and again and again.

"Bastard. Bastard. Bastard."

Now end it. Do it now. You've suffered enough.

It was a question she'd asked herself numerous times during this ordeal: would oblivion be preferable to the occasional benefits of consciousness? It was a matter of weighing and balancing. Previously, there was just enough hope and goodness in her life for the answer to be no. This episode though had tipped the scales. She floated towards the front door. The alarm still screaming in the background.

The streets were paved in ice and mist. Dressed in only her nightdress, the elements didn't bother her for a second. She couldn't feel a thing.

Where shall I go? The motorway? The train station? No, I know where I'll go. I know where.

She moved towards the lake. A place of classic childhood scenes: family picnics on long summer days, mucky dogs and lemonade, daisy chains and dragonflies.

She began climbing the fence backing onto the banks of the lake. To her left, a man teetered on the edge of his doorstep, picking up his milk and paper. He rubbed his eyes. This type of thing doesn't happen around here. She smiled at him, hoping he would bring her to her senses but he'd already shut his door.

The perimeter of the lake was dotted with wooden hutches filled with hay and somnolent wildfowl. Some of the ducklings were stirring, struggling to keep their heads up. The swans were already out on the lake, traversing its depths with majestic ease.

The traumatic, uncertain, screeching madness that she understood would mark such moments was absent. She was in complete control. Her life finally in her own hands.

She pictured him sunbathing on this very bank. His blue sailor's hat pulled down over his eyes; his belly bronzed and bulging. She smiled. He was a beautiful man. At least now he would never know what she'd been through.

The plumes of mist were now kindly mermaids beckoning her to dive in. It spoke to her of one of her favourite films, *The Water Babies.* And this is what she would now be: a riverine princess, living amidst the water lilies with all the other innocents.

She waded in. Her dad used to say that when swimming in cold water the trick was to take the plunge right away, give yourself no time to think about it. Then after a minute or two of hell, acclimatisation and then pleasure would follow. She took his advice. He always gave good advice.

18TH JULY 2002

She told him that every time her eyes closed he was there, surrounded by a coterie of nymphs, his bald head littered with lipstick kisses. She told him that in every man she saw his face – top lip curled in contempt, and in every woman she saw her rival. She told him that she'd removed every mirror in the house. Was she going under? Was she breaking down? Under no circumstances. Not on his watch.

"Hi Mum, are you still up?"

"David? What's the matter? What time is it?"

"It's late. You said you hadn't been sleeping. I was just ringing to—"

"Check I was asleep? David, it's half past two in the morning. For your information, I was dead to the world until you bloody woke me up."

"I was just worried about you."

"Go to sleep, David."

I fuckin' wish.

The alarm on his mobile ended another night. He'd lived it from beginning to end. The land of Nod as distant as the North Pole; the sound of dawn birds and rickety milk floats like a boot to the bollocks.

He took a swig from his Evian and limped towards the window.

Look at those bastards all bright-eyed and bushy-tailed. God, I'd give anything to be one of them.

The weather had changed, pitch-black clouds overshadowing the sky. In his sleep-deprived state, they reminded him of the clear plastic bags that as a kid he would fill with tadpoles from the brook behind his house. His mind replayed the time he showed his mum one of these and it burst, soaking the kitchen floor in putrid water. How his dad ran in to investigate and slipped on his backside. That they laughed until their jaws ached – even his dad stifled a giggle. Happier times, but only just. Even so, it triggered a volley of tears.

The sound of an incoming text interrupted his distress. He grabbed his mobile from under his pillow.

Sorry about being sharp last night, love. Know you're looking out for me. You're a son in a million xx.

He pulled himself together and rang Harington.

"Ian, are you awake?"

"Yeah, just brushing my teeth."

"Good lad. What time are we meeting Rose?"

"Half ten."

"Right listen, I've got a few things to sort out. I'll meet you outside the entrance to the pier around ten. Oh, and put a twenty in the Mondeo."

"Sure boss."

They sped through the damp streets. A gleaming spaceship traversing another planet.

"Fuck Dave, we need a break – some names, some contacts."

"Are we left or right here?"

"Right I think. Yeah, right."

"Okay, what was you saying?"

"That we need a break. We're pissing in the wind."

"Well, if we get the names and addresses of the people she mentioned last time, it shouldn't be that difficult. One lead could create another and another."

"Dave, it was thirty-odd years ago. They've probably fucked off, or are dead or fuck knows what. She said that herself."

"I know Ian."

"It's going to be a proper needle in the haystack job."

"Ian, I know, okay. What do you want me to do?"

"Alright mate. Calm down."

"I'm calm mate. Let's just have a bit of positivity eh?"

"If you say so."

"I do say so Ian."

The Mondeo stopped outside Rose's house concurrent with a deathly figure dressed in a heavy winter coat limping through her gate.

"What do you reckon Dave? He looks a bit weird doesn't he? He's been to hers as well."

"Looks like it. C'mon, let's have a word with him ...Go on then Ian, before he fucks off."

They bounded from the Mondeo and gave chase.

"Sir, excuse me, sir."

The man ignored them, limping faster, his silver walking stick propelling him forward.

"Jesus, it's like the fucking Paralympics."

"Sir, have you got a second? Sir, if you could just wait a second. Sir ..."

Progressing into a semi-sprint they finally caught up to him.

"Sir ... sir, my name is Detective—"

"What? God, you scared me half to death. Who the bloody hell are you?"

"It's okay sir. There's no need to be alarmed. My name's Detective Sergeant Wrench and this is my colleague Detective Constable Harington. We are here to see Mrs Lundy. We noticed you'd just called to see her."

"Well?"

"Well, we're looking to track down people who knew Mr Gordon Lundy. I wonder, have you just got five minutes for a quick chat?"

"I can't, I have an important appointment to attend. No, I'm sorry, I've got to go."

"Sir, I'm sorry for any inconvenience, but this will only take a second. Did you know Mr Lundy?"

"What? No, I've never met him."

"Okay, what's your relationship to Mrs Lundy, friend? Family?"

"I'm from her church, that's all."

"Okay sir, so you've never met Mr Lundy then."

"No, never."

"Are you sure?"

"What do you think I am, senile or something? I said no."

"Right, okay that's fine sir. I was just checking that's all. Could I just take your name please?"

"My name, why?"

"There's no reason. Sir, are you okay? You seem really jumpy."

"Yes, I'm fine. You shocked me, that's all. I suffer with my nerves. My name is James Anderson."

"Okay, thank you Mr Anderson. Could I just get your address please?"

"Twenty-two Springtown Gardens. Just down the road, opposite a row of shops; one is a florist, the other a newsagents."

"Right sir, that's great, thank you. Here's my card. If you need to speak to me, don't hesitate to call that number. Also, we may need to contact you again in the future."

"I hope not, I'm a busy man. I've told you I never knew Gordon Lundy."

"Okay sir, well you never know."

"I do, goodbye."

The man struggled onward, as if tethered to a ball and chain.

"What a fucking weirdo, Dave."

"I know, yeah. Thought we'd cracked it there for a second – one of Gordon's old muckers."

"I know."

They walked back to Rose's house. Their first sight of goal coming to nothing.

"Proper oddball though wasn't he?"

"Aye but unfortunately Harington, there's no crime against that."

"No, I suppose not. Maybe Light will come up with one."

"Yeah maybe."

Dave knocked on her door.

"Hello boys."

"Hi Mrs Lundy, how are you?"

"Not too bad. Come in."

"Thank you."

"You've just missed Mr Dolby."

"Who?"

"Mr Dolby, the man who was trying to get in touch. Remember he'd been trying to ring me, he passed a message on to the boys?"

"The guy in the black coat, the thin guy?"

"I know. I told him, you must be boiling. He's quite slight though, as you say. He must feel the cold. Anyway, it was lovely of him to call. Did you see him?"

"Yeah, we had a brief chat with him. And he is definitely called Dolby?"

"Yes, James Dolby. He is a lovely man. He's really given me a tonic by visiting."

20TH JULY 2002

"There it is, Rutland Manor Retirement Home." Harington veered the Mondeo left onto a long gravel path. Sentinel trees shadowing either side.

"Beautiful place eh? Especially on a day like this. Wouldn't mind ending my days here myself."

Dave did not answer. The old woman had returned. A persistent childhood vision, her skin practically vulcanised, her breath condensing on the front room window. Like most people, he'd rationalised the figments that had once plagued his night hours. The bogie man climbing the stairs was the sound of the wind buffeting the back gate; that wicked witch cackle the result of boisterous neighbours and paper-thin walls. The old lady though remained a mystery. There was no explanation for her, other than she was real.

They crunched to a stop in front of an oblong grey-bricked building, swathed from head to toe in ivy.

"Fucking hell Dave, it's like *Brideshead Revisted*."

"Yeah."

"That old dear in the tea shop said it used to be one of the biggest boarding schools in England."

"Really."

They climbed from the Mondeo; Ian stretching as if he'd flown in via long-haul.

"Yeah, proper establishment conveyor belt. Hey Dave, look at this mate. Charms your heart, eh?"

"What?"

From the rear came two older men in admiral jackets, arm in arm with a couple of blue-suited carers.

"Heroes getting the care they deserve."

"Heroes? I bet the shit they got up to would make your eyes water. Dividing and conquering, raping and pillaging – the fucking lot."

"Shit Dave, you sound like a fucking student."

"Fuck off."

"I'm surprised at you."

"Yeah."

"Can I help you gentleman?"

A large middle-aged black woman in a white nurse's uniform with matching hat and plimsolls strode towards them.

"Oh, hello, we're from Greater Manchester Police. This is Detective Constable Ian Harington and I'm Detective Sergeant Dave Wrench. We rang the other day about seeing Mr Dolby. Here's our ID, please ignore my picture."

She peered over rimmed glasses at their credentials before handing them back and shaking their hands.

"Of course you did. How are you? My name is Abe, I am the home manager. Come with me, we can talk in my office."

"Right you are then."

"We were just saying, Abe, what a beautiful place you've got here."

"Thank you, Ian. We try our best."

"I could imagine it costs a few bob."

"Well, yes, but you can't put a price on quality care and piece of mind."

"I bet."

She led them through an oak door into a marbled porch.

"Could you just sign in the visitors' book please. It's for health and safety."

"Sure, no problem."

"Please excuse the mess. These girls spend a fortune on clothes and then can't be bothered hanging them up. The younger generation are so untidy."

"No it's fine. A messy workplace is a busy workplace. That's what my mum used to say. Right, done."

"Not mine Dave. She'd take a stick to us if our rooms weren't spotless. Right, it's just in here."

They followed her into a tiny office.

"Take a seat gentlemen. It's a bit cramped but I'm afraid it's the best we can do."

"It's fine Abe."

"Right, before we start would you boys like a drink?"

"I could murder something cold."

"Okay. Ian?"

"Yes, me too thanks."

"Orange juice?"

"Yes, that's fine."

"Victoria …Victoria, where are you? I need you to come and get us some drinks. Victoria, come here please …Victoria! Sorry about this gentlemen, these girls are everywhere but where you need them to be."

"Don't worry Abe, they must be very busy."

"Here she is …Victoria, where have you been? These men have travelled a very long way and they're desperate for a drink. Now come on, two orange juices please."

A young girl in a green pinafore, her black hair yanked backwards into a high ponytail, accepted her orders with a brusque nod.

"Thank you."

"Yeah, thanks love."

"See what I mean. I blame those magazines they all read."

"You may be on to something there Abe. Anyway, before we get into why we're bothering you today, I just need to reassure you that it's nothing to worry about. It's just some basic enquiries about the murder of a local man."

"That will be Mr Lundy."

"Er … yes that's right. How did you hear about that, Abe?"

"It's been in the papers that his body was found in Manchester. They say he lived around here and his wife still does. And you're from Manchester police too."

"You've missed your way, Abe."

"That's what my husband says. When we're watching a mystery film, I'm always the first to spot the killer."

"I bet. Well, like I say Abe, it's just enquiries. We know Mr Dolby to be a former acquaintance of Mr Lundy and we just want to ask him some questions, that's all."

"Okay. That's fine."

"Isn't he a bit young to be in here?"

"Absolutely Dave, he is one of our younger residents. I will get his file and tell you exactly how old he is."

She pulled open the top drawer of the filing cabinet and rummaged through its contents.

"Here we are. Right let's see … he was born on the 15th of March 1936, so that must make him … sixty-six. He is sixty-six years of age. Yes, he's our youngest resident."

"And what's wrong with him, is he ill?"

"Well, he had a stroke a couple of months ago. He was lucky, it was only a small one. He can still walk but he's physically weak. He stays in his wheelchair most of the time. But that's more down to laziness than anything else."

"How long has he been in here for, Abe?"

"Only recently, just after his stroke. He just walked in and said he wanted someone to look after him."

"Does he have visitors, any family?"

"No one. He is … how can I put this, not a very nice man. God forgive me, I should not speak ill of one of my residents but he is a nasty man."

"In what way?"

"The way he talks to people. However, I see sadness in his eyes. Maybe he never found happiness. I don't know. He's angry."

"Okay, well we're going to see him now … if that's okay? We won't be long."

"Okay. No problem. I will show you to his room. Here's Victoria, late as ever with the drinks. Come on girl."

"That's fine Abe. We'll have them when we come out."

They walked up the varnished staircase; pictures of small Victorian girls playing with small Victorian dogs, or slight variations on that theme, covering the walls.

"Here's his room. Shout me if you need me."

"Thank you."

Dave knocked on the door. There was no reply so he knocked harder.

"Well."

They shrugged at each other and stepped inside.

The room was vast. The paucity of its contents – a bed, small table, wardrobe and a wheelchair-bound Dolby – enhancing its capaciousness. He was sitting in front of a three-paned bay window. The manor's undulating greens stretching out in front of him.

"Hello sir."

"Who are you?"

"Mr Dolby, my name is Detective Sergeant Dave Wrench and this is Detective Constable Ian Harington we are from Manchester CID and we're here to ask you some questions about a friend of yours: Gordon Lundy."

"I've already spoken to you about this. Why are you here again? This is harassment."

"Well, the problem is that the last time we spoke to you, you weren't called Mr Dolby then, you were called erm … just remind me Detective Harington."

"Mr Anderson."

"Yes. That's right, Mr Anderson. Now what we have been trying to figure out is why you would have lied about your name."

"I can't remember."

"And why did you say you didn't know Gordon Lundy when we have it on very good authority that you knew him pretty well. Given all this confusion, I'm sure you can understand why we wanted to have another little chat with you. Mr Dolby? Mr Dolby!"

"Don't raise your voice to me. I heard what you said. I barely knew Mr Lundy, maybe I have been in his company on one or two occasions, that's all."

"Why the false name then?"

"It's the stroke. I get confused."

"To the extent you think that you're someone else?"

"Yes, on occasions."

"Bit far-fetched wouldn't you say?"

"Sorry, I didn't know that you're a trained doctor."

"Well no, I'm not. It would be interesting to hear a medical opinion though. You certainly seem okay to me. Does he seem pretty sharp to you Ian?"

"Yeah, sharp as a tack Dave."

"It comes and goes."

"Really? That's a new one on us but as you say, we're hardly experts in that particular field. I am though interested in one thing you said …That you've only met Mr Lundy a couple of times. Is that right?"

"Yes, that's right."

"So why does Mrs Lundy have a different opinion to you of how close you were to her husband?"

"I don't know; you'll have to ask her."

"Oh we did. And she says that you were pretty tight – Territorial Army pals, weekend manoeuvres. Proper bosom buddies."

"We may have been, like I say I can't remember."

"You sure about that?"

"What?"

"That you can't remember."

"Yes, I'm fucking sure."

"Okay, just checking. Just want to be clear about things. I believe you were a successful business man Mr Dolby."

"What's it to you?"

"I was just wondering, have you always been based in Hastings or have you ever lived anywhere else?"

"I can't remember."

"No?"

"Yes."

"You sure?"

"Yes, I'm fucking sure."

"Okay, let me try another one. Were you ever aware that Mr Lundy engaged in any extra-material affairs?"

"I can't remember."

"Were you ever involved in any of the affairs?"

"Who with?"

"Mr Lundy."

"What, I'm no fucking queer."

"I never said you were Mr Dolby. I meant you, Mr Lundy and another person."

"No, absolutely not."

"Right. I must say you remembered that okay."

"Look, wherever you're going with this you can stop right now. This is a disgrace. It comes to something when a law-abiding man, a man who's served his country, who is now very poorly, is subject to an interrogation."

"C'mon Mr Dolby, it's hardly an interrogation now is it?"

"Well, that's what it bloody feels like. I have had a stroke. I cannot remember. What part of that do you not understand? And to cap it all, you're calling me a bloody queer. I think you better leave."

"Look Mr Dolby, we know that Gordon Lundy had voiced concerns that he and another man had been ill-treating a girl. We're merely enquiring do you know who this man could be?"

"Are you implying that man could be me?"

"I never said that."

"I am going to be putting in a complaint about the both of you. You will regret the day you harassed me. When I was a young man, you could set your watch by the boys in blue—"

The fallen picture frame again caught Dave's attention and with Dolby preoccupied with his rant, he scooped it up from the floor.

Fucking hell. I've hit the motherlode.

"Leave that alone. That's my private possession that is."

Within the splintered frame was Dolby standing in front of an orange-clad building underneath a bubble-lettered sign reading *New Direction Catalogues.*

"Now this is interesting Mr Dolby."

"Do you mind, did I say that you could look at that?"

"Ian, check this out, it's Trafford Park."

"Shit, it is as well. I drive past there every morning."

"You never said you worked in Trafford Park, Mr Dolby."

"Put that down. I know my rights; you need a warrant for this."

"How long did you work in Manchester?"

"Nurse! Get me a phone. I need to ring my solicitor."

"C'mon Mr Dolby, we're just intrigued by the coincidence aren't we Ian?"

"Yeah, it's a small world."

"It certainly is. So go on sir, how long was you in Manchester for?"

"Bloody long enough."

"Presumably you lived there as well?"

"No, I fucking commuted from down south every day."

"No need for expletives sir. Did you forget that as well?"

"Forget what?"

"That you lived and worked in Manchester."

"How many times, I'm an ill man."

"Did you ever meet up with Mr Lundy in Manchester?"

"No. Absolutely not."

"What was your address in Manchester?"

"I can't remember."

"So the only thing that you can remember about Manchester is that you never met Gordon Lundy there."

"Yes, if you like."

"I think your bad memory is covering up a multitude of sins Mr Dolby."

"My bad memory is none of your bloody business."

Dave now stepped back and with a nod ushered Ian to the fore.

"C'mon Mr Dolby …Look, we're pretty sure you had nothing to do with this, it's just that you're raising our suspicions with these lies and this nonsense that you cannot remember things."

"I can't. How many times, I can't."

"All we want is for you to tell us the truth about your connection to Mr Lundy and we'll leave you alone. Won't we Dave?"

"Absolutely, just tell us the truth and we'll leave you—"

His bedroom door crept open, introducing an older woman dressed in a green floral frock. Her face like crumpled paper, her eyes full of empty space. Just as Dave had pictured.

"No. No. Fucking get out, fucking bitch."

"What are you doing? I live here. Get out of my house. This is my father's room."

Dolby grabbed a glass of water from the table and threw it towards her.

"Nurse! Nurse! She's in here again! Fucking bitch, get out."

She shuffled towards them. Slow and unsteady.

"You must all leave immediately. My father will be home from work soon."

He burst from his wheelchair, Ian holding on to him by his fingertips.

"Stay there Mr Dolby. Please sit down. Hello …Hello, nurse … We need a nurse in here. Stand in front of her Dave. Dave, wake up man!"

"What?"

"Stand in front of her."

"Yes, right."

"Who are you? Get out of my house."

"It's okay love …Nurse, we need help in here."

The woman lifted her left hand – its veined circuitry resembling pure cartography – and launched it towards Dolby's face. Ian dived in front of him, intercepting her attack.

"It's okay love, nice and calm."

"Fucking die. Fucking die. I'll fucking kill you."

"Calm down Mr Dolby. For fuck's sake Dave, get her out. Where are the fucking staff?"

A young broad-shouldered carer with mousy blonde hair ran into the room.

"Lilly, Lilly. No. No. This is not your room sweet. Come with me Lilly. Come on love."

She gently grabbed her elbow and guided her away from the scene; the intonation of her voice dousing Lilly's fire. Dolby though was still burning.

"It's your fucking job to keep her out. Your fucking job. If I hit her, it'll be your fault."

"Now Mr Dolby, don't overreact. Don't get yourself worked up. Lilly meant no harm."

"You'd fucking want that wouldn't you? You want me to hit her. Liven up your day, a change from cleaning up piss and shit."

Dave had heard enough.

"Mr Dolby, I'd appreciate it if you did not use that kind of language. You need to calm down right now."

"I'm here an ill man, a disabled man. I have these morons from bumblebee-land interrogating me about nonsense and you, you useless fucking bitch, could not do the one task afforded you – keeping this fucking crank out of my room. Why couldn't you do that? Are you that stupid?"

"Mr Dolby, I don't care if you're ill, you will not talk to people like that."

"It's okay sir. Mr Dolby is a very grumpy man but it must be hard for him. He told me he was once very important and successful. It must be so very hard for him, now that he is here with Lilly and all the other ladies."

Her words hit him like a tranquiliser dart. He attempted a riposte but it was too much and he slumped back into his chair.

"Will you please all just get out. Please, leave me alone."

Abe came into the room.

"Gabby, take Lilly away. Please officers, I think you should leave Mr Dolby now. He needs rest. Dave you need to go."

"Okay Abe, no problem. I think we've got all we need for today. Thank you Mr Dolby, we really appreciate your time. We will be in touch soon."

They turned and left the room.

"Ian, it's her."

"What?"

"No sorry. I mean it's him. It's him. He's our man."

11TH FEBRUARY 2002

In the small windowless room there was not an empty seat to be had. A circle of concern, including his social worker Mary – her silver hair and red Doc Martin's glinting under the lights – and his psychiatrist Dr Murray, the remnants of his lunch adorning his long grey beard.

"Hi Adam, you know me don't you …Dr Murray?"

'Course, I know you. I've met you every week for the past year. I'm not a fucking retard.

"Yes, doctor."

"Well do you know why we're all here today?"

"Because I want to leave."

"Well, it's not so much that you want to leave. I mean, you've made great strides since you've been with us; you've finished your treatment and you're an informal patient. You can leave. It's just where you want to leave to that worries me. Mary, what's your view on this?"

"I have to say that I share your concerns Doctor. I've spoken to Adam about a couple of options that I think would be better for him – supported accommodation, a stepping stone place-ment … A short-term tenancy to reintegrate him back into the community. But he's turned them down. He wants to go back to his own home."

And why fucking not? Isn't that where you go every night?

"Adam, why do you think these types of placements are not for you?"

"I've nothing against them Doctor. It's just that I want to go home, I'm ready to go home."

"You'd have access to staff twenty-four hours a day, Adam. You wouldn't have that at home."

Why do you think I want to go fucking home.

"I know Doctor but I'll keep in touch with my nurse this time. You have my word on that."

"Adam, I've spoken to Unicorn Housing. They have some reservations too—"

"They can't kick me out Mary. I'd fight it all the way. Over my dead body."

"No, they're not kicking you out Adam but they would like you to consider other options. The options I've mentioned."

"But I have considered them. Long and hard. It's just that it's better for me to go home. Where everything's familiar and to hand."

"Yes, like all those bad memories."

"Mary, my memories will haunt me no matter where I go."

"I know that Adam but they don't need any encouragement."

She's right. They'll all be there waiting for me. In every wardrobe and behind every door. So will their kryptonite though. Uncle Smirnoff. Pure white spirit.

"You'll need to be diligent in taking your medication, Adam."

"Oh, absolutely Doctor. Every day like clockwork. You don't need to worry about that."

"Well Mary, there's not a lot we can do. He's making an informed decision, albeit in my opinion an unwise one."

"I agree Doctor."

"Listen folks, you don't have to worry about me. I'll be fine. I'm not daft. I'll look after myself. No offence like, but I don't want to end up back in here."

3RD MARCH 2002

He stopped dead outside the wooded entrance. The branches of the attendant oak trees had breached their demarcations and joined together. A union bathed in twilight, overseen by febrile bats and a constant owl. *Fuck man, it's like a tunnel. A portal into another world.*

From nowhere, a window shut. He spun around, a picture of vigilance, and faced the baffled glare of a curtain commando in one of the surrounding cottages. *Whose idea was this again?*

The tribute came to mind after draining his second bottle of Vodka – he did all his best thinking when barely able. The placing of a memorial crack pipe and lager can at the spot where Flames fell. A man who in life he couldn't stand but in death loved like a brother. It was also the perfect riposte to him. Returning to the scene of the crime for the first time. Fronting out his fears. (Although his stance was somewhat sullied by ringing Tat and confirming Bailey had definitely said he'd left town.)

He marched onward.

"If there's anybody out there who fancies their chances ... bring it on. But ask yourself first how mad must I be to walk through the woods in the dead of night? Yeah that's right, I'm fucking certifiable. Come and have a go if you fucking dare."

A pair of yellow eyes ran across his path before stopping and fixing him an ultraviolet glare.

"What are you looking at?"

The eyes stood firm for a couple of seconds before darting off.

"Yeah, yeah, go and tell your crew. There's a human in the wrong part of town. I'm ready for the fucking lot of you. You ain't got a fucking clue what I've been through."

He rummaged in his pockets for his cosh.

"Say hello to my ...Oh for fuck's sake."

Naked on the battlefield, he debated turning back but he had come too far.

He'd been striding forward for at least an hour but still couldn't find the spot. It had to be around here somewhere. If only it didn't all look the fucking same.

There's the fence, isn't it? Yeah, that's got to be it. This is definitely it, near the lake. The place where I saw through time. My shit enlightenment. Fuck, it seems like an age ago.

In a Pavlovian response, pools of sick began welling in the back of his throat. *Oh, please no. Not again. I can't do it again.* He extended his arm, steadying himself against a tree before bending over and vomiting.

"Jesus fucking Christ."

After a couple more expulsions, he straightened and wiped his mouth with his sleeve, panic subsiding in conjunction with his nausea. He felt a lot better. So much so that he pulled Flames' can from his coat pocket and tore it open.

"For Flames! Oh shit ... I'm—"

He toppled down the steep embankment like a felled chimney.

A cascade of piano notes nursed him from sleep. The sound

of a beautiful mobile in the world's comfiest crib. *Fuck, I feel amazing. Completely rejuvenated. Have I died and gone to heaven? Judging by the used syringes, probably not.* He sat up, shielding his eyes from the disco-ball illuminations shimmering through the bracken. *What the fuck* ...He climbed to his feet and shook his arms and legs. The theme tune to *Close Encounters of the Third Kind* playing in his mind's ear.

He inched towards the light. *Shit, what if it's that bastard? He's back and burying people by floodlight. No, it's too beautiful for that. I can feel it in my bones.*

The steps leading towards the lake were wet and slippery but he practically ran down them. *Who the fuck is that? It looks like ...No, it can't be. It's the spit of her though. Oh my God, it is her. It's fucking her! The girl in the newspaper cutting. The girl who died. Sarah. Sarah Gregory. She's so ... beautiful.*

He was right; it was she. Ensconced in a luminous bubble, dancing across the lake's sodden banks in a gleaming white nightdress, her hair a golden ocean.

I feel no fear. I have no words.

He rubbed his eyes and looked for a camera or some kind of projector. Nothing. It was all real. He tiptoed behind an adjacent oak tree. A safe place to watch the show of a lifetime.

The songs of the early birds told him how long he'd been there. Their serenade was the finishing touch. Could this scene get any more perfect? It had the opposite effect on Sarah though: her eyes igniting in terror, her body flailing, tearing at invisible constraints as if a desperate diver.

"Sarah, what's the matter. It's okay. I'm here."

Her aura though was rapidly fading and by the time he'd climbed onto the embankment, she'd disappeared into thin air.

"Sarah, don't go. Sarah, please come back."

26TH JULY 2002

The Mondeo weaved through the morning traffic. Nominally marshalled by Dave, his phone glued to his ear.

"It's an absolute game changer, Mum. The heat this investigation has brought down on them. I mean, did you not read it in the paper? It was damming, absolutely damming – 'A culture unwilling or unable to manage complex investigations.' The *Evening News* are running with it too. Word is Jakes is fielding daily calls from the Chief Super. There's even talk of drafting in other forces. This is my time, Mum. I'm riding the zeitgeist. I'm back in fashion. Mum? Mum? Don't cry Mum. It's going to be okay. Please, Mum."

The mountain of stairs to Jakes' office was no match for him today – just another obstacle to conquer – and he burst into the office as if proclaiming a fire. From his left, Tracy from payroll approached. They had a bit of a thing going in '97. Or did they? Who cares. He lifted his hand in readiness for a high five but she looked at him as if he'd just pissed on her shoes. Her loss.

He steamed into Jakes' office.

Right, you fucker. How do you like me now?

"Whoa, knock why don't you, it's only my fuc— Oh, Wrench it's you."

"Certainly is sir. Live and exclusive."

"Er, yeah, good. Well, you certainly sound chipper. How was Hastings?"

"Okay sir. Yeah, really good."

"It's a beautiful part of the world, isn't it?"

"It sure is sir."

"How was Harington?"

"Good, okay. He's a good man to have along."

"Yeah, he'll be an asset."

"Yes, he will. Sir, the visit was pretty fruitful—"

"Yeah?"

"Absolutely sir. We've got a name. A real lead."

"I know we have. It's great news. Quite a turn up isn't it? Light's just interviewing him now over at Strangeways."

"Who, James Dolby?"

"Who? Never heard of him. No, Terry McVeigh."

"What, THE Terry McVeigh?"

"Oh yes, just when you thought he couldn't go any lower."

"Seriously?"

"I know, I know, you don't have to tell me, it's crazy. Light's been over there with him since half seven."

"What have we got on him? Any forensics?"

"No, he's coughed to it."

"What. Why? What was his motive?"

"Clear his conscience apparently. Word is he's not well. Do you know he is sixty-nine? He's probably worrying about meeting his maker. I've seen that a few times, evil bastards desperate to make their peace. Sorry, you mean his motive for the murder. Well, it appears that him and Lundy were acquaintances but fell out over some women. Same old story. And as you know, McVeigh needed no second invitation."

"What were his connections to Lundy though? I mean McVeigh knocked about in the gutters of Manchester, Lundy's clique was on a different level. He mixed with business men; he wouldn't be seen dead with the likes of McVeigh."

"What can I say? He liked to get his hands dirty now and again."

"Sir, it doesn't fit. Let me tell you about a suspect I found in Hastings. I think it's a lot more credible than McVeigh."

"You can't get much more credible than a full confession Dave."

"Just hear me out sir."

"Okay. Go on then."

"Thanks sir. One of Mrs Lundy's church friends put us on to a Reverend James. He's the local vicar, he's getting on a bit but he's as sharp as they come. Just prior to his disappearance, Lundy confided in him that he and another man had been involved in the abuse of a young girl. Sounds nasty and don't ask me why but the good Reverend didn't report it, penitent privilege or something like that he said – don't worry I gave him a right bollocking about that. Anyway, the Reverend said that Lundy was really guilty about his actions and wanted forgiveness. His daughter had been taken away from him or something and he thought God was punishing him – very strange if you ask me but there you go, religion does strange things to people. Anyway, the Reverend also said that he appeared scared stiff of his accomplice. Apparently, Lundy was a real nasty piece of work so he was a bit surprised by this. Then he disappeared."

"Is that it?"

"No, when we visited Mrs Lundy, we saw a suspicious-looking guy leaving her house. When we stopped him to ask him his name, he gave us a false one."

"How do you know it was a false one?"

"When we spoke to Mrs Lundy seconds later she confirmed that the guy wasn't who he said he was. His name was really James Dolby."

"Who?"

"James Dolby. Are you sure you've never heard of him sir?"

"Doesn't ring any bells."

"Okay. Well anyway, we managed to track this guy to a nursing home in Hastings. He denied knowing Lundy but we've got info from Mrs Lundy that they were good mates, Territorial Army buddies apparently. Also, when I asked him whether he had ever lived or worked outside of Hastings he said that he hadn't, but then I saw a picture in his room of him suited and booted outside the offices of New Directions Catalogues. Me and Harington clocked straight away … it was Trafford Park! He was lying. He then starts saying that he suffers from memory loss and that's why he denied knowing Lundy and working outside of Hastings. I mean it was farcical really."

"I'll be honest, I'm not hearing much here, son."

"Think about it sir …Lundy, guilty about how he and Dolby treated the girl and high on religion threatens to go to the police and Dolby shuts him up. I know I'm right about this sir. I can feel it."

"Look Dave, you know me, I always respect a coppers' nose but all I'm hearing is a lot of supposition and not much else."

"Why would he lie about his name? What about all the other stuff?"

"A multitude of reasons. Listen, I admire your passion on this one son but think about it, how does what you've got compare to a full confession?"

"I know but c'mon boss, do you really think that this has the hallmark of McVeigh? It's nothing like him."

"Why not?"

"Well for a start, his MO is completely different. McVeigh always strangled his victims."

"Light was saying that McVeigh's given details of the murder weapon and it's consistent with Lundy's injuries and none of this info has got out to the press. Serial killers don't always stick to the same method either son."

"I know but—"

"Look at Jessica Byrne, he didn't strangle her."

"We only suspect him of the Byrne murder. He's never admitted it and we've never come anywhere near charging him for it."

"Aye, but there's good evidence that puts him at the scene Dave. I'm not the only one who thinks he's responsible."

"Okay, why has he admitted to this but not the Byrne murder? Why is he admitting to anything at all? He's never admitted to any of his crimes. Why now?"

"That's a good point. As I say, age can do strange things to a man. I wrote the fucking book on that one …Listen, you need to speak to Light when he gets back. He seems pretty sure that McVeigh's our man and with the level of scrutiny on us he'll need to have a watertight case to get it past the DPP and, well, he says he has. Speak to Light, he should be back soon."

"Don't make me laugh."

"I'm sorry?"

"C'mon sir, you know."

"I know what exactly?"

"Watertight, with him in charge."

"And what's that supposed to mean son?"

"Sir, don't you find all this a touch suspicious?"

"I don't know what you mean."

"With the greatest of respect boss, this is a murder case, not some tin-pot burglary investigation. Do you think it's appropriate to fudge this one?"

"What do you mean fudging? Who's fudging? People don't confess to a murder for nothing."

"Sir, he's old, he's given a full confession and he's already a lifer. Isn't it just a touch too convenient?"

"So that's a reason to confess? You're losing your critical faculties on this one Dave."

"Have you any idea how many people Light has bribed to admit to crimes that they've not done. He's a master at it, you must know that. God knows what he's bribing McVeigh with but I would imagine it has to be more than his usual price – the odd conjugal visit in that fucking rank B and B he uses. Look sir, we're supposed to be serving the people and if we're not, what end are we serving? Not justice that's for sure."

"What are you talking about?"

"Boss it's wrong, you know it's wrong, but it doesn't have to be. Let me look into Dolby, a full belt and braces job. He is our man. I'm sure of it."

"Wrench."

"If you could just have seen Mrs Lundy's face, sir. She's old and tired. She deserves justice but she ain't going to get it is she? She's not is she? You know that as well as I do …We're going to cheat her."

"Wrench."

"Boss, he's corrupting the whole team. Why did he ever—"

"Wrench. Shut the fuck up! Now you listen to me you self-righteous little shit. Light's a fucking very good detective and if he's sure then I'm sure. Just because McVeigh is already a lifer doesn't mean it's the wrong call. I desperately hope for the good of our force it is the right call but mostly I hope it's the right call to save his poor cow of a wife more trauma. But you wouldn't want that would you lad? You want your day in the sun. You want a big trial, a real cliffhanger. It's all about you."

"I only want justice."

"Bollocks."

"I'll blow the whistle. I'll speak to the top brass. I know they're crawling up your arse on this one.

"Here, I'll dial the number for you and while they're on I'll tell them you're fucking losing it; that you lost out on promotion and are now trying to destroy the man who beat you fair and square to the job. I'll also tell them that you are a mentally un-stable, insubordinate, fucking liability."

A series of images spun across his mind: his passing out parade; the breathless calls to Mum announcing another promotion; the look on the faces of the victims after another scumbag bites the dust. *Fucking fat corrupt cunt. Fucking fat corrupt cunt.* He lept from his seat and booted an empty chair. *Oh, shit no. The wheels. The fucking wheels.* It span into an adjacent coat stand sending Jakes' black windbreaker and the mounds of copper hidden in its pockets crashing to the floor.

"Sir, I'm sorry—"

"Get out of my office. Get the fuck out right now, you little shit."

"Sir—"

"Get out before I kick you out. You're fucking finished son."

25TH MARCH 2002

She wasn't eating her lunch; he'd calculated as much. A café so greasy it named its specials after types of coronary heart disease was no place for a social worker. Not this one anyway. He figured it a win-win: she doesn't get to see his squat and he gets double dinners. The university of life.

He put down his knife and fork and wiped his chin with a pre-stained napkin.

"You not eating your fatty artery, Mary?"

"Sorry?"

"Your fatty artery …That's what they call fried egg on toast here."

"I asked for boiled egg on brown toast and I get this."

"Ha, Bernie's never poached an egg in his life."

"When I asked him, he nodded and smiled."

"He was probably just humouring you. He's a character."

"Yeah, he looks it. I'd take it back if I didn't think he'd stab me with that butter knife."

"Shit, don't do that; this is him on a good day. Two rules for coming in here – never complain about the food and always clean your plate."

"You better finish it then. But if we ever do this again, I'm choosing where we eat. Or even better, you can make me something at your place."

She slid her plate over to him.

Like taking candy from a baby.

"It's a deal. You could have come around to mine, no problems. To be honest, I just wanted a break from the place. And it's always pretty quiet in here, so it's nice and private."

"I can see why. Anyway, how's the medication going?"

"Yeah, no problems."

"Sure?"

"Cool, yeah."

"No side effects?"

"No, no. All good."

"You are definitely taking them Adam?"

Like fuck.

"Defo Mary. Every morning religiously. I'm not daft."

"How's your symptoms?"

He slurped his tea.

"Not bad. Yeah, all good."

"No voices?"

"No, no."

"Visual hallucinations?"

"No, nothing. I'm in a real good place at the minute."

"That's great Adam. You deserve it."

"Thanks Mary. Like I say, I feel like I'm coming out the other side."

"That's great news Adam. Whatever you're doing, keep doing it."

"Well, to be honest Mary, I'm seeing someone."

"A relationship? Oh, right. That's good."

"Yeah, it's going really well."

"Where did you meet?"

"We just bumped into each other. She's called Sarah. She's lovely."

"Is it serious?"

"Well, I think so. I've never felt this way about anyone else."

"Really?"

"Yeah."

"Right…"

"What's up, Mary?"

"Nothing, I mean, it's great Adam. And I'm delighted for you but …"

"What?"

"Well, relationships can be stressful too. I know I sound negative but you're not long out of hospital and … I just want you to be careful."

"No, you don't understand. She's great for me. She's my one constant. Whenever I need her, she's always there for me."

"Well, okay. If you're sure."

"I've never been more sure of anything in my life, Mary."

He placed the poem and a bunch of wild flowers on her verdant stage. He used to write prolifically but had retired in disgust after his entry into a school poetry competition, a satire on Eighties individualism called *Knuckle Shuffle,* resulted in a month's detention. Sarah though had reignited his musings and so many other things.

He retired to his usual seat and covered himself in an avalanche of blankets. Right on cue, she emerged from nowhere, dancing through eddies of mist like a Cold War gymnast. At first, the bundle failed to capture her attention. She was too busy playing hopscotch and performing ramshackle handstands. What could he do to make her see? He had to make her see. Fumbling in the undergrowth, he picked up a branch and lobbed it towards her as if it were an ignited firework. She stopped dead; studying the dark of the audience, before bending down and gathering her bounty, her face aglow with wonder.

Her eyes scanned the page.

Sarah, though you dance alone,

You are not alone.

I share your space but you cannot see me,

I share your pain but you cannot feel me.

I know you but alas, you do not know me.

The silent witness to your ordeal.

The unfortunate one to survive.

Therefore, again I watch you, your faithful audience.

Rapt with wonder and joy,

Waiting for your call.

She tiptoed to the edge of the bank, casting her gaze left and right, up and down. She stepped backwards, a wide smile covering her face. She'd finally found her man. She beckoned him forward. A pantomime star requesting audience participation. They embraced, her spectral hands wiping away his tears, before morphing into a staccato waltz, as if two figurines in a music box.

5TH AUGUST 2002

With their snow-white shirts, zany ties, slicked-back hair and pitch-black trousers and shoes, their fellow regulars at the Discotheque Royale called them "the twins." It was an apt description. From their first day at Cop College, they were inseparable. Work, rest and play. They even kept romantic liaisons within the family – dating a pair of bubble-permed sisters from Wythenshawe.

The first chink of light between them came after passing out. Dave went to North Manchester – leaving him and returning to the Midlands was never an option. Geoff though, for reasons he never clarified, chose the south of the city. A betrayal compounded when within a year he'd quit the force and gone travelling with his new bird.

"I'm just not feeling it Dave."

"Feeling what? What is there to fucking feel?"

He came back a year later and joined the prison force. Their relationship though never recovered and they drifted apart like litter on the tide.

Today's meeting was the first time they'd seen each other for years. Dave had asked him to arrange an unauthorised visit with Terry McVeigh. He figured he owed him.

Look at him. Who the fuck does he think he is. 'Do you want a brew mate?' Why doesn't he just come out and say it: 'I'm such a big shot

I've got my own office with my own fridge and kettle. No communal bullshit for me. I'm special.' Fucking line manager. He's cheating a living.

"Biscuit?"

"Nah mate. I'm right."

"You sure? They're bourbons."

"Yeah, I'm fine thanks."

"I can't resist them me."

I can tell pal.

Geoff placed the silver tea tray on their table positioned overlooking the Victorian exercise yard.

"Cheers mate. Is that Paul Cauty?"

"Where?"

"There, on the other side of the yard."

"Yeah, that's him."

"What's he in for this time?

"What do you think?"

"Jesus, he doesn't get any better does he."

"Post Office in Leyland this time. An old guy, proper have-a-go hero, knocked him on his arse."

"Fucking hell."

"Yeah, it never ends."

"Tell me about it."

He sat down, shuffling his ample backside into its arse groove.

"So Wrenchy, you think it's all bent then?"

"Sorry mate?"

"The case, you think it's bent?"

"Oh yeah, classic Jakes and Light this one."

"Are you sure?"

"One hundred percent. I know who's fucking done it, I've just got to prove it. A guy in Hastings, a real piece of work. James Dolby, you heard of him?"

"No mate."

"Yeah, it seems like he's gone right under the radar."

"Some do. It's only when they get caught that their trail of devastation comes to light."

"Yeah, I suppose so."

"We see quite a lot of it."

"Hmm. What I can't get my head round is why McVeigh would do this. With the heat on this one, press and all that shit, what could Light give him to take the rap, to go through all of this shit?"

"That's the point though isn't it ..."

"What is?"

"That's his motivation ...The kudos, the fame."

"Nah, for a murder charge?"

"Yeah, of course for a murder charge. What else? It's always been a sticking point for him. Sutcliffe, Nielson ... fucking Copeland, everybody's heard of them right? McVeigh? Who the fuck's heard of McVeigh? No one. He's small-time, Dave, and I know for a fact this fucking pisses him off—"

"How do you know that?"

"'Coz he's fucking told me. He was watching one of those shit crime documentaries one night. I tell him it's lights out and he says to me 'If I'd butchered some birds down South instead of fucking Collyhurst they'd be making documentaries about me.'"

"He said that to you?"

"Yep, more or less, and maybe he's got a point. His crimes are small town. They ain't got a narrative or some warped fucking ideology. Now this is big fucking news. Now he'll get his documentary. Just you wait and see."

"I know but still, it's a big fucking ask."

"Well, there is something else you should know about."

"What?"

"We found some stuff in his cell. We were baffled at first because his only visitor is his mum and that was too sick to contemplate. But it's starting to make sense now ...Jesus, if it was him, he's one on his own that Light.

"What are you talking about?"

He jumped from his seat and opened the bottom draw of his filing cabinet before throwing a black bin-liner onto Dave's lap.

"Get a load of these babies."

Dave dipped into the bag and pulled out a handful of DVDs.

"Glamour Flower?"

"Oh yeah. We found a load on a routine inspection of his cell. Got a thing for nylon and chiffon has our Terence. Or rather, watching people doing unspeakable things in nylon and chiffon to other people in nylon and chiffon."

Dave dived back in and pulled out a bunch of tights.

"What are these? Oh God, they're not what I think they are, are they?"

"Ha ha. They sure are. He's got loads in his cell. We've not washed 'em either by the way."

"You bastard."

"Ha ha. Fucking twisted, isn't it?"

Who's directing this? Who's fucking with me? What have I ever done to them?

Dave's particular thing was for silk scarves, those robes of pure femininity. Since the unfortunate incident with Janice, he'd remained largely abstinent before falling off the wagon the other night with a spider-silk shawl.

As a child, his auntie – *my own flesh and blood for God's sake* – had playfully whipped his bare torso with one on a hot day in her back garden. His body shook with sensations. Feelings seared onto his brain, resulting in a constant, overwhelming desire to recapture those forbidden tremors.

This compulsion mortified him; for he knew that of all the psychological states it was sexual desire that shone the most probing light into the window of our souls – those strange peccadilloes that really make us tick. And this was what made him tick. The soiling of silk with all its connotations of hate, freedom, and motherly love. And now he had a friend in fabric who was a homicidal maniac. What did that make *him*?

"You took this filth off him I hope?"

"Some of it for research purposes. The rest we left with him."

"Fucking hell, how come?"

"Because Dave, we'd end up in fucking Strasbourg."

"That's political correctness gone mad."

"Alright mate, calm down. You forget we've got to live with 'em."

"I know but—"

"But nothing. Spend a weekend on our Cat A landing and trust me, you'll be glad of anything that keeps them quiet."

"It's not right."

"Yeah, yeah. Listen, what's the point of all this Dave? He's hardly likely to cough to you."

"I know. I just need to know."

"Know what?"

"That I'm right, I suppose."

Geoff ushered him into a small box of a room with school-dinner furniture and neon strip lighting. The perfect ambience for what he had in mind.

McVeigh shuffled in after him wearing grey track pants and de rigueur teardrop tattoo and skinhead. A screw pushed him into the seat facing Dave and retreated umpire-like towards the corner of the room.

"Hello Terry."

"Who are you?"

"My name is Detective Sergeant Wrench and I'm just here to speak to you about Gordon Lundy."

McVeigh glanced towards the guard.

"Why? What more do you want to know?"

"I just need to clarify a few things about Lundy."

"What things?"

"Just a few things, nothing to worry about. I'll be done in ten minutes."

"Go on then."

"How long did you know him for?"

"Er ... years, about seven years. I've been over all this with Detective Light. Speak to him."

"I'm sure you have but we need to go over it again. Were you close?"

"Yeah, I suppose you could say that. He got too cocky in the end though. Had to pay the price. You see he—"

"Where was he from again?"

"What?"

"I said, where was he from, where in the country was he from?"

"Down south somewhere …I don't fucking know."

"You don't know where?"

"Like I said, down south."

"And where did you meet him?"

"In the clubs in town."

"What clubs?"

"You know, Slack Alice and all that fucking stuff."

"What did he do for a living?"

"How am I supposed to know? I was his mate, not his fucking bird."

"Well, I would have thought you'd know a bit more about him."

"Well I don't know that. We never talked about work, it was more about pleasure. Going out, socialising and that."

"And in all that time, in all those nights out, he never said what he did and where he was from?"

"He may have done, I can't remember, like I say I wasn't his bird."

"Okay. Why did you kill him?"

"'Coz he pushed his fucking luck."

"Go on."

"Because he thought it was a good idea to shag my woman."

"So, you killed him for shagging your woman."

"I did, yeah."

"How?"

"What?"

"How did you kill him?"

"Stabbed the cunt didn't I?"

"Where?"

"What?"

"Where did you stab him? In the chest, the groin, where?"

"Everywhere. He fucking deserved it too."

"Tell me where."

"In the fucking chest …In the neck."

"What else did you do to him Terry?"

"I just stabbed the cunt, alright."

"Nothing else?"

"No, just the blade."

"You see that—"

"Oh, and a rock, I hit him with a big fuck-off rock."

"A rock?"

"Yeah, a proper fucking boulder."

"You pulled that little snippet right from your bootlaces, eh Terry?"

"What?"

"Nothing. Why did you confess to this one Terry and not Jessica Byrne?"

"'Coz I didn't murder her, smart arse."

"Oh, come on Terry. The whole world and his wife knows that you murdered that poor kid, shot her right in the head if my memory serves. She was only fourteen."

"If you say so."

"I do say so Terry."

"What's your fucking game kid?"

"No game Terry. And anyway, I could ask you the same question."

"You're fucking nuts son. Guard, I want to go back to my cell … Guard?"

Dave banged his hands on the table.

"You're going fucking nowhere till you answer my questions."

"Fuck you."

"Oh, but you already are fucking me, aren't you Terry."

"You need locking up pal. You're fucking mad."

"Tell me about the night you killed him."

"What?"

"The night you killed him, tell me about it. Had you been out together?"

"Yeah that's right."

"Where?"

"What?"

"Fucking hell Terry, do you not clean your ears out? I said where did you go?"

"We had a few drinks in Slack Alice's and then went back to his place."

"Where was his place?"

"Somewhere in the town centre."

"Town's a big place, be more specific. What street?"

"I can't remember."

"Was it near Oldham Street, Market Street, Deansgate …?"

"I told you, I can't remember."

"You can't remember."

"I was pissed. We both were. We went to his flat in town, that's all I can remember."

"A flat?"

"Yeah, a flat."

"Hmm, it doesn't quite fit does it Terry?"

"I don't give a fuck whether it fits or not, that's how it happened."

"Did you bury him straight after you killed him?"

"Yeah, that night."

"In the woods?"

"Yeah, in the woods."

"How far are the woods from Lundy's flat?"

"Not far."

"How far? Far enough for you to carry him there? He was a big man, wasn't he? Be a bit of a struggle I suspect."

"I put him in the boot of my car."

"Right, okay. Then I'll ask you again, how far were the woods from Lundy's flat?"

"About five or ten minutes."

"Five or ten minutes."

"Yeah, more or less."

"The woods are at least eleven miles from the town centre."

"It was late, I put my foot down."

"Bullshit. You haven't got a clue what went on the night Lundy died have you?"

"Fuck off."

"Because it wasn't you, was it?"

"You're fucking nuts. As if I'd confess to a crime I didn't commit. Why the fuck would I do that?"

"I believe you've recently obtained some new viewing matter Terry?"

McVeigh began rocking on his chair.

"I'm not listening to anymore of this, no fucking comment."

"Exciting stuff, Terence. Where did you get that little lot from?"

"No comment."

"A little reward perhaps, for services rendered?"

"No comment."

"I mean, for a man with ACAB plastered all over his knuckles, you're certainly a good friend to us boys in blue."

"No comment."

He jumped from his seat and got right into McVeigh's face. His noxious breath a professional hazard.

"You didn't kill him, did you?"

"No comment."

"You didn't, did you? Tell me the fucking truth."

"Fuck you."

"Say it, you didn't kill him."

"No comment."

"You didn't kill him, did you? Say it."

"No comment."

"Tell me the fucking truth."

"I killed him for fuck sake!"

The guard intervened.

"Keep your voice down McVeigh."

"Well, it's this fucking idiot …Does he not realise I'm the one doing you lot a favour?"

There was an explosion of silence; his face rupturing into red.

"What did you say?"

"Nothing."

"What do you mean you were 'doing us a favour?'"

"Nothing. I'm not saying anymore. Guard, take me back to my cell."

"Tell me, what did you mean? You didn't do it did you?"

"Guard. Guard!"

The screw inched towards McVeigh.

"Guard, don't fucking move. I've not finished with him yet."

The screw stopped dead.

"Sir, what did you say?"

"You heard me, stay there."

"Are you going to let this bit of a kid talk to you like that?"

"Shut up, McVeigh."

"What's this favour Terry?"

"Guard. Guard. Guard!"

"Shut up. Tell me. Fucking tell me."

"Fuck off, pig."

Bastard. Fucking dirty bastard. I'll fucking kill you.

Dave went for his throat like a banned pitbull.

"You didn't kill him did you? Fucking tell me you fucking pervert. Tell me."

"I ... help. Help!"

"Say it you bastard. Say it."

The guard slammed the red emergency alarm button and rushed to McVeigh's aid. He'd seen a lot in his time but nothing like this.

"Tell me. Fucking tell me."

The door flung open, Geoff leading an army of screws.

"Jesus, Dave. What the fuck are you doing?"

1ST APRIL 2002

They were inside each other. Their knotted bodies veneered in perspiration. His face ecstatically crumpled. Her eyes rolling like lines on a slot machine. A symphony of flesh nearing its crescendo.

"I love you so much Sarah it hurts."

"Me too, don't stop. Please keep going."

"Never leave me Sarah."

"Never will. Oh my God, that's beautiful."

"You're everything to me."

"Oh my God, I'm coming…I'm coming."

"Me too …Me too."

They exploded together like a pair of dying stars.

He sat on his deceased couch cradling his morning bowl and bottle. Vodka and cornflakes can be deemed rock 'n' roll except when it isn't. And in Adam's case, it wasn't. It was the only way to assuage his heaves and tremors – which although hellish, were nothing compared to the sweated bed sheets and searing convulsions that marked his dark hours. After last night though, his tail was very much up. It wasn't only a dream but an advert for intimacy and like all the best commercials it had him sold from the start.

The TV displayed an older woman whose kindly face had the texture of partially kneaded dough. She was hosting a phone-in program on shyness. Could this be a further sign? A sad man from Gloucestershire called John had rung in. He had a thing for a colleague but was in his mid-twenties and had never even kissed a girl. This was right up her street and she inched closer to the screen, her eyes filling with tears.

"Now dear, as you can tell, I'm old. In many ways, I'm blessed. I've got a nice house and husband, a couple of kids and a beautiful grandchild and of course, a good job here, which I love. But in another way, I'm poor – bereft if you like. I live with regrets you see. Not things I've done you understand, but things I haven't. And trust me there's nothing more painful as memories of words left unsaid and deeds left undone. Seize the day, John …Grab life by the throat. Tell her how you feel, show her how you feel. And that goes for you Adam too. Trust your heart. Be brave. Sarah loves you, she loves you deeply. Don't let her slip through your fingers."

He picked up his vodka bottle and studied its label before glancing towards the mantelpiece where his meds bottle stood unopened.

Fuck it.

They danced under the moon's mirrored-ball, the tin man and her. At least tonight he had an excuse for his lead-footedness and sodden palms.

When should I move? Will she be into it though? What about my teeth? And my breath? And my…No, I'm too ugly to kiss, I'll scare her away. Jesus, the fucking state of me – and after all the years I've fretted about being single. Be careful what you wish for. Oh shit, what am I doing? I'm going… I'm going in, two-footed.

He lurched towards her with puckered lips. She recoiled backwards, arms extended, eyes wide open. He went in again; leaning forward like a novice dartist requiring the bullseye. This time he met no resistance and fell right through her, his only kiss the floor.

He climbed onto his knees, wiping the grass from his nose. His Disney dream debased. Fairy tales though are powerful things and with her expression now deadly serious, she urged him upward. The biggest moment of his life. They stuttered towards each other, their lips finally meeting for the briefest of seconds.

I love her and she loves me. She loves me and I love her. She fucking loves me and I fucking love her. Hang on … I'm happy. Shit, I'm actually fucking happy. Well, maybe not happy but nowhere near as unhappy as I usually am and what is happiness if not the decline of unhappiness? Definitely, this is the best I've felt since Mum … Absolutely. No doubt about it. There it is again …What is that fucking noise?

A rumble, like an avalanche of distant rocks or a terrible marching band, interrupted his celebration.

It ain't ending; it's getting louder. It's getting nearer.

"Don't worry babe. It's nothing to worry about, I'll check it out. Just keep calm."

He moved to the front of the stage; snatches of light, flashing and manic, breaking through the wooded mass.

What the fuck is it?

As it got closer, a threshing, snapping sound augmented its thunderous roar; trees and foliage falling like dominoes.

It's like a fucking robot T-Rex.

He covered his ears with his hands while Sarah cowered like a stray animal on bonfire night.

"It's okay Sarah. It's like some kind of machinery. It'll be gone soon, it's nothing to worry about. Sarah? Sarah, where are you? Sarah, where have you gone? Sarah!"

He knelt in the dirt. Hidden by an embrace of ferns; sawdust tears streaming down his face. This was the worse moment of his life – even worse than losing his mother.

Those brutal bastards. Those fucking monsters. Her stage …Her home …Our kiss …How can they do this? Well they're not getting away with it. Not on my fucking watch.

He marched towards them; shouting and gesticulating like a wronged footballer but they just shook their heads and pointed to their ear defenders.

He jumped up and down as if extinguishing embers but they refused to budge. Finally, one of them turned off his electric saw and pointed towards an older guy studying a pile of blueprints.

Oh, so he's the big boss man. King of all he surveys. And then destroys. I'm your worst nightmare pal.

They had words but not the shards of righteousness that Adam had in mind; wild, pseudo words falling from his mouth like broken teeth.

Oh my fuck, I can't speak.

When the dust finally settled, he sat alone on a mound of soil. Gnawing at his nails; dying to see what the night would bring.

It didn't bring her but it brought other things: Dolby, blooded whip in hand, corralling his scrapbook victims into a constant circle. The blond, broad-shouldered man, doused in blood, screaming in agony.

Unperturbed, he came back every night. The gauntlet of horror nothing compared to the fear that the one time he didn't show, she would. It never happened. He couldn't blame her though: she'd been in enough war zones in her life.

18TH JUNE 2002

An ensemble of shit music and machinery shook him from his slumber. Another night over. The same outcome achieved. This time though his disappointment came with a jagged edge. The wick leading to his mind full of dynamite ignited and burning.

I am a panther, a patient panther waiting for my moment. Because I hate all you bastards. I hate your denim cut-offs, your stupid fucking jokes, I hate your whistling and your radio and your tabloids. But most of all, I hate you because of her...My Sarah. You bastards. I'm a patient panther, but my patience is running out. I'm a panther that's going to attack. Attack. Attack. Attack.

He dragged himself through the bush, slipping down the small embankment to the edge of the camp, where the protestors stood.

Hey big boss man ...You evil old fuck. I'm coming for you mate. No second chances. No more Mr Nice Guy.

"Alright pal? I've not seen you for a while."

He dragged a ball of flem from the bottom of his feet and spat it on the floor.

That's what I think of you, dickhead.

The foreman made towards a group of builders surrounding the edge of the pit. Adam followed him. The time was now. He was going to do it now. The foreman climbed a muddy hill before pausing and conversing with the protestors. His face transmuting into different people from Adam's past lives – the angry lollipop man on his school crossing; Slabhead, a lower-league bully who once assailed him with a cricket bat; and finally, the king of them all, his father. *You're all the fucking same.* He burst into a sprint but a commotion stopped him in his tracks.

24TH FEBRUARY 2003

The hospital's revolving doors span him around and spat him out. No welcoming crowds or tearful goodbyes – Mary didn't even turn up to his discharge meeting. Just eight months of treatment and a conclusion of incorrigibility; that there was nothing else they could do.

As he passed through the walled entrance, the winter rain brutal and unyielding, he bent down and pulled a white paper bag from his holdall. A month's supply of Quetiapine, Sertraline and Diazepam; exactly as the doctor ordered. The clinical packaging piqued a succession of images in his mind: test tubes, white coats, violated mice. A wholly uniform ideal of sanity. Everybody in their right place.

"Fuck that."

He tossed them into a passing bin before grabbing them out and throwing them back in again.

No, after everything I've seen, everything I've been through, I don't need them. I'm a warrior. I stand on my own two feet. Fuck the chemical cosh, it's time to put it all behind me. To have a good time …To have some fucking fun. And that's what I'm going to do now. I'm going to have some fun. I'm going to have a party. I'm going to call Wendy Fingers.

And that's just what he did.

Eccles precinct sat in the centre of Eccles and mostly consisted of single-floor shops. To protect people from the elements, a jutting rim of about three feet in width traversed its contours. Hence on rainy days, which were not uncommon, people stuck to the sides. Walking in single file, they resembled an automated conga, regimentally filing off into shops such as *Kevin's Towels* and *Sophisticated* – which provided a nice line in faux *Burberry* mini-skirts and *Chanel* handbags.

When he was a kid, Adam's next door neighbour, Mrs Stevenson, used to give him and his mum a lift to the precinct every Saturday morning. Mrs Stevenson worked in the pawnbrokers and parked her car in the multi-story car park that loomed over the precinct like a large grey cloud. The banks of cars concertinaed into those endless bays fascinated Adam. Unfortunately, in the new world, no one came to the precinct anymore and like a box with all its contents taken out, the car park was now full of empty space.

Adam certainly did everything he could to avoid the place. Especially its main street – a carnival of smacked faces, drunken clowns and moustachioed strongmen; where a desperate morning rush to the pub would be translated as a "quick half before I start my shopping" and a badly swollen arm the result of "some mad fucking flea bite." He often wondered whether people in more salubrious postcodes knew how the other side was living. If they did, they would surely do something?

Tonight though, despite himself – or perhaps because of – he'd gone to Eccles. He had a date with the greatest grafter in town and he wouldn't have missed it for the world.

Her and Adam went way back. She was brought up across the street from him and they wasted many days together. In fact, he traced his uplift in victimhood from when she moved away at the age of fourteen. (Flames had kept his distance from her mainly due to her perennial skinhead and *Action Man* scar – the result of her dad's sharp-edged sovereign.)

Fingers wasn't her real surname. That was Cockburn. She'd

earned her epithet because of her talent. And what a talent. However, as she would often caution, what is aptitude without hard work. Sweet Lady H may have been her motivation but it was planning and dedication that propelled her to greatness. No job too big or too small. The shoplifters' shoplifter.

As her bounty increased so did her horizons. She began robbing to order, sub-contracting the spadework to a trusted gang of protégés. This proved a decent earner but it was diversifying into drug dealing that really projected her into the big time.

She would source the gear herself; the middleman well and truly taken out. The risk of capture was large but it was more than offset by the margins – especially since it was Mrs Fingers', with her grey hair and headscarf, "poorly" sister in the Netherlands and cavalier approach to jail time, "a change is as good as a rest," who actually smuggled the gear over the North Sea.

There were other risks though. Without the army of intimidation an organised firm provides, she was wide open to the type of direct taxation levied with a sword up the arse. Ergo, she kept on the move, purchasing a battered mobile home that would rarely park in the same place twice. Her customers would text their orders and she would give them her position.

Despite their shared history, Adam was no different. She'd ordered him to present on the third storey of the big grey cloud not a minute before or beyond seven thirty.

He stood in front of her mystery machine; its exterior a battered orange, a barrage of stickers showing where it had been, a bullet hole illustrating where it had now arrived.

That can't be roadworthy.

Bang on cue, the door swung open and she emerged onto the

front step. Layered in smoke like a *Top of the Pops* performer; her smile as wide as it was toothless.

"Well well, if it isn't my old mate Grimo. Where have you been hiding, stranger?"

"Oh, you know, various psychiatric institutions."

"I bet, you ginger weirdo. Come in dude."

He walked into another world.

"Fucking hell, did you win this on *Bullseye*?"

"Fuck off, you cheeky bastard."

"I'm only messing, it's cool as fuck. Check out the fucking woodchip."

"I know yeah, it's fucking mad isn't it?"

"And the psychedelic seat covers."

"They sealed the deal, to be honest."

"I'm not surprised. Fucking stinks though."

"What, the covers?"

"Well, everything."

"What of?"

"Weed."

"That my little bundle of orange is because I sell the finest herb known to man."

"I've heard."

"I'm sure you must have."

"Yeah, you were the talk of Orwell Ward. You were top of everybody's discharge to-do list."

"Don't even joke about that shit."

"Who's joking?"

"You're a fucking mad-head. Right, c'mon sit down. I want you to check this out."

"Okay."

He scooched around the oval table while she rummaged in her jacket.

"You've not still got that fucking Fila jacket?"

"There's nothing wrong with this jacket."

"You've had it for fucking years. You had it in Hartington Road."

"I know yeah, but that's the beauty of it, it's never out of fashion ...Perry Boys, to B-Boys and fucking Brit Pop. It always comes back around and due to the old brown keeping the pounds off, I ain't never going to grow out of it. Anyway, who are you, Trinny and fucking Suzanne? Now are you having some of this, or what?"

"It smells like rocket fuel."

"It fucking is mate. White Widow, all the way from the 'Dam."

"Go on then, I'll have a tenners."

"Good lad. Shall I roll us one for the road?"

His visit was supposed to be a fleeting one. However, due to the incapacitating effects of her weed he was still there at 10:00pm, shapeshifting from mammal to vegetable and back again.

"Fucking hell Grimo, I forget to mention to you about fucking Flames. That was a bad one, wasn't it?"

"Er, yeah."

"I was shocked, man."

"Yeah, same here. Terrible."

"What a fucking hypocrite, eh?"

"Yeah …What?"

"A fucking hypocrite. The way he used to go on about smack – when he smashed Wogga when he found out he was digging? And the next thing you know he's overdosed in the fucking woods."

"It wasn't like that."

"What?"

"Nothing, change the subject."

"No, what do you mean?"

"Nothing, like I said change the subject."

"Hark at you, Mr Fucking Nowty-arse."

"I didn't mean it like that. It's just that it wasn't his fault."

"No one fucking forced him to put the needle in his arm. "

"Wanna bet?"

"What's up with you? Do you know something I don't?"

"Nah, I'm fucking around. I'm just stoned. That weed's mad.

"You're telling me. We'll both be sharing a bed on fucking Orwell Ward if we carry on."

"I know yeah."

"Get some decent meds though …Proper mind twisting shit."

"To be honest, they're not all they're cracked up to be."

"Fuck off you mad-head. Hey, do you know what?"

"What?"

"I'm sure I've got a picture somewhere of us in Hartington Road. I found it when I moved into here. And I've got the famous *Fila* on."

"Yeah?"

"Give me a sec."

She flopped into the driver's side and began rummaging in the glove compartment.

Just what I need. Rub my nose in it why don't you.

"It's in here somewhere."

Shit, I can't feel my legs. I can't feel a thing. I'm pure fucking jelly.

The door rattled like a morning drunk.

Fucking hell.

"There's someone at the door ...Wendy, there's someone at the door."

"What?"

"There's someone at the door."

"What?"

"The door. There's someone there."

"Answer it then. I won't be a sec."

"Me?"

"No, the bloke next to you. Yes you."

"Fucking hell ..."

He clambered upward, inching towards the door like an arthritic dog.

Fuck me, she could be getting taxed or anything

"If I take a bullet for you, you owe me big time."

"What?"

"You heard."

He gradually opened up.

"Oh, fuck."

A beat bobby. His cap perched just above his nose, his ripped arms sleeved with shit Celtic tattoos.

Adam slammed the door shut pressing his knee into its

middle.

"Wendy, it's the law. It's the fucking law. We need to move it, we need to get rid of it all."

The door banged again, twice as hard this time.

"Fingers open up. What the fuck's going on?"

"I don't fucking believe it. The law. The fucking law. "

"Adam for fuck's sake calm down."

"He's the law!"

"I know, I know. He's come a bit early that's all."

"You're expecting him?"

"Just give us five minutes please, Adam."

"You what?"

"It's fine. He's sorted. Just give me five minutes."

He'd stood in the shadows for the past twenty minutes. What was happening? What the fuck was going on? He crept towards the window – she could be in trouble – and peered through a gap in the dirt.

Fuck me. She's got them on the pay role. She's paying them off. She's big time.

With her cash firmly deposited in his top pocket, the copper turned and scuttled out of the van.

"What are you looking at druggie?"

"A bent copper."

"What did you say?"

"Nothing, nothing at all."

"Yeah, that's what I thought you said."

She popped her head through the door.

"Sorry about that mate."

He re-entered the van.

"You've finished then?"

"Yeah, all done, all sorted. The look on your face …Listen mate, you've got to keep the gendarmes sweet."

"Really."

"Yeah, you may have noticed I ain't got much in the way of traditional muscle."

"Personally, I wouldn't touch them with a barge pole. They're all corrupt fuckers."

"Ooh, you've changed your tune."

"How do you mean?"

"Remember that argument we had in The Lamb – years ago it was. I was slagging them off and you were defending them. Typical you and your way with words, you called them 'essential umpires.' I always remember that."

"Did I fuck."

"You know you did."

"Well that was before."

"Before what?"

"Nothing."

"Adam is there something you're not telling me? Are you in trouble?"

"No, of course not."

"C'mon mate, I've known you since I was a kid. I know when you're bothered about something."

"Honestly, there's nothing."

"Fuck off mate, it's written all over your face."

He rubbed his eyes.

"Right, you can't say owt? If I tell you, you've got to keep it quiet."

"Of course, I will. On my mum's life."

"Promise."

"Yes, I promise. I promise."

"Remember that body they found in the woods."

"The recent one?"

"Yeah, last year."

"Yeah, I saw that documentary the other week. That geezer did it ... McCain."

"McVeigh, Terry McVeigh. That's the problem, he didn't do it. Someone else did it. I've told them that."

"Told who?"

"The law."

"You told the law?"

"Yes, on multiple occasions."

"Who did it then?"

"A sick fucker. James Dolby. Used to be a manager of that company in Trafford Park, New Directions."

"And you know this how?"

"I used to work for him. He beat the shit out of me. Flames and I burgled him—"

"You burgled him with fucking Flames! What the fuck were you thinking?"

"He made me do it, Flames made me. I wouldn't have dreamt of doing it otherwise. You know me. Honestly, he made me."

"Okay, calm down love. I know, he was a bullying fucker. I know that's not you."

"We found a scrapbook. We saw his picture – Lundy, the guy

that died. Dolby's crew did it. A big grufty bastard, he beat the shit out of me. He killed my fucking girlfriend too and poisoned Flames. He poisoned me as well but I survived. I—"

"He killed Flames?"

"Yeah, forced a cocktail of shit down our throats and let us loose in the woods. It was horrible. Like hell. Fuck that ... it was hell. The last time I saw Flames he said metal spiders were attacking him. Then he collapsed. Then he died."

"And he killed your bird?"

"Yeah, as good as, back in the seventies. Around that time anyway. I went to the law, stood right at the desk in the fucking cop shop."

"What did they say?"

"Weren't fucking interested. It was only when I went back a second time and wouldn't leave that I got to speak to the head of the case, Detective Inspector Light. What a cunt he was."

"Why?"

"He threatened me with slander and said he'd charge me with burglary, if I didn't leave him alone. A confession was a confession, he said."

"Right. And where's this Dolby now?"

"Fuck knows. Not where he should be that's for sure. One of the guys I used to work with said he'd fucked off down South."

"I see. That's mad, really fucking mad. It's interesting too as in that documentary they all seemed pretty convinced by his confession. I mean, I wonder why he would confess."

"I haven't got the answer. How could I have the answer? I just know what I saw, what I've been through."

"Are you sure though?"

"What do you mean?"

"Well, like you say, I know you've been through a lot. What

with your mum and that …I know you've had some problems."

"You think I'm mad. You think I'm making it up."

"No, I don't think that. I just think that the weed is strong and —"

"I don't believe this. You think I'm mad, that this is all in my head. You think that I've lost it."

"Of course I don't."

"Liar, fucking liar …You're as bad as them."

"Adam love, I don't think you're mad but if I did, could you really blame me? You said that he killed your girlfriend in the seventies. How old were you seven? Eight?"

"She was a ghost, okay?"

"A ghost? Adam have you heard yourself? Listen, I think that you need some help."

"No, you're wrong. You're dead wrong. I don't need some fucking shrink. What I need is justice and if no one is going to give it me then I'm going to get it myself."

25TH FEBRUARY 2003

O h fuck, no. Leave me alone. Give me some peace."

She was finally engaging; striding across the supermarket car park towards his patrol car, her greying hair and Gore-Tex jacket reminiscent of a total rambler. He pushed down his peaked cap and sank into his seat. Inconspicuousness was vital in his previous role but his new one required the opposite: a strong presence in the community. Protecting and serving. He could've called it a vocation if they hadn't forced him to do it.

She knocked on his window.

Big smiles.

"You okay love?"

"Is it PC Wrenchy?"

"Wrench."

"Oh, I'm sorry love."

"That's okay, Wrenchy's my stage name."

"Really?"

"No, I'm only kidding."

"You had me going then."

"I'm sorry love. What can I do for you?"

"I never got a chance to thank you."

"Thank me?"

"My mum, last week."

"I'm not following."

"You brought her home last week – the confused lady in the beret. She gave your shins a good couple of whacks."

"Mrs James …The lady from the care home."

"That's it. I played hell with them you know. Fancy not locking the bloody door."

"I know yeah. Too quick for 'em, they told me."

"Too quick! She's ninety-eight and she had her bloody slippers on."

"Well, I'm not the quickest myself."

"You're not that bloody slow …No one is that bloody slow. Anyway, I was too busy giving the manager an earful to thank you properly. The staff said that you were lovely with her. I asked for your name but they couldn't even get that right. I was going to pop into the station to thank you but I don't need to now."

"Ah, that's lovely. That makes it all worthwhile."

"No problem love. It's the least I can do. You're a credit."

"Thank you."

She pulled away from his window and looked left and right.

"Eh, are you here for those bloody muggers?"

"Well …"

"Don't worry if you can't tell me. I know sometimes you can't, I'm just curious."

"Let's just say I'm keeping an eye out."

"That's good. The bloody scumbags got my neighbour for her pension last week. Beat her black and blue they did."

"You said it right, they're scumbags. Trust me though, we'll get them. We'll put them away."

"God bless you. You're an angel."

"No problem. Like I say, it's people like you that make all the crap we get worthwhile."

"Not from me love. I sleep a lot easier knowing you're out there. Now you be careful, we need you in one piece."

"Will do."

"See you now love. God bless."

"Thanks again. Bye now."

I am a man of the people. The Salfordian Serpico. I bet he drove to work every day sobbing too.

He pawed at his supermarket sandwich. He was impressed: it takes real effort to make something as inedible as this. He brought it to his lips as if it were a shotgun. *I suppose it'll fill a hole for a while. The story of my fucking life.* As he further inspected its contents, a loud buzzing sound emanated from his glove compartment. "Here we go." He threw his sandwich to the floor and pulled out his phone. "You little beauty." It was her, she'd replied.

Hope you like the pic.

"Wow!"

His fingers blurred as they punched the silver keys of his Nokia.

U are stunning. You must work out. Super fit. Here's one of mine. Hope u like it.

He lifted his head and scanned the car park. The tracksuited cadavers were conspicuous by their absence. Even if they weren't, what would he do? For once, he wasn't sure.

Another buzz.

Thank u. I like swimming and boxercise. U look fit 2. Nice abs!!

It was time to reel her in.

Cheers, I like to do yoga, keeps me fit and flexible. Anyway, when are we meeting up?

His right index finger hovered over the send button. Was he really going to do this? It certainly felt right. It felt brilliant. But did that make it a good idea?

"Fuck it, you only live once."

Within seconds that familiar sound.

You're a bit forward aren't you? We will see.

"Oh, we'll see alright."

A scream of static burst from his radio.

"Echo Mike 17, do you read me, over?"

"Shit."

"Echo Mike 17, do you read me, over?"

"For fuck's sake."

"Echo Mike 17, are you there, over?"

"No. No. No. No."

"Echo Mike 17, can you read me, over?"

"No, I can't."

"Echo Mike 17, are you there, over?"

"Okay, okay, keep your hair on."

He yanked the mic from its holder.

"Echo Mike 17, sorry I couldn't get my radio to work. Can you hear me, over?"

"Loud and clear. Can you confirm your location please, Echo Mike 17?"

"Walkden Town Centre, ASDA car park, over."

"We've received a report of a potential assault from the foreman of that housing development in Worsley Woods. The suspect is reportedly a white male, approximately five feet nine inches tall, wearing a black cagoule with blue jeans. Suspect is reported to be unarmed but heavily intoxicated, over."

"I'm staking out the muggers, over."

"Sarge says he wants you to attend this one. We've no one else in that area, over."

Of course he did, the fucking prick.

"Copy that, I'm on my way, over."

He reached for his phone.

Got to go, called out on a job. As for being forward, if you don't ask you don't get.

The deeper he strode into the woods, the darker it became; the scene covered by a veil of heavy, dank foliage. Eventually, after a bad twenty minutes, he fell through a horde of bushes and confronted an island of completed and partially completed houses. The builders were standing at the far end of the site, huddled around an old guy sat on a deckchair. Dave trudged towards them. His shoes mired in shit.

They don't have much luck these guys. First a body and now this …A pissed-up eco-warrior? Nah, probably just another casualty of the mind.

"Hi, my name is PC Wrench. I believe someone has reported an assault."

"Yeah, it was me mate. I'm Terry Mason, site manager.

With the help of his workforce, he stood up and proffered Dave a mud-caked hand.

"I would say nice to meet you but, you know …"

"No, I understand. How are you doing, sir?"

"I'm a bit shook up to be honest."

"Right, I'm sorry to hear that. What's happened? What's gone on?"

A voice came from the group of builders.

"He finally fucking flipped didn't he? He wants fucking locking up, so he does."

"Alright Murphy, I'll deal with it."

"Who wants locking up Terry?"

"It's this guy. He's like a vagrant. A bit of a tramp, like. He's defo a few sandwiches short of a picnic, if you know what I mean?"

"Yeah?"

"Yeah. The first time I saw him was the first morning we came here. We were moving the hardware in and I see him. He's standing there, pretty much right on that spot, pretending to smooch and dance with someone. It was bizarre. It scared me at first but to be honest we kind of got used to him."

"What, so he was here a lot?"

"He practically lived here mate. He used to sleep in the bushes where that house is now."

"Really?"

"Yeah, I mean we knew he was there but the last thing we wanted to do was engage with him coz he would have never left us alone. A few of the lads did think about calling a doctor or a nurse or something but we never got around to it. I mean, we've got a tight schedule and we also had a load of protestors to deal with by that time."

"I see they're still here. Do you think they had anything to do with this?"

"Who, the Women's Institute? No, definitely not their style."

"Did they ever speak to him?"

"Nah, like us they kept well clear.

"So, has there been any build-up of hostilities to explain all this. Any indication he was escalating his behaviour?"

"No, we ain't seen him for a year or so. In fact, the last time we'd seen him prior to today was on the morning that we found that body. He came down and stood next to the protestors. He looked like a man on the edge to be honest with you."

"How do you mean?"

"His eyes were on fire, his head had gone. Just like today."

"And you hadn't seen him for a year did you say?"

"Yeah, we just presumed he'd been committed or something. I mean we mentioned him to you boys but that's the last we heard of it. "

"You did?"

"Yeah, I spoke to some detective and so did a couple of the other lads."

"Right ... anyway talk to me about what happened today."

"Well, Murphy spotted him striding towards us. When he realised that we had seen him, he snuck back into the bushes. We thought that was a bit weird, so we tried to keep an eye on him but we lost sight of him. Then the bastard came at me from behind."

"Where?"

"From behind that mound of dirt ...I've got my plans on that table, going through 'em and luckily one of the lads spotted him right at the last second. I turned around and the bastard rugby tackled me. Then he smashed me in the face a couple of times."

"I can see the marks."

"Yeah but the lads were soon on the scene and he got up and

ran off."

"In which direction?"

"North, towards the motorway bridge."

Dave opened his note pad.

"And he was wearing a ... black cagoule and blue jeans. Has he got any other distinguishing marks, hair colour?"

"Boss, he's over there."

"What?"

"He's there. Look he's there."

"Forget about the description, he's over there."

"Sorry?"

"That's him, arm in arm with that protestor. There, just on the ridge. The kid with the ginger hair."

"Are you sure?"

"Absolutely, that's definitely him."

Dave moved into a half-jog.

"Excuse me ... oi you, stay where you are. Don't move, stay there. Stop. Police!"

26TH FEBRUARY 2003

A n interview room: the scene of his demise. Not this one though, another one. A long time ago, when he was a very different beast.

He put down the Noxia and stifled a cheer. *See, she doesn't think I'm going too fast. That I'm desperate as fuck. I mean I am but not in that sense.*

His smile morphed into a grimace as the Ginger Ninja scraped his chair across the floor.

"For the purposes of the tape, as well as closing his eyes and putting his hands over his ears the suspect has now turned his back on me and is facing the wall."

Dave scratched his head. He'd not had one like this for a while.

"Look this isn't helping your situation you know. You're looking at serious charges here. Common assault is no laughing matter. You need to tell me what went on. Let's start with what you took because you definitely took something didn't you? What did you take? They said your eyes were like saucers."

The man began rocking back and forth.

This guy is properly fucked.

"Adam, if you don't stop that you'll fall off the chair. You don't want that do you? You don't want to hurt yourself?"

He rocked harder.

He's gone. La la land. Full bed and board.

"You need to talk to me. I can't help you if you won't talk to me."

I'll ring the psych. Dougan will moan but fuck him. Better keep her ticking over first though.

He grabbed his machine and turned up the heat.

If it's a special night then, I better get you something nice to wear. Maybe something to play with 2?

Back to the real world.

"For the purposes of the tape, I am pausing this interview at 11:15am …Right, I need to speak to someone about this. See Adam, I think you're unwell. I think you need some help but I can't help you if you won't talk to me."

His silence was loud and clear.

"Okay wait here, I won't be long. Don't worry, I'll only be a minute."

Dougan's sledgehammer tones dominated the corridor. The Picasso of obnoxiousness. Dave paused and swallowed hard.

Now you know he's going to contradict you but that's not your problem that's his. Bitter old bastard. Any chance to kick the fallen one …Get in fucking line, pal.

"Sarge—"

"Ah Wrench, just the man. These two ladies have come in to talk about the chap you're interviewing. That's right isn't it ladies?"

In the custody suite stood two silver hairs, dressed in big coats and hiking boots, their faces stained with the ruddy hue of outdoor living.

"Yes, we were the ones that found him. I'm Claire and this is Ruth. We're two of the protestors from the woods."

"Oh right, found him you say?"

"Yes, in a terrible state, writhing in a clearing. We didn't know at this point what he'd done and we struggled at first to get any sense out of him but then he—"

The other lady spoke.

"Can we discuss this somewhere a bit more private?"

"Yes, that would be better."

"Er, yes of course, we got any rooms free Sarge?"

"Interview Room C is free, for the time being at least, they tend to fill up pretty quickly."

"Thank you, we shouldn't be long. I hope you don't mind, it's just a bit sensitive that's all."

"No problem, take them down Dave, if you pardon the phrase ladies."

Everyone laughed apart from Dave.

They sat at the interview table. As incongruous as belly laughs at a burial. As they eyed the posters of vigilance, Dave entered the room, his bony arse propelling the door open.

"Oops, sorry about that. Here you are ladies, it's hardly *Starbucks* I'm afraid."

"As long as it's wet and warm."

"Just about."

"It'll be fine."

"Sorry about the wait, I had to get someone to sit with our friend."

"How is he?"

"Not great."

"It's a shame. He's sickening for something that boy."

"Sorry?"

"There's something badly wrong with him."

"And some."

He sat down and opened his note pad.

"Right, anyway, how can I help you ladies?"

"Well, the thing is officer although as we've just said this lad is obviously poorly, some of the things he said were very vivid and troubling. We know it could be rubbish but we thought we better tell someone."

"Okay. That's fine, thank you. What type of things was he saying then?"

"Pretty graphic stuff and he said it with such conviction. I mean the tears were streaming down his face, weren't they Ruth?"

"Absolutely, it was pitiful to see."

"Right. Go on."

"Well, as we said, we found him having some kind of breakdown, so Ruth and I went to help him."

"Had you seen him before, ladies?"

"Some of the other girls had said that they had, but we hadn't had we Ruth?"

"Some of the other girls knew him as the local tramp."

"So I've heard."

"So, we asked him if he was okay and he just started ranting and raving – going on about how the builders took 'their special place away.'"

"Their special place?"

"Yes."

"Any idea what he meant by that?"

"Well, I presumed he meant the carnage they've reaped down there. All the flowers and wildlife, it's a disaster zone."

"Do you think that was a motive for the attack?"

"Maybe, I mean everybody's upset about it aren't they Ruth?"

"Absolutely."

"You said he said 'their special place' implying two people."

"Yes, Sarah he said her name was. He kept repeating that 'she had suffered enough.'"

"He kept repeating that over and over."

"Who's Sarah?"

"We presumed it was his girlfriend, or some sort of friend."

"Did he give any other details about her?"

"He said she had died in the lake. Raped and drugged, he said. Said he'd seen the pictures with his own eyes."

"Pictures?"

"We didn't push it. The mind boggles."

"What pictures?"

"Like I say we didn't push it."

"We didn't have chance; his mouth was going a mile a minute."

"That's right Ruth. I mean the next thing, he's saying is that the person who killed this Sarah was the same man who killed that chap they found in the woods."

"Gordon Lundy?"

"Yes, that's right."

"Go on."

"Well then he said that this man beat up and drugged him and his friend, and his friend died."

"His friend died?"

"Yes, that's what he said."

"At the hands of this same bloke?"

"So he said."

"Did this mate have a name?"

"Oh, what did he say his name was Ruth? It all happened so quickly."

"Was it something like Sparks?"

"It may have been."

"Sparks?"

"Yes, it's a nickname, obviously."

"Yes obviously. Right, let me summarise then …He said his girlfriend was drugged and raped and was killed in the lake. Or, he'd seen the pictures – whatever that means – and the man who did this was the same man who killed Gordon Lundy and also killed his mate."

"Yes, that's right."

"Right …"

"It's a lot to take in, isn't it?"

"I mean it is, and it's interesting stuff and all, but the thing is ladies Terry McVeigh has been inside for years, so he wouldn't have been around to do half of this stuff."

"But that's just it officer. Ruth's been following the body story —"

"I'm the morbid one of the group you see."

"Oh right."

"So she mentioned Terry McVeigh's name to him and he starts shouting that he's not the man who did it. I mean, he was going mad by this stage."

"So who did he say did it then?"

"Just a minute … as you've probably guessed our memories are not what they were, so I wrote it down when we got back to the car. It's just in my bag."

"Was it James Dolby?"

"Yes, that's right; do you know him?"

His suspect lay prone on the desk, cradling his head in his hands. A broken waxwork in a chamber of horrors. Dave sat down and cleared his throat. This was personal: no pad, pen or tape recorder.

"Adam, does the name James Dolby mean anything to you?"

He lifted his head up.

22ND MARCH 2003

He pulled down his bags and applied the complementary face cleanser. It could be the warm lights of the bathroom but their darkness appeared to be fading. He leant deeper into the mirror. Another revelation. His hair really had issued a moratorium on any new strands of grey. *Fucking hell, I'm getting younger by the minute.* He grabbed the monogrammed dressing gown from its hook and draped it around his glistening torso. His moment of victory.

"Have you got lost in there, Dave?"

"What?"

"You've been in there ages."

"I'm coming now. I was just putting my face on."

"Finally you're out. I've never known anyone spend as much time in there as you do."

"There's nothing wrong with having pride in your appearance. You wrote the book on that."

This was self-evident. Reclining on silk sheets, she resembled a mahogany goddess, her hair a shower of black pearls, her dressing gown loose and open.

"My mum used to say there's a fine line between pride and vanity."

"Yeah and you're pissing all over it."

"I'll swing for you Dave."

"I'm joking, I'm joking. Of course, you're not vain. Although with your looks you have every right to be."

"Okay charmer, I'll let you off … this time."

"Thank you."

"So then …"

"So then what?"

"So then."

"What? What are you looking at me like that for?"

"Do I have to spell it out?"

"I've no idea what you're talking about."

"When are you going to give it me?"

"Pardon me?"

"My present, when are you going to give me my present?"

"Present?"

"Yes, you promised me 'something nice to wear.'"

"Who did?"

"Dave! You did."

"What?"

"You promised."

"No, I'm only kidding. I was going to wait till after dinner though."

"I want it now. Give it to me now."

"Oh you do, do you?"

"The present I mean. Jesus, you've got a one track mind."

"Okay, okay, you win."

"Yes!"

He sauntered over to the dressing table and pulled out a silver box tied with a red ribbon.

"Right, close your eyes then."

"Oh, Dave …"

"No, come on, let's do it properly."

"Okay, okay."

He placed the box in her outstretched arms.

"Right you can open them now."

"It's a box."

"God you're observant. Open it then."

She carefully untied the ribbon and opened the box.

"Er …It's a scarf."

"Woah, hang on, this isn't just 'a scarf.' This is a Connaught Silk scarf, it's top of the range. The cream of society wears these you know …Royalty, the lot."

"No, it's beautiful. It really is."

"Are you sure?"

"Yes, of course. It's so pretty and soft. It's just that …"

"What?"

"Are you sure it's my style? Will it suit me?"

"Of course it will. Wear it for dinner."

"Do you think it will go with my outfit?"

"It'll go fine."

"I won't be overdressed."

"Oi, this is the Wood Horton Hotel, of course you won't be overdressed. You'll look fantastic."

"If you say so babe. Ahh, that's lovely Dave, thank you. Come here."

She planted a kiss on his cheek.

"You're welcome, babe."

"Right, I'm just going to jump in the bath then."

"You've not tried it on yet."

"What? I'll put it on when I get dressed for dinner."

"Just try it on now. See how it looks, see if it fits."

"Dave, it's a scarf. Of course it's going to fit."

"Just try it on and see."

"No, later."

"Please, I paid a pretty penny for that and I just want to see it on you."

"Okay, if I must."

She moved in front of the mirror and wrapped it around her neck.

"It feels gorgeous."

"It looks beautiful on you."

"It doesn't look bad, if I do say so myself."

He came from behind and wrapped his hands around her waist, rubbing his crotch into her backside.

"Oi tiger. After dinner."

"Take the dressing gown off."

"Dave! You're a right little stud muffin."

"Take it off. Take it off, now."

"Oh, I love it when you're all assertive. Okay then, just for you."

"Leave the scarf on though."

"What?"

"The scarf, leave the scarf on."

"What if it gets messy?"

He spun her around, pushing his tongue into her mouth.

"It's alright, I've got another two in my bag."

"What?"

He placed his Champagne glass on the bedside cabinet and turned the volume down on the remote.

"Tonight's the night for love and romance. Tonight's the night if you give it a chance. I can be your lover. I can be your wife. I can give you the night of your life."

"Oi Kylie, keep it down in there."

"What?"

"Keep it down. Think of the neighbours."

"Sorry, I always sing in the bath."

"Is that what you call it?"

"But don't make me ask you twice. If you want me to be nice."

He smiled. He liked her. It was a shame it had to end this way.

"How long till dinner, Dave?"

"About an hour or so babe."

"What are you doing?"

"Just watching telly. Don't worry; enjoy your soak. I'll shout you when you need to get out."

"Okay."

He grabbed her Samsung from the bedside table and searched for his mobile number before punching in his message.

Hi baby, I've got a nice surprise for u. I've booked a hotel room at the Wood Horton. Posh eh? Just for me and u baby. Got lots of nice things 2 wear. Don't keep me waiting. I'm in room 252.

"Babe, I've had an idea."

"What?"

"Shall we have dinner in our room?"

"Ah Dave, I wanted to dress up."

"No, hear me out. I'll order us a snack, with some champagne, and we'll snuggle up and watch a bit of telly and then we'll go to Alfonso's in town."

"Alfonso's really? Can you afford it?"

"For you, no problem."

"Okay babe. You're really spoiling me you know."

"You're worth it. You're worth every penny. What you've done for me cannot be quantified in money."

"Really Dave? Do you mean that?"

"Absolutely, every word."

"Aw thanks babe. You really know how to make a girl feel wanted."

They lay entwined on the bed. Dave clad in pinstripe boxer shorts; her dressing gown now complemented by a toweling turban. He lifted his Rolex from the bedside table. It had been at least an hour since he'd lit the fuse and still nothing. The best laid plans of men and monsters? No, it was going to happen. It had to happen.

"This is lovely Dave. I'm living the dream here."

"It's not bad is it?"

"Dave?"

"Yes babe."

"Now don't get me wrong, it would be lovely to go to Alfonso's but we could always ..."

"What?"

"You know... stay here and get more comfortable."

"I thought you wanted to dress up and go out"

She whispered into his ear.

"Maybe I've changed my mind. Maybe I think it's better we stay in and I dress down. Or even better, don't get dressed at all."

"Mmm, I like the way you're thinking."

"Like the song says, 'I can give you the night of your life.'"

As they launched down each other's throats there was a loud knock on the door.

"This will be my other little surprise. Open the door babe."

"What 'little surprise?'"

"You'll see. If you thought the scarf was nice, wait to you see this."

"What is it?"

"Go and find out."

"Really?"

"Yes really."

"Dave, you're spoiling me. I can't believe it."

"Well you better open the door then. Go on."

"But I'm not dressed."

"You've got more clothes on than I've got."

"I know but …"

"Go on, you're alright. Trust me, they've seen a lot worse."

"Thanks!"

"You know what I mean. Go on, before they go."

"Okay, okay."

She made for the door.

"God, I'm shaking."

"Open the door!"

"Right, I am, I am."

She grabbed the handle and swung it open.

"Private Wrench here, present and correct, ready to receive his orders."

"Gerry. What are you doing here?"

"You texted me to come—"

"No I didn't."

"Of course you did."

"I don't know what you're talking about."

He joined them in the doorway.

"David. Why are you here? What are you doing half-undressed?"

"Do you two know each other?"

"We do unfortunately Jayne. In fact, we all know each other. I know my cheating spineless scumbag of a father who I have disappointed from the day I was born; and you two know each other as you are the woman he left his wife of nearly fifty years for, destroying her in the process; and of course I know you Jayne because you've been shagging me behind his back for the past couple of months in blissful ignorance of the fact that I'm his son …Now isn't this nice and cozy? Come in and have a drink, Dad. Make yourself comfortable. Champagne?"

"Oh my God."

"You bastard. You bloody bastard."

"Stings doesn't it Father?"

"You knew how much she meant to me."

"I know. Sorry about that Dad but you see I just couldn't compromise my feelings any longer."

4TH APRIL 2003

Adam was just a kid when he first travelled by train. A British Rail special offer allowing him and his mum to visit a distant aunt on the South Coast. The promotional leaflet showed a group of families riding carriages of fifty pence pieces. The realisation then that trains had two sides and a roof was somewhat of a disappointment. Nevertheless, this trip ignited his passion for train travel and by the age of eleven, he was bunking carriages across the North West. His technique was genius in its simplicity: as soon as the guard approached, he would hide in the nearest toilet. Maturity though had refined his method and he now skipped the carriage and headed straight to the bogs. On this occasion, he'd been in there for the past four and a half hours. He had little idea where Hastings was but concluded it must be somewhere near the end of the world. That or he'd missed his stop.

My arse is gone. Completely fucking dead. Can't feel a thing.

He shuffled on the seat; raising his left then right buttock like a crap yogi.

"Oh shit, the note."

He thrust his hand into his back pocket.

"Thank fuck for that."

He pulled out a stained-yellow stickie and ironed its creases on his knee. He could just about understand it. The address that is; not why the copper gave it to him. That was still a mystery.

A loud bang shook the toilet door. *Here we go. Time for the old routine.*

"Sorry mate. I'm going to be here a while. I'm a slave to my bowels, unfortunately."

"Pull the other one son. You've been in there ever since we left Piccadilly. I'm wagering that you don't have a ticket, right?"

"No mate, I've got a ticket. I'll show it you when I'm done. I've just got a stomach bug that's all. I can't keep off the toilet."

"Yeah, right. Have you any idea how often I've heard that?"

"No, straight up. It's pouring from me."

"Well I can't smell anything?"

"What?"

"I said, I can't smell anything."

"Well I thought you were a shite inspector but that's ridiculous."

"Right, open the door. Let's see your ticket."

"Only joking mate. I've told you, I'll show it you when I've finished."

"Open it now."

"Just give me ten minutes. I'll be out in ten minutes."

"Okay, I've given you every chance."

The silver lock ratcheted left then right.

"Whoa, hang on, hang on. I'm on the toilet—"

Adam pressed his knee into the middle of the door.

"Fuck off will you."

"Stop resisting. Leave it!"

"Fucking stop it man."

"Open it or I'll force it open."

"No. I told you ten minutes."

His patience ran out; his black boot nearly separating the door from its hinges.

"You lying bastard. You've got your pants on."

"Okay, okay, so I've not got the shits. I'm sorry for lying to you."

The guard, middle-aged and moustachioed, grabbed the neck of his polo shirt.

"Come on, you're coming with me."

"No, please."

"Come on, time to go."

"Don't touch me. Don't touch me. Leave me alone."

"If you don't like it, don't bunk the bloody train. Everybody else has to pay, why shouldn't you?"

"Taylor, the tubes please. John, the medicine if you will."

"No, Mr Dolby, please don't."

"Don't cry Adam, it will be over soon. I'm not the bad guy here. You and your friend brought all this on yourselves."

"No, please. You don't have to do this."

"Nooo!"

His fist hammered into the guard's spare tyre causing him to convulse backwards into the grey corridor wall.

"Argh, you bastard."

"I told you not to touch me. No one touches me. Not anymore."

He cocked his right hand and smashed it into the guard's throbbing temple. He fell to the floor like flour from a shute; his hat spinning down the corridor.

"Help!"

"I warned you, I fucking warned you."

He pulled back his foot and booted him as if a pile of autumn leaves.

"Hey, stop it gentlemen…This isn't on."

A bespectacled man, a wailing kid wrapped within his tweed suit, sounded the alarm.

"Leave him alone. Can someone help me here? They're fighting …"

Their gaze collided. Him and the kid. Within his fledgling eyes a terrible storm: a whole new world unfolding before him.

Adam didn't feel a thing.

I'm a stone-cold killer.

Concurrent to the cavalry arriving, the train began to slow. A flurry of trees, hi-vis vests and frustrated faces filled the stained window. A stop. Not his intended one but good enough to make his escape.

He pulled on the door handle and disappeared into the exiting throng.

His chauffeurs to Hastings were a study in opposites: the taciturn Polish truck driver with his hanging crucifix and mullet, a picture of Lech Walesa glued to his dashboard and then Mick, a non-stop cockney, his balding plate barely visible over the wheel of his bronchial Datsun.

As he dropped him off on the empty country lane with a beep of his horn, Adam pictured his reaction.

I picked that geezer up on my way down from the smoke. I'm renovating some B&B's like – on the seafront. Hitchhiking on the exit lane of the service station, he was. We talked about hating do-gooders and the French. Seemed like a nice guy. Just goes to show, eh?

He sat under the Rutland Manor sign on a grassy hillock. The spring sunshine nourishing everything within its gilded stare; the long gravel path to the house stretching out in front of him. He opened his Discman. There was a time and place for *The Court of The Crimson King* and this wasn't it. He rummaged in his rucksack and pulled out his only other disc – *80's Synth Hits.* His hidden pleasure. He cued track nine: Its foreboding synths and strangled arpeggios closing his eyes. Its bass and drums clenching his fists. *I Ran* by a Flock of Seagulls. This time though there was no chance of that and he skipped towards the manor whistling like a milkman.

"This is what it must feel like. Living life at the sharp end. No margin for error. Death or glory."

He pressed the intercom on the heavy wooden door.

"Hello. Is there anybody there?"

"Hi, Abe speaking; can I help you?"

"Yes, I wonder if you can. I'm an old friend of Mr James Dolby. I'm in the area and just wondered if I could pop in and see him."

"He's just had his tea. He's pretty sleepy. Can you not come back?"

"Oh, right. It's just that I'm only in town for the day. I'm back at work tomorrow, in Manchester, you see."

"It's getting late."

"Just past six …I'll only be ten minutes or so. Just show my face."

"Hmm, okay but you can't stay too long."

"No, that's fine, no problem."

The door opened.

"You better come in then."

"Thank you."

He followed her into the building's hallway.

"Can you sign in please?"

"Sorry?"

"Just print and sign your name in that visitors' book. It's just for health and safety; so that if there is a fire we know how many people are in the building."

"Okay. No problem."

He pulled the pen from its stand and signed as John Fleming.

"Right, all done."

"Okay, come with me please, just up these stairs."

"Right."

"How long is it since you last saw him?"

"Oh, a while. Maybe two or three years ago."

"So, have you heard about his strokes?"

"Er, yes. It's really sad."

"His first one wasn't too severe but the second one has been really bad. His mobility and speech have been badly affected. I would prepare yourself for a shock."

"Oh dear, that's terrible."

"It is, but he's in the best place here. We make sure he is as comfortable and as pain free as possible."

"I'm sure you do. I bet you're doing a fantastic job."

"We try our best. How do you know him? If you don't mind me saying he's a bit older than you."

"No, that's fine. He was my old boss."

"Really?"

"Yeah."

"My God, what was he like?"

"Er, you know, hard but fair."

"I could imagine he was a real tyrant."

"He could be but I was his blue-eyed boy. He let me get away with murder."

"I see. Well here we are."

She knocked on the door and slowly opened it.

"He can't answer but I always knock out of respect."

"Yes, of course."

"Tut, he's asleep. Oh dear. Well, I suppose if you're only here today, I could wake him up."

"No, you mustn't do that. If he needs his sleep then he needs his sleep. I'll just sit with him for a bit. If he doesn't wake up, I'll write him a note or something."

"I'm not sure that he will be able to read it. It's hard to say how badly his brain has been affected, as his speech is so bad. We'd read it out to him though."

"Great, I'll just sit down here then."

"Yes, okay. I must say you're a good friend. I'm not sure what he's done to deserve a friend like you."

"Ha, he's done plenty. He's done it all."

"That's nice. Anyway, if you need me, press that red button over there."

"Okay, will do, thanks."

He pulled a chair from the corner of the room and sat on it back to front. Just like he had.

Jesus, look at him: bent and retracted, slavering like a dog. How the mighty have fucking fallen. I almost feel …Nah, fuck that. All he's done. All he's destroyed. He deserves all he has and all that's coming to him. You can't escape justice. No one is above the fucking law.

For the past thirty minutes, he had revelled in his every twist and turn. Flipping the paint encrusted Stanley knife he'd stolen from Mick's van between his fingers. Playing God.

Would killing him be too kind? Nah, not the way I'm going to do it.

As he jumped to his feet, that Polaroid burst onto the scene again. He couldn't rid it from his mind. Sarah lying on a four-poster bed. Though incapacitated her eyes wide open. Them sat either side of her. Sweating and half-naked, as if footballers celebrating a cup final victory.

"You're going straight to hell pal."

He leaned over him and rattled his shoulder.

"Wake up. I want you awake for this. Wake up you evil bastard. Wake up! Don't fucking ignore me."

He pinched the skin on his wrist, turning it from translucent white to angry red. His eyes flickered open then immediately closed.

"Yeah, you know me, don't you. I'm the last person you expected to see. But he told you remember? He said, 'we'll fucking haunt you' and here I am. You should have killed me when you had the chance. I'm going to savour every minute of this."

He ran his blade over his cheek. Nothing. Not even the slightest spec of blood.

How do I kill him? Where are his veins? He's like a vampire. Full of fucking dust.

He dug deeper, harder, until his blood began streaking down his face like rain on a window pain.

One hundred and eighty. Now it's time to paint the fucking walls.

He eased his head to one side and tapped his neck. The faintest trace of a jugular vein. He hovered the blade over his target; marking his incision like a school kid dissecting a worm. Then he stopped dead. "Who's there? Who is it?" There was another presence in the room. He could feel it.

"Oh my God."

Standing within a lucent cocoon was the love of his life. Arms outstretched, tears flowing.

"Oh my God, Sarah, it's you! You've come back. I can't believe you've come back."

She beckoned him forward; silent entreaties falling from her mouth.

"Sarah don't be upset. This is for you. This is for us. This is for all the people like us, for all the people like him. I'm putting down a marker. This ends here."

She shook her head.

"Don't worry about me, I'm ready for this. I'm ready to take the blame. No, really I am."

She clasped her hands and shook them in supplication.

"But I'm doing it for us, Sarah."

She leant forward and caressed his cheek while her other hand took the knife and threw it across the floor. There would be no need for it now. A wide smile lit up her face. She attempted a kiss but he pulled away.

"But Sarah. The things he did to you. The things he did to me. The things he did to Flames …"

She took his hand and offered him the floor. Just for old time's sake.

"We have to fight back. Beat the bastards at their own game."

For once, he was on form and they floated around the room in complete symmetry. From the bedsit to the boardwalk.

"He can't get away with it. You know what they say – bad things happen if good people do nothing. I've been kicked around my whole life. I'm not going to take it anymore …

I mean, why should we fucking take it? We've done nothing wrong!"

She brought a finger to her lips and then kissed him. It felt different from last time; firmer with a distinct hint of permanence. Could she be back for good?

"I can't believe that you've come back to me Sarah. I never thought I'd see you again. I didn't tell you properly last time but I love you. I never thought that word existed until now. Sarah, we are one. I feel your bones in my body; your blood in my veins; our hearts beating as one."

She pressed her finger to her lips again and kissed him. This time though it felt as intangible as ever. Like petals on the breeze. She moved to his right and whispered into his ear.

"Stand with the angels not the apes."

"Sarah, you spoke to me. That's the first time you've ever spoken to me. That's unbelievable. That's amazing. You've no idea how much I've dreamt about this moment …Sarah, what's happening? No, don't fade. Sarah you're fading. You're disappearing. No Sarah, don't go. Please, I need you. Please no …Sarah, don't leave me again. Please. I love you. I can't live without you!"

He collapsed into tears. Curled in a half-circle on the linoleum floor; wailing like a winter storm. He stayed like this for a good half-hour before rising to his feet and rubbing his eyes. He wouldn't let him see him like this. Once maybe but not now.

"She's right. I thought I needed to beat you at your own game. But I see it now. I don't need to change. We don't need to change. You need to change. Every last fucking one of you."

He moved towards the door. Before he left the room, he turned and faced him for the final time.

Is he smiling at me? He's smiling at me. The bastard is smiling at me.

He strode down the red-carpeted stairs; a farrago of relief and regret. From below came two men dressed in matching pin-stripe suits negotiating the steps in a blur of flapping hair and ice-white socks.

"Alright?"

"Sorry, excuse me. Thank you."

As they reached the landing, the man on the left pulled a hammer from the inside pocket of his suit.

"Twenty-six. There it is."

Twenty-six? That's Dolby's room.

He followed them back up the stairs.

"Hey, what are you doing? What are you doing with that?"

The man with the hammer turned and faced him.

"God's work. We are here to do God's work."

He left them to it.

ACKNOWLEDGEMENTS

A massive thank you to Sam, Grace, and Mum for your love and support. I couldn't have done it without you.

Thanks also to Gaffer, Marika, JR and AC who have supported me to keep sane during this process.

And finally to my Dad, who I think about every day.

Printed in Poland
by Amazon Fulfillment
Poland Sp. z o.o., Wrocław